THE VALLEY OF THE THREE FORKS

LOOK FOR THESE EXCITING WESTERN SERIES FROM BESTSELLING AUTHORS WILLIAM W. JOHNSTONE AND J.A. JOHNSTONE

The Mountain Man
Luke Jensen: Bounty Hunter
Brannigan's Land
The Jensen Brand
Smoke Jensen: The Early Years
Preacher and MacCallister
Fort Misery
The Fighting O'Neils
Perley Gates
MacCoole and Boone
Guns of the Vigilantes
Shotgun Johnny
The Chuckwagon Trail
The Jackals
The Slash and Pecos Westerns
The Texas Moonshiners
Stoneface Finnegan Westerns
Ben Savage: Saloon Ranger
The Buck Trammel Westerns
The Death and Texas Westerns
The Hunter Buchanon Westerns
Will Tanner: U.S. Deputy Marshal
Old Cowboys Never Die
Go West, Young Man

Published by Kensington Publishing Corp.

THE VALLEY OF THE THREE FORKS

WILLIAM W. JOHNSTONE
AND J.A. JOHNSTONE

PINNACLE BOOKS
Kensington Publishing Corp.
kensingtonbooks.com

PINNACLE BOOKS are published by

Kensington Publishing Corp.
900 Third Avenue
New York, NY 10022

PUBLISHER'S NOTE: Following the death of William W. Johnstone, the Johnstone family is working with a carefully selected writer to organize and complete Mr. Johnstone's outlines and many unfinished manuscripts to create additional novels in all of his series, like The Last Gunfighter, Mountain Man, and Eagles, among others. This novel was inspired by Mr. Johnstone's superb storytelling.

All Kensington titles, imprints, and distributed lines are available at special quantity discounts for bulk purchases for sales promotion, premiums, fundraising, and educational or institutional use.

Special book excerpts or customized printings can also be created to fit specific needs. For details, write or phone the office of the Kensington Sales Manager: Kensington Publishing Corp., 900 Third Avenue, New York, NY 10022. Attn. Sales Department. Phone: 1-800-221-2647.

First Pinnacle Books Trade Paperback Printing: September 2026

ISBN: 978-0-7860-5155-7

ISBN: 978-1-4967-5224-6 (ebook)

10 9 8 7 6 5 4 3 2 1

Printed in the United States of America

The authorized representative in the EU for product safety and compliance
is eucomply OU, Parnu mnt 139b-14, Apt 123
Tallinn, Berlin 11317, hello@eucompliancepartner.com.

THE VALLEY OF THE THREE FORKS

Chapter 1

Logan Trent poured whiskey for a prospector named Wiley Phillip, then corked the bottle and reached under the bar for his sawed-off twelve gauge, or his "Peacemaker," as he called the old stagecoach gun that had been used by many shotgun messengers here in Big Creek in the shadow of the Absaroka Mountains, Montana Territory.

It had cut many a man in two and in even smaller pieces. Amazing how much damage a seasoned shotgun messenger could inflict with such a weapon when the chips were down, and it was his job to keep "his" strongboxes out of the hands of trail scum.

Wiley Phillip saw the move and grinned, showing a mouthful of whiskey- and tobacco-stained teeth. He'd seen it before and knew that trouble was on the horizon. Trent owned the Stray Dog, here in Big Creek, having purchased the saloon nearly five years ago, and he was known to cut trouble off at the pass, so to speak.

Or nearly cut it in two with a double load of double-ought buckshot to the belly.

Wiley glanced over his shoulder. Trouble was on the horizon, indeed, for a big Swedish woodcutter, Lars Holstrom, had nabbed one of Trent's bar girls, Miss Clara. He had pulled her onto his lap and was nuzzling her neck against her ever-loudening protestations. She struggled to free herself from the woodcutter's brawny arms, but Holstrom was a big, powerful man. He was also drunk, as he usually was, and wasn't of a mind to let the girl go.

Wiley returned his gaze to Trent and saw rage building in the saloon owner's eyes. Logan Trent was a big man, too, nearly six-six, none of it tallow, and he ruled the Stray Dog with an iron fist . . . *er*, with the iron Peacemaker, which still had old bloodstains on it from past violence. Truly, the twelve gauge had known violence in its day. Wiley Phillip had a feeling, judging by the ever-building darkness in Trent's eyes, it was going to get another round of it soon.

Sure enough, when Miss Clara squealed, "Oh, won't you please leave me alone—you're *hurting* me!" out came the Peacemaker from under the bar, and the apron-clad Trent, dark-haired and dark-eyed, with a severely chiseled, handsome face, pushed through a swing door to Wiley's left and marched over to the table where the big Swede was molesting Trent's eighteen-year-old serving girl. He held the savage popper straight down along his right leg.

He stopped six feet from the Swede's table and said quietly but tightly, "All right, Holstrom, you've had your fun—let her up."

The Swede pulled his face out from the girl's neck, where he'd been nibbling the girl's right ear, and said with casual defiance and a jeering grin, "Nah. Don't want to." He laughed and went back to chewing the girl's ear.

"I don't care what you want," Trent said with quiet menace. "You either do it, or I'll smash your face in. If that doesn't work, you'll get buckshot to the belly, and you will not be walking out of here."

The smile left the Swede's bearded face. There were maybe a dozen other drinkers in the rough-hewn place. Now they all went quiet, swiveling their heads toward the scene of the trouble, until there were only the sounds of Miss Clara's protestations.

The Swede glared up at Trent.

Trent glared down at the Swede.

Holstrom flared his nostrils, face reddening with rage. He said in his thick Swedish accent, “Who in the hell are you, Logan Trent? No one knows a damn thing about you. You show up five years ago on that big roan of yours and you don’t say a damn thing about yourself!”

“If I wanted you to know, you’d know. Now let her go.”

“You know what I think?” Holstrom said. “I think you’re *hunted*! I think you’re a *wanted man* hiding out in Montana!”

“You think what you want, but if you don’t let that girl off your lap, you’re going to get your face caved in.”

The Swede’s lips quivered as he hardened his jaws.

He threw the girl off his lap and straight into Trent, who dropped his shotgun as he caught her. The Swede leaped out of his own chair, charging like a bull buffalo at Trent. Trent threw the girl into a chair an eye blink before the Swede, who was two inches taller than Trent, barreled into the saloon owner, knocking him flat on his back onto a table that was vacated quickly by the two miners who’d been sitting there playing poker.

The Swede slammed a ham-sized fist into Trent’s face, scrambling the saloon owner’s brains. The Swede pulled his fist back and slammed it forward once more, but it got only halfway to its target before Trent, suppressing his aching head and blurred vision, reached up and wrapped both hands around the woodcutter’s big fist, stopping it. The Swede’s gray eyes widened in renewed rage, but he yelled out in pain when Trent head-butted him twice and slammed a knee into the man’s groin—maybe not a sporting move, but this was no sport.

It was survival.

The Swede groaned and fell off the table to the floor.

Trent bounded off the table and picked up the Peacekeeper from the floor. He turned to see Holstrom bounding toward him once more, roaring like a gut-shot griz. Trent flipped the shotgun around and slammed the butt into his opponent's face. The man's nose and mouth exploded like a ripe tomato.

The Swede staggered backward, clutching his nose in both big paws. As he did, Trent slammed the shotgun's butt against the man's forehead. That dropped Holstrom like a poleaxed bull. He lay groaning, writhing, and glaring up at the saloon owner.

Trent flipped the Peacemaker again, drew back both rabbit-ear hammers, and aimed down the side-by-side barrels at Holstrom, the muzzles a foot from the man's face.

"*No!*" the Swede begged, turning his head to one side, steeling himself for two rounds of double-ought buck.

Trent started to draw both triggers back.

"*Logan!*" a man shouted.

The saloon owner looked up to see the Big Creek town marshal standing between the saloon's batwing doors, gazing warningly at Trent.

The lawman, Lou Gentry—tall, gray-mustached, and gray-headed under his high-crowned black Stetson—gave his head a single admonishing wag.

"Turn around, Lou," Trent said. "You don't want to see this. Not gonna be *pretty*!"

Gentry released the batwings and walked into the saloon.

He stopped seven feet from where Trent stood, still holding the shotgun's barrels close to the terrified Swede's bearded, bloody face. He looked at Trent. He didn't say anything, didn't even shake his head again. He just stared at the saloon owner, who, after several seconds, gave a frustrated chuff, depressed the shotgun's hammers, and raised the gun until its barrels were aimed at the ceiling.

Trent kept his eyes on the Swede, whose nose was turned sideways on his face, and said through gritted teeth, "Get the hell out of here. You ever come back, not even Gentry will be able to save you."

Gentry said to Holstrom, "I won't even try."

The big Swede gained his feet heavily, miserably, grabbed his whiskey shot off the table, threw it back, and slammed the glass down hard. Glaring at Trent and Gentry, he set his feathered canvas hat on his head, then stomped across the still-silent saloon and through the batwings.

Immediately a low roar of conversation rose from the other drinkers.

Gentry looked at Trent and jerked his head toward the bar. "Buy ya a drink, Logan?"

"I'll buy."

Trent pushed through the swing door, set the shotgun on a shelf behind the bar, and, as Gentry leaned over the bar and entwined his hands on top of the scarred mahogany, filled two shot glasses, sliding one to the aging lawman he considered a friend. Gentry lifted the glass, said, "That was close," and threw back the entire shot.

Miss Clara came to the bar, set her tray on it, and said, "Thanks, Logan."

"Why don't you take the rest of the night off? I can handle it to closing."

"Thanks."

When she was climbing the stairs, Gentry glanced at her bodice, corset, and matching skirt, then said to Trent, "Pretty girl. Ever seen others of that cut . . . from where you came from . . . ?"

"Oh, sure, sure." Trent smiled, knowing the lawman was probing him for secrets.

"Where is that, Logan?"

Trent shrugged and refilled the lawman's shot glass. "Here an' there."

"You sure keep your cards close to your chest, Logan."

"Never thought of it that way." Trent threw back his whiskey.

"Oh, I think you have, Logan. And it's not just because you're a man of few words."

"Why, then?"

Gentry grimaced, deeply curious. "Can't figure it out."

Trent left the lawman to pour drinks. When he returned, he finished his shot and refilled both their glasses.

"I'll figure it out," Gentry said.

"It's not worth it, Lou."

"I got me a feelin' it is. Just to satisfy my curiosity, of course." The marshal raised his glass in salute.

Steeling his voice a little, Trent said, "Let it go, Lou. You'd just be bored."

"Ah, another clue." Gentry sipped his whiskey. "When a man rides to town on a fine horse, buys a saloon, and doesn't seem to have a story—at least, none he wants to talk about—it makes people curious. Makes people think he's got a past he's runnin' from."

"People should mind their own business." Trent threw back his shot to try to temper his annoyance. He didn't like sharing much about himself with anyone—not even with his only friend in town. Gentry was a former cowboy and shotgun rider before age caught up to him and he became the lawman of a small, mostly peaceful town in the Montana mountains.

Trent knew Gentry's story, but that didn't mean Gentry needed to know his.

Gentry refilled his glass from the bottle on the bar and removed his hat, putting it down on the bar beside him. He winced and scratched the back of his head. "Seems to me, if I remember right—I've had the memory of an old man for years—when I was trailing owlhoots over in Idaho, I heard a story about some trouble down in the Valley of the Three Forks of the Wolf River."

Trent just stared at the man, squeezing his empty shot glass. Warm blood rose in his face.

"What was it now?" Gentry said. "I don't think I got the whole story, just that some deputy sheriff was accused of killin' some young man from a wealthy ranching family over a woman in a town called Three Forks. He went to trial, but the jury said they couldn't convict him because they didn't have enough evidence. I guess everyone in the county figured he did it because this deputy and the dead man were blood enemies. Feelin' disgraced and wantin' to spare his family further scandal, this deputy fled town soon after the trial."

The lawman shook his head, as if he didn't know what to make of the tale.

"Crazy story," Trent said.

"A sad one, too. Especially if he was innocent, with everyone believing him guilty."

Gentry sighed resignedly and set his empty glass on the bar. He put his Stetson on his head. "Reckon I best get back to my night rounds. Have a good night, Logan."

He tapped his knuckles on the bar and headed for the batwings.

"You too, Lou."

The lawman had taken only two steps when he stopped, turned back around, and pulled a small leaf of yellow paper out of his pocket. "Almost forgot—you got a telegram earlier. Ain't it a coincidence? It came from a place called Three Forks in the Idaho Territory. Imagine that!"

He laughed as he put the note on the bar, then started once more for the batwings.

Trent stared down at the penciled telegram addressed to *Logan D. Trent of Big Creek, Montana Terr.*:

LOGAN, YOU'RE NEEDED AT HOME. TROUBLE—DAD

Chapter 2

Three days later, in Hell's Canyon in southwestern Montana Territory, he sat astride his big roan, Wolf, so named as the horse had been born on Trent's family ranch in the Wolf Mountains near Three Forks. He stared down into the muddy offshoot of the Jefferson River, which he and Wolf had traversed minutes ago. He and the horse were soaked, but despite the river's strong current, Wolf had gotten them across safely.

As soon as they'd gained the opposite bank, Wolf lifted his head high and whinnied. From experience of fording previous waters with the roan, Trent knew what was about to happen. Quick as lightning, he leaped off the horse, landing flat-footed, just before the big stallion shook himself so violently, ridding himself of the river water, that he shook off his saddle, as well as his bridle. Trent's saddle scabbard, in which lay his Winchester "Yellowboy" repeater, went flying with the saddle, saddlebags, and bedroll wrapped in his rain slicker.

Trent turned to the horse, the light of mischief in the mount's eyes, and said, "Doggonit, Wolf—why do you always have to do that?" The horse took one step forward, whinnied shrilly, and did it again, showering Trent with water from his soaked roan hide.

Trent used his sleeve to swab his big, chiseled face, spiked with three days' growth of dark-brown beard stubble. He knew how the horse felt, however. His own denims, a good strip of his shirt, and his vest were soaked from just above his cartridge belt. His pants hung heavy on him, clinging uncomfortably. The Jefferson was deep, and it flowed rapidly, violently in places, so when horse and rider had plunged into it from the bank on the opposite side, the current had swept them downstream as the roan had fought his way to freedom. They'd been in the river for several long minutes, however—always a bit of a harrowing maneuver. Trent wouldn't have tried it with any other mount, but only with a tall, tough, determined stallion like Wolf.

The horse turned to him now, craning his neck, and that devilish glint remained in his eyes. There was pride there, too—oh, make no mistake! He was a ham, Wolf was, and he enjoyed showing off for his beloved rider, who loved him back in every way.

"You suppose I can put your saddle back on now, ya ornery cayuse?" Trent said with fake frustration. "We best keep movin'." He glanced at the sky, where clouds were building. "I think we're gonna get rain in a coupla—"

Trent cut himself off. Just then he spied a foreboding glint from atop a low rise, maybe a hundred yards to the north. He cast his gaze to the ridge crest just as the crown of a hat dropped down behind the ridge. He'd been watched, surveyed through a spyglass or field glasses. He'd be damned if he hadn't been. He was a veteran of the long coulees, having been an outlaw of petty sorts as a much younger man, before his father, owner and operator of the Wolf Mountain Ranch in the foothills of the Wolf Mountains, had put the kibosh on that, threatening his youngest son with a bull-whipping and being stripped of his considerable inheritance. Ben Trent had taken the hangdog, humiliated Logan Trent to the town of Three Forks and had coaxed its sheriff, Dan True, into giving his firebrand son a job as deputy sheriff.

He cast his cautious gaze again to the top of the ridge.

Who'd been eyeing him?

Could just be range riders wanting to know who was crossing their range. On the other hand, many men salivated at the sight of the handsome roan. Whoever was up there might be following him and Wolf, hoping to get their hands on the horse. Many men were killed for their horses and long rifles, whatever coin or greenbacks they had in their pockets. The West was largely still a wild, untamed frontier.

Trent quickly resaddled and bridled the roan, getting everything strapped back into place. As he did, he kept a watchful eye on the crest of the low ridge to the north, not wanting to get drygulched. He stepped up into the saddle, loosened his Winchester in its sheath, and cast another cautious glance at the ridge, relieved not to see any more hatted heads and, best of all, no rifles trained on him.

When he was a good mile away from the crossing, threading his way between long, sloping rises, spiked with the sage and pines that made him know he was in Montana, he began to let his guard down a bit.

"Prob'ly just a cattle puncher keeping an eye on his boss's range." Rustlers were a dime a dozen out here.

After he and Wolf had gone another quarter mile, Trent looked up. Lightning flashed as purple clouds built and a coolness touched the building breeze. Thunder rumbled throatily, and the smell of rain grew stronger.

Time to seek shelter.

He surveyed a pair of stony dikes rising around him. In the one on his left, sitting atop a grassy apron slope peppered with pines, he thought he spied a notch cave beneath a stone overhang. Perfect . . . if the cave wasn't already occupied by some mountain lion or some other wild beast that wasn't looking for company. He swung Wolf off the trail and heeled the mount into a gallop.

Wolf took the slope easily, weaving around the pines and occasional aspens. They wound their way through the forest in about three minutes. When they came out on the other side, the high sandstone dike rose before them, its face sheer. The cave was near the bottom, at the top of a gravelly low rise sheathed by two large boulders sitting about fifteen feet out from the dike's wall. They, too, were shielded from above by a stone overhang.

Perfect place to shelter Wolf.

Now, if only the cave itself was unoccupied.

Trent slid his Yellowboy from its sheath, swung his right leg over the saddle horn, and slid smoothly down from the saddle. He racked a round into the Winchester's action, then moved to the cave, crouching, peering inside, which was nearly all shadow. With his right gloved index finger snugged against the cocked rifle's trigger, he stepped up to the entrance and crouched even lower, poking his head inside to give the place thorough scrutiny.

Empty.

There was the sweet, wild smell of some animal of the forest that had recently occupied the cavern, with bits of rabbit fur and broken bones scattered here and there, but it was empty, all right.

Quickly Trent leaned his rifle against the face of the dike and went to work, unsaddling Wolf and laying out his gear in front of the cavern entrance, under the stone overhang, which would be a good place to build a fire, if he could find dry wood before the storm hit. When he'd secured Wolf between the boulder to the left of the cavern and the dike's front wall, ground-reining the well-trained horse, he hurried off on foot back down the slope, gathering two good armloads of fallen pine and aspen branches. He'd just returned to the cavern's entrance when he felt the first drop of cold rain.

He built a fire ring from surrounding stones, beside the pile of branches, and had a smoking fire going just as the rain began to fall in earnest, the thunder building now to the tone and volume of kettledrums. Trent hauled his speckled tin coffeepot out of his burlap possibles bag, filled it from his canteen, set it on an iron claw in the fire, then sat back, enjoying the soothing warmth of the crackling flames as the water began to sigh and gurgle.

When it came to a boil, Trent pulled a handful of ground Arbuckles' from a small burlap sack, then pulled the pot out of the fire and dropped the coffee into the water. He set the pot back on the claw. When it came to a boil again, the bubbling dark-brown brew gurgling out of the spout and steaming in the fire, he pulled it off the claw with a worn leather swatch, lifted the lid, and added cool water from his canteen to settle the grounds. He then filled one of his two white-speckled black tin cups, which he'd also pulled from his possibles sack, and sat back with the steaming cup in both hands.

A contented man.

He looked over the fire at the rain curtaining down off the overhang six feet away from him. It smelled like minerals, forest, and mountain rain. Rain smelled different in the mountains. In his thirty-four years, he had spent time in both the mountains and plains, and he knew the difference.

It was good to be back in the country. Mountain country.

He'd grown up on a mountain ranch, as beautiful a place as a man could ever see, and he'd preferred it to town. He'd punched cattle from dawn to midnight, and he'd broken horses for his father. But, to no one else's fault other than his own, he'd spent a good many years working as a deputy sheriff in Three Forks and then as a saloon owner in Big Creek. He yearned for the wide-open spaces again. Running a saloon entailed a lot of responsibility, but he thought it would help him blend in with the rest of humanity. He supposed he could have lived like a mountain man, but that was a lonely life. A life where he'd have bitten off more than he could chew. He could no longer break horses, because he'd been nearly stomped and thrown to death more times than his body could tolerate. He may have been only thirty-four, but he often felt ten years older than that. When he'd come to Big Creek and bought the saloon, he'd wanted to hide from his past.

But now with one thin yellow scrap of paper with seven simple words scribbled on it, he was about to ride back into the past he'd tried so many times to forget.

He may have been a grown man, but he could not defy his father.

He could not defy Ben Trent.

His aging, crippled-up, leonine-headed father, shorter by several inches than Trent and stove-up from tangles with wild horses and dangerous and mercurial bulls and heifers—he'd even been attacked by a grizzly once and had been near death for two months—still made Trent feel like that eighteen-year-old firebrand his father had hauled out of bed by his ear.

He wondered what the trouble was.

But for his father, the only one who knew of Trent's whereabouts, to have summoned him home, it had to be for a good reason. Probably not one that Trent even wanted to hear about, but hear about it he would.

Dread touched him, tempering his enjoyment of the coffee, the fire, the rain. . . .

He was glad for the storm, though. It slowed his progress along the trail back to Three Forks. He was in no hurry to arrive in that cauldron of ancient trouble, though he knew his father was waiting for him and he'd had a damn good reason for calling his boy back to where he'd endured so much strife and scandal, dodging the bullets of many men who'd been out to kill him and even kill the woman he'd loved.

Still loved.

Clarita Ortiz . . .

The sound of her name, the image of the beautiful Mexican saloon owner in his head, bit him deep.

He sipped his coffee, lowered the cup, and shook his head, staring through the curtain of rain once more at what was a very thin curtain on his past. “Damn, Pa,” he said, witches’ fingers of lightning forking nearly right above his head, his voice nearly drowned by the thunder and the rain. “Why . . . why . . . why . . . ? Liable to get me killed. Liable to get others killed as well. You have to know that.”

Still, Logan Trent, whose past was a yoke on his shoulders, was on his way home.

“Hello, the camp!” a man’s deep voice rose distantly, muffled by the storm.

Instantly, one of Trent’s two Russian .44s was in his hand, his coffee cup lying on the ground between him and the fire.

His heart was a war drum in his chest.

Chapter 3

To Trent's right, between the boulder and the dike, Wolf whinnied. The horse shook his head and pawed at the ground with one front hoof.

Trent said, "Your instinct trumps mine, boy. Who do we have here?" He rose, the Russian in his hand. Quickly he broke open the piece and filled the chamber he usually kept empty beneath the hammer so he didn't accidentally shoot off anything he couldn't live without. He stared through the rain curtain and saw movement in the forest that began roughly fifty yards down the slope from the dike.

Trent called, "Name yourselves!"

The man's voice returned, "Just three weary pilgrims, mister!" They emerged from the forest—three stocky, bearded men in gray rain slickers and battered Stetsons. They spread out in front of the forest and the man in the middle—big, potbellied, round-faced—yelled, "We seen your fire from the trail below. We had a feelin' you had mud, an' we sure could use a cup. We been battlin' this storm for an hour now an' we're chilled to the bone!"

A stretched silence.

The younger man to the left of the man who'd spoken—thin and hawk-faced under a low-crowned black Stetson with a chin thong—said, "You mind? It's kinda the way o' the country, ya know. To offer hospitality to strangers."

"No need fer that gun, mister," yelled the man to the right of the first who'd spoken, pointing up the slope at Trent. "Ain't no need fer that hogleg. Why, that's downright unpolite. We ain't no threat. Just trail-weary market hunters." He was old, with a craggy face and long gray hair hanging down from a battered canvas hat.

Trent yelled, "If it's just hospitality you want, ride in. But keep your hands where I can see them. I can be hospitable . . . in a pinch. As long as no one's out to kill me for my horse."

Again, to Trent's right, Wolf whinnied and shook his head.

The newcomers looked at each other and laughed, then heeled their horses ahead. The rain funneled off their hat brims.

Trent tilted his head to his left. "Picket your horses over here. They'll be out of the rain."

"Thanks, mister," said the first man who'd spoken, as all three swung their mounts to Trent's left, their right. "Sure do appreciate it. A mite soggy out here and I spent the winter battlin' the flu!"

"You can leave your rifles in their scabbards," Trent ordered, sitting down by the fire, his back to the slot cave behind him.

When they'd loosened their saddle cinches, slipped their horses' bits, and tied their reins to roots humping up out of the ground, they fished coffee cups out of their possibles sacks and came over to the fire, lining up on the other side of it from Trent. They stared down at him as though they were waiting for him to pour. Trent tossed the leather swatch to the beefy, bearded man who'd spoken first.

"Help yourselves," he said. "Be careful—it's hot."

"Sure, sure," the beefy man said.

The other two sat down and crossed their legs, Indian style. The beefy man crouched to lift the smoking pot off the rock near the flames, where Trent had set it. Now he poured himself a cup of the brew, set the cup down before him, then handed the pot to the other two in turn so they could fill their own cups. He wasn't a damn butler, galldangit!

Trent smiled.

When the other two had filled their cups, sighing their eager anticipation—nothing made coffee taste better than a cold, wet day—the older gent, with the long gray hair, returned the pot to its rock. When they'd all settled in, legs crossed, and had taken their first tentative sips of the hot brew, Trent said, "Where you fellas headed?"

The older gent, who had a high-pitched, womanish tone, said, "Crazies. We're gonna shoot us a coupla elk and head to Livingston. The saloons there are payin' top dollar. Lots of miners and railroaders in there these days."

"And cattle buyers, too," said the younger man with the hawkish face, holding out his right hand and rubbing his thumb and index finger together.

"I see, I see," Trent said, and took another sip of the coffee he'd just refilled his cup with.

"Where you headed?" the beefy gent asked.

Trent shrugged as he held his cup on his knee. "Here an' there. I drift until I find something interesting enough to stop for."

"You ain't no drifter," said the older man, scowling at Trent beneath his shaggy gray brows. "Why, you own the Stray Dog in Big Creek!"

Trent chuckled dryly. "You got me, you got me. I just got tired of town and decided to drift for a few days, maybe bring a deer or two back to the saloon. Gets sort of tight in there. I have good folks workin' for me an' they can hold down the fort for a while."

The younger man said, "You got some nice-lookin' girls workin' there!"

Trent smiled.

"You like good-lookin' girls, do ya?" the older man asked.

"Who doesn't?"

They all shared cackling chuckles at that, like it was the funniest joke they'd ever heard.

"You must make purty good money," said the beefy gent, sitting cross-legged to the left of the other two. "Whenever we're in there, the place is filled to the rafters."

Here we go, Trent thought, right hand on his right thigh near the bone grips of the Russian holstered on his right hip.

"High overhead," he said, "but I do all right. Enough to get away now an' then."

"You got purty women workin' fer ya," said the older man, shuttling his gaze to the left where Wolf stood between the boulder and the dike wall, "and you sure ride a purty hoss!" He whistled.

The other two grinned as they stared at Trent, dropping their chins a little, threat touching their gazes as their hands slid slowly to the six-shooters strapped to their waists.

"Forget it, fellas," Trent warned, holding his coffee up in his left hand, splaying his hand across his upper right thigh. "Sure is an awful wet, dreary afternoon for dyin'."

The older man turned, staring at him over the dancing flames. "Oh, is it, now?"

"In case you hadn't noticed, mister," said the beefy man, whom Trent took to be the leader of this motley trio, "you're outgunned."

"I'm just sayin'," Trent said, returning the man's gaze with a hard one of his own.

All three stared at him.

Trent could almost hear the wheels turning in their dull but wanton brains.

Seconds passed. Nearly a minute. The fire cracked and popped, the breeze from outside hitting them sideways.

The man cut his eyes to both sides, subtly signaling the others.

His hand whipped to the Schofield .44 holstered for the cross draw on his left hip. The barrel had just cleared leather before Trent's Russian spoke loudly, smoke and orange flames stabbing from the barrel. The Russian spoke again, its deafening roar for two seconds drowning out the thunder and the hammering rain of the storm. The other two, whose gun barrels had also just cleared leather, flew backward through the rain curtain. They grunted as Trent's .44 bullets tore through their bellies.

They lay groaning, dying hard, as did their leader, who lay back down against the ground, the rain curtain splashing on his face. He looked up at Trent with pain-bright eyes, one hand on the bloody wound in his bulging belly.

"D-damn," he wheezed, and stretched his lips back from his teeth with a pain spasm. "You're . . . fast . . . fer a saloon owner."

To Trent's right, Wolf whinnied and pawed the ground excitedly. The stallion hadn't seen action like this in a long time. He was ready to shed some stable green, though Trent had taken the horse out often for hard runs, to keep him trim and to satisfy his wild spirit. Trent had to admit he felt the same way. Though he was able to bust some heads or fill rowdy men with buckshot now and then, the saloon life was too confining.

Suddenly he was ready to hit the trail to Three Forks again.

The trail to whatever trouble his father had waiting for him.

Trent raised a knee, cocked the Russian, rested his forearm atop his knee, and aimed down the barrel at the forehead of the beefy man.

"Oh, God," the man said, wincing and closing his eyes. "Oh, God . . ."

"Just let me ask you this," Trent said, looking at the other two, holding in their guts over the holes in their bellies. "Was it worth it?"

The younger man swallowed as he stared back at Trent. "Mister . . . we . . . we didn't expect you to be that fast. You're just a . . . a . . . *apron*!"

Trent's Russian roared, the bullet drilling a puckered blue hole in the beefy man's forehead, slamming his head back hard against the ground.

Trent shifted the Russian slightly. The older man screamed. The scream was cut off by the Russian's roar.

"No!" bellowed the younger man.

Trent finished him as well.

"Oh, yes," Trent said. "You play poker, you gotta be ready to lose."

All three lay dead, half in and half out of the curtain of rain.

Trent never carried an empty gun. Old habit. He replaced the spent shells in the Russian with live ones from his cartridge belt, holstered the hogleg, and dragged the dead vermin out, away from his camp, not wanting to attract four-legged interlopers.

Then he came back, sat down by his fire, and freshened his coffee cup, causing the fragrant steam to rise. He rested back on an elbow. He could still smell the cordite from the Russian's blasts.

He smiled.

He might have been cooped up in a saloon for the past five years, but he still had it.

And . . .

Yeah, it's nice to be back in the high-an'-rocky country again.

He spent the rainy night by the fire.

He cooked beans and fatback from his possibles bag, brewed another pot of coffee, and washed the beans and fatback down with the fresh mud. The rain slowed gradually and then died; the thunder continued for a while, but grew quieter as the storm pushed on toward where he was headed, the Bitterroot Mountains and the Idaho Territory beyond.

Once you leave the southern Bitterroots, you climb a divide and then, in a broad valley below, you see the Valley of the Three Forks, the three forks of the Wolf River sort of cradling the town of Three Forks—a motley, sprawling bastion—cabins, houses, a broad main street sheathed in one-, two-, and three-story business buildings of log, ripped wood, and brick.

Corrals and privies and lumberyards arranged with no planning, for the town had been founded by miners, prospectors, and ranchers up from Texas—Trent's own grandfather had hazed a herd of longhorns up from Texas just after the brunt of the Indian wars, along with Trent's father, who'd been in his late thirties at the time. Trent's grandfather had been found hanging from a stout pine branch. No one knew exactly who had hanged him, but it had probably been Donovan's men.

Likely, men from their rival ranch owned by another Texan—"Big Ike" Donovan. The surly frontiersman hated the Triple T, as the Triple T hated the Circle Double D, Donovan's spread. Each was finding their own men dead on their land, and they attributed those deaths to each other's men.

Also, each man was greedy—land hungry, as most ranchers were. They wanted the other's land. But even beyond that, they just plain lived too close together. Neighbors just made enemies, that's all. Familiarity coupled with monetary interests had probably bred trouble back when men were dancing around leaping fires between notch caves to the drumming of tom-toms.

Trent's grandfather had been found dead on Circle Double D graze, where he'd probably gone to haze back Triple T beef that had strayed. Cows did not recognize property lines. Texans didn't either when they could get by with it. No Wolf Mountain Texan, neither Ben Trent nor Big Ike Donovan, would resort to the savagery of Glidden wire, or "barb wire," in the frontier parlance.

They would resort to the savagery of gunning men down when found outside their own ranches' boundaries, but that was just the cost of doing business in the beef industry. At least, unlike with barbed wire, no horses or cattle were injured, no money lost.

The old man, Trent's grandfather, had shot and hanged many men himself. On the day he was killed, he'd likely run across one or two of Donovan's men he'd run afoul of in the past. They'd likely had words. Zeke Trent had been a man of few words, but he was always crossways with somebody. His killers on that day had likely decided to give him a taste of his own medicine. He'd been shot through the shoulder and then strung up. He'd been hanging from that ponderosa for two days before Logan's brother, Dev, and several Triple T men had found him, looking no better for what the birds had done to his face.

Devon Trent had always vowed revenge. He himself had hanged . . . and still did hang . . . every rustler he and his men came across, hoping that one of those he hanged was the one—or one of the gang—who'd hanged his grandfather. No way of knowing for sure. Rustlers were a tight-lipped bunch. They knew if they weren't, they'd likely get a bullet in the back from one of their own.

Having hunted as a boy, and then as a young man, with his father, his father's longtime foreman, Clancy Reed, now deceased, and his older brother, Devon, Trent knew the Bitterroots as well as he knew his own Wolf Mountain Ranch headquarters and the Wolf Mountains, in the foothills of which the ranch sat. He automatically followed one canyon after another into the range's higher reaches, pausing at certain places to remember the deer, elk, moose, and even the several grizzlies they'd shot. For two nights, he camped in their favorite camping spots, usually under the cover of large spruces and boulders and towering stone walls that flamed to spectacular life just before the sun fell in the west. Then as it continued to drop, taking its light with it, he watched the slowly dimming color changes at the tops of those majestic peaks.

In the Bitterroots, the past came alive.

Not the dark one he'd left behind when he'd abandoned Idaho to become anonymous in Montana, but the one with Dev shouting with unabashed joy when he'd pulled a large, fat golden trout out of No-Name Creek. Logan had heard the heavy footsteps behind him and then smelled the sickly sweet stench of some wild animal, just before he'd turned to see a mammoth bull grizzly rise up behind him and bugle a gut-wrenching cry. The feeling of being so certain he was about to die turned his spine to jelly.

Then, hearing the cracking reports of two large-caliber rifles issuing from the rocks on both sides of him, as well as the grizzly's last roar as he fell forward, Logan stumbled backward, tripping over his own feet. He fell just seconds before the grizzly had fallen, so the griz's big head, heavy as a small boulder, landed on his chest, slamming the breath out of him.

The grinning Devon, blond, muscular, and devilishly handsome, laughed down at his younger brother and said, "Kid, you owe me an' the old man a few shots of red-eye."

Laughing and cocking a fresh round into his Sharps Big Fifty, Ben Trent had emerged from the rocks, his high-crowned black Stetson on his head, which was nearly as big and square as that of the bear. "He's too young to drink!" the eldest Trent had admonished his oldest son.

"Not no more he's not," Devon had returned. "When you get that close to death, you're all grown up and ready to take on the world"—he'd winked at his younger brother—"including a saloon and a brothel or two!"

Chapter 4

The incident with the bull griz had been a terrifying experience, but one Trent smiled at now as he continued riding down the south side of the mountains, following a steeply sloping canyon that became a torrent of snowmelt in the spring. To know a fear like that jolted a person out of any dolor that he might have, taking life for granted, and propelled him into the heart and soul of life itself. Devon had made sure of it, soon taking Trent into Three Forks and introducing him to the "ladies" of the most notorious parlor house in town.

As old as he was now, Trent still blushed at the memory of that night.

After his second chilly night high in the Bitterroots, he rose, shivering and stepping into his boots, pulling on his buckskin mackinaw, and building up his fire for coffee and to reheat his beans and fatback of the night before. He, his father, and his brother had camped in this very place, in a shallow canyon between high, craggy peaks. They'd stayed awake listening to the bugling of the elk in the higher reaches. Now he ate his breakfast, drank his coffee, gathered his gear, secured it on Wolf's back, mounted up, and headed off on the final stretch of his ride home.

His ride back to trouble, most likely.

He found that even more likely as he was riding through a canyon in the lower southern mountains and heard the telltale screech of a bullet, felt the curl of warm air off his right ear and the loud *thunk* as the bullet plowed into a stone wall behind him and on his left. He'd been anticipating this, so he reached down quickly to shuck his Yellowboy from its scabbard and leaped out of the saddle before slapping Wolf's hip, sending the stallion galloping, buck-kicking angrily, on up the trail to safety.

As another bullet screeched toward him to hammer the same stone wall as the first, he ran crouching to the canyon's western wall, to his right. He pressed his shoulder to the wall as the thunder of the rifle that had fired the second bullet reached his ears. There was a notch in the wall to his right. He ran to it, climbed a few rocks, doffed his hat, and peered up the forested western ridge from which the two shots had come.

Another bullet caromed toward him to slam into the lip of the canyon inches from his head. As the ripping report of the rifle echoed around the ridges, he saw the puff of powder smoke hanging on the thin, still air. He cocked and raised the Yellowboy, pressing the butt plate to his right shoulder. He aimed just beneath the wafting powder smoke and squeezed the trigger.

The Winchester leaped and roared in his hands.

He saw where his round kicked up sand and gravel from the top of a shelflike ridge bulging out from the side of the pine-clad ridge a hundred yards away. He didn't think he'd hit his assailant, but the man or men had to know he was going to give it back as good as he received it.

Rage burned in him.

He hated bushwhackers.

Who was this bunch? More greedy varmints after his horse, his saddlebags, and his prized Winchester? Something . . . old instinct . . . told him no. This was another set entirely. He was only about twenty miles from Three Forks, sitting at the base of the Wolf Mountains, which were a southwestern offshoot of the Bitterroots. South of there was all barren ranch country, but with the ermine-tipped peaks of several separate mountain ranges ensconcing it in a complete circle, from horizon to horizon.

Ranch country.

His father's own ranch sat in the foothills of the Wolf Mountains, just west of the town of Three Forks surrounded by its forking rivers and grassy meadows, a playground for the beaver, deer, elk, and the occasional bear wandering through to pause to fish for succulent trout and eat the rich berries that grew along the banks of the forks.

Could someone not want him to return home?

The idea was solidifying in his mind when another bullet came buzzing over his head to slam into the wall of the canyon behind him.

He had to find out who was after him and why. They needed to die—so they couldn't try it again.

He turned away from the notch, set his hat on his head, and ran back down the canyon in the direction from which he'd come. He'd seen another break in the canyon wall a hundred yards away. He reached it, climbed rocks up through it, and ran crouching into the pine and fir forest. He ran straight up the mountain, a steep climb, especially for a man who'd been confined mainly indoors for the past five years. When he gained the top of the mountain, he stopped, crouched, placed his hands on his knees, and took several deep drafts of the cool mountain air.

His head ached and his ears rang.

He was not accustomed to the altitude anymore, either.

"Are you a man or a mouse?" he asked himself, breathless, repeating his father's old saw when either of his boys showed weakness. "Keep going, you damn tinhorn!"

He straightened, held the Yellowboy low in his right hand, and ran across the top of the wooded ridge toward the south. He ran for maybe a hundred yards when, out of breath once more, he stopped and bent forward again to catch his breath. The move saved him from getting his head blown off.

The bullet screeched through the air where his head had been an eye blink before.

Trent straightened instantly and racked a live round into the Yellowboy's action. The man who'd fired the shots was twenty feet away, moving up the mountain through the pines on his left; he was angrily stretching his lips back from his teeth. Trent fired straight out from his right hip, once . . . twice . . . three times. The man cursed, groaned, dropped his own weapon, fell, and rolled a good twenty feet down the slope before slamming up against the base of a large boulder.

Trent looked around.

More movement in the forest below him. Another man with a rifle appeared, lifting a pine branch and ducking under it. His gaze landed on Trent and he jerked his rifle up. He fired an errant round and ejected the spent cartridge, but before he could get off another shot, Trent drilled two rounds into him, sending him flying backward down the slope. In the corner of his right eye, Trent spied movement downslope and on his right. He dove to his right and rolled up behind a broad-boled spruce just as a bullet blasted into the side of it, spraying bark and wood slivers in all directions.

Trent snaked his Yellowboy around the right side of the spruce trunk, then saw the rifle, face, and hatted head of a man lying behind a fallen pine. Trent fired three quick shots, blowing the man's hat off. The man's head jerked back. He'd caught a bullet in his forehead. He flopped backward and rolled, dead before he ended up against a stout aspen.

Trent drew his head back behind his covering spruce once more, holding the Yellowboy straight up and down before him. He winced, expecting another bullet. When he'd fired that last shot through the forehead of the man who'd fired from behind the downed pine, he spied more movement in the woods a little farther down the slope, a man running from one covering tree to another.

Trent waited for another bullet.

None came.

An angry squirrel chittered.

The breeze made a soft whispering noise, scratching limbs together.

Those were the only sounds.

Then another sound came to Trent's ears.

The distant rataplan of galloping hooves. They dwindled quickly to silence.

There'd been a fourth dry-gulcher. He'd fled. Heading in the direction of Three Forks.

Trent walked down the slope and stared at the third man he'd killed. Open, sightless eyes gazed up at him. His heart quickened. A Donovan rider. Big Ike Donovan was the father of the man Trent had been wrongly accused of killing more than five years ago, which was the fuse that had set off the powder keg his life had become after that. So it was back, the old trouble. Big Ike had somehow known Trent would be returning to Three Forks and had intended to literally cut him off at the pass.

Old grievances died hard.

Trent checked out the second man he'd shot.

Another Donovan Circle Double D rider.

Trent cursed.

He approached and kicked over the first man he'd shot and who had rolled up belly down against the boulder. When he saw the face staring up at him, eyes and mouth still wide with horror, Trent's knees turned to mud. The mountain pitched around him until he thought he'd pass out.

The face staring up at him was another Donovan son.

Pete Donovan, Big Ike's oldest boy.

* * *

Trent found the dry-gulchers' horses tethered to branches on the back side of the mountain. He led the three remaining mounts up the mountain, lifted their dead riders over their saddles, tied the bodies ankle to wrist under the horses' bellies, then gave each mount a slap with the rear stock of his Yellowboy.

They galloped off down the mountain in the same direction the fourth man had galloped.

They'd see their riders home.

To the Donovan Circle Double D.

That's where they all were from. Trent had recognized each man, and the brands burned into the horses' hips corroborated his knowledge that Big Ike himself had sent these men, including his oldest son, to interrupt Trent's return to Three Forks and his family's Triple T Ranch. Big Ike wanted him dead.

Not for the first time.

But how had he known he'd be coming?

As Trent whistled for his own horse, heavy brows mantled his dark eyes. Even darker now since he'd left Big Creek. The trouble he was riding into was even more massive than he'd imagined. It was so large and dark that even Big Ike knew about it and knew that Trent would be lured back to it.

Movement in the forest, below where Trent stood atop the ridge. A horse snorted. Shod hooves thudded. Wolf climbed the ridge to him, reins trailing along the ground. The roan came up to Trent and lowered his head, sniffing his rider as though to make sure he was alive.

"I'm still standing, boy," he said, running his hand down the roan's long snout. "Got through that rough patch, but I got me a feelin' there's gonna be plenty more as long as Big Ike believes I killed Buck."

Wolf blew, shook his head.

"I know, I know," Trent said, tightening the horse's saddle cinch. "But that's how things are stacking up. In the old way."

He had to ride out to the Triple T and talk to his father.

He had to find out why he'd been summoned. He didn't like all the signs. Didn't even want to think about what it was all about. But he'd find out by the end of the day. And then his life was going to change once more in a very big way.

Darkness consumed him as he stepped into the leather, then booted the roan down the mountain. He left the mountains an hour later and crossed the last broad valley, mounting the last dike and stopping to stare down at Three Forks in the elk meadow below. Not much had changed since he'd been gone. The rustic town sat between the tines of the Valley of the Three Forks, with the Wolf River sliding down out of the bastion of the Wolf Mountains to the southwest. His family's ranch was a third of the way up those sprawling mountains, under the white tips of the craggy, higher ridges. At least, what remained of his family—his mother long since gone delivering his youngest brother, who had died then, too.

Smoke unfurled from the chimneys of the cabins and business buildings of Three Forks, ensconced in pines, firs, and spruces. Wagons entered and left the town by the two trails giving access to it. Beyond the town, to the southwest, was the placid jewel of Elk Lake, nestled in foothills and surrounded by evergreen forest and gray granite crags the mountain goats liked to climb. A great fishing lake. Trent and Dev had pulled many trout out of there, simply cleaning them and cooking them whole in a cast-iron skillet on a hot fire, taking swigs from a bottle of Spanish brandy they'd stolen from their father's study.

Smiling at the memory—all the memories of his life converged here, the good ones and the bad ones—he rode into town after traversing the wooden bridges of the Wolf River forks and reined up at the small log jailhouse on the broad street's right side. The wooden sign jutting into the street read only JAIL, just as it had when Trent had left five years ago in shame. The letters were a little more faded now, the windows of the building a little more opaque with time. As he reined up at one of the two hitchracks fronting the place, the office's rickety front door opened and a black cat ran out and across the porch, meowing.

It ran down the three porch steps and sat at their base, staring up at Trent, meowing some more.

"Thunder!" Trent said, smiling. "Glad to see you're still kickin'. It's been a while!"

Meow. Meow.

Trent swung down from the saddle, picked up the long, sleek black cat, and cradled him in his arms.

Meow.

"Did you miss me?"

"He's about the only one who has," a man's voice answered for him.

With the cat squirming in his arms, thrusting its paws up toward Trent's face, Trent looked up to see his old boss, Sheriff Dan True, standing at the top of the steps, staring down at him, a loosely rolled quirley between his lips, a look of disgust on his mustached face.

"Don't doubt it a bit," Trent said.

True was in his sixties, ready to retire, with a face like a mountain crag and a hard belly bulging out from his cracked brown leather vest, a five-pointed star pinned to his shirt. Like most frontier lawmen, he'd been a cattleman first. True had been a stage driver, shotgun messenger, and town mayor. He was the sort of man who died the same day he was buried, with little fanfare.

"What am I doin' here, Dan?" Trent asked, still cradling the cat in his arms, bouncing him lightly. They were old friends.

"You talk to your father about that," True said, drawing on the cigarette and blowing the smoke out his nose.

"I killed Pete Donovan." He just blurted it out, seeing no reason for preamble.

True stared at him, drawing on the quirley between his lips. His eyes darkened as though a lamp behind them were turned down.

"So it's already started," he said finally.

"What is it?" Trent asked. "What's started?"

"Hell has started."

"What started it? Pa called me home, but he didn't say why."

"You talk to him." True walked in his heavy way toward the jail office door. He glanced at Trent over his shoulder. "You know I always loved you like a son. But you stay out of town. I don't want your trouble here . . . and I don't want to watch you die."

He went inside and closed the door.

Trent stood holding the cat and staring at the lodge's closed door.

His heart thudded. His guts rolled in his belly.

He reached up and set Thunder on the jailhouse porch.

"Later, good fella. Keep the mice runnin'."

The cat arched his tail and meowed at him. He was likely the only being that was happy to see him in these parts. Trent doubted his father would be. But Ben needed him.

Why?

He didn't want to think about it.

He swung up onto Wolf's back and continued toward the eastern end of town. Passing the three-story adobe-brick saloon and hurdy-gurdy house, the Yellow Flower, he stopped abruptly. The saloon's owner stood leaning against the front of the building to the right of the batwings, one foot resting up against the wall, smoking a black cigarillo, regarding him a little inquiringly through the smoke wreathing her lovely, dark-eyed face.

Clarita Ortiz.

She blew out a smoke plume and said in her husky, sexy, Spanish-accented voice, "Nothing to say to me, Logan?"

He studied her for a time, feeling the old pull of her. He shook his head finally, said, "Don't see the point," then booted Wolf on down the street to the east and then swung west and south toward the darkening mountains, long shadows spreading over the Valley of the Three Forks and the pines and spruces lining them.

An hour later, after traversing several creeks that fed into the Wolf River, and climbing through pine-enshrouded canyons, he trotted into the Wolf Mountain Ranch surrounded by forest with the big log house to the right, the barns, stables, corrals and other outbuildings to his left.

He pulled up in front of the three-story house and sat staring at it, dread climbing up and down his spine.

"Logan!" a man yelled behind him.

He turned to see his father's bunkhouse cook, Morgan McCallister, jog toward him, a dirty white apron wrapped around his ample waist. "Figured I'd see you again before my allotment was up!" He stopped beside Wolf and stared through blue eyes set in a round, pale, fleshy, middle-aged face. "Just didn't want it to be like this."

Morgan had always worked in the bunkhouse and in the chuck wagon during roundups. He hunted the game he liked to cook . . . and eat. Trent's father had had a few cooks and housekeepers up at the lodge after his wife had passed. The man who currently ran the house was a Lakota Sioux named Lone Dog, who'd also taken on the chore of keeping boisterous young men in line—in Lone Dog's customarily laconic way, of course.

Now, Morgan McCallister's broad face, with gray muttonchops and chin whiskers, was cast in sadness.

"Like what?" Trent asked.

When the portly cook only lowered his head and shook it, Trent asked again, "Like what, Morg? What's happened?"

A man's familiar throaty voice rose from the porch above Trent. "Your brother's dead."

Chapter 5

Jake Coffee galloped hell for leather down the last slopes of the southern Bitterroots. He crossed the broad, flat-bottomed valley between the Bitterroots and the lower stretches of the Wolf Mountains.

He followed a two-track, winding trail into the sierra and after a half hour's ride from the valley floor, he swung right onto a secondary trail, which took him through more evergreen forest, under the Circle Double D portal, and into the ranch yard itself. There weren't many men in the headquarters this time of the day. Most were out moving the herds from one part of the range to another and brush-popping calves and their lowing mothers from deep thickets, but those that were here swung their heads to Coffee, regarding him expectantly.

They likely hadn't officially known the task Coffee and his now-deceased compatriots had been assigned. But they knew, all right.

Cards were never held too close to the chest in a ranch bunkhouse. Information oozed through pores.

Coffee checked the black-and-white pinto down at the hitchrack fronting the ranch's big main lodge. He started up the porch steps, but stopped when the front door opened and Big Ike Donovan himself stepped into the doorway—a gray-headed large man with thick, gray muttonchops framing his darkly tanned, craggy face. He wore a black string tie over a burgundy corduroy shirt. His blue eyes were dark, fateful. He tossed his head back to indicate the foyer behind him and said, "Come on."

He turned and disappeared inside the lodge, which was age-silvered and three stories tall, added onto several years after Big Ike had first settled here thirty years ago, meaning to raise a whole passel of kids. He and his beloved wife had had time for only three. Donovan had married a local woman, the daughter of a Lutheran minister. Soon after a buggy accident, Leona Donovan had passed away from her injuries, leaving behind the children and a bereft husband.

With his heart hammering, Coffee felt his feet grow leaden. He suddenly wished he hadn't come here but had galloped on out of the county to start a life elsewhere. The news he was about to deliver to Mr. Donovan was tragic. The man, who'd already lost one son, was not going to take well the news of having lost another one. And Jake Coffee was the man who was going to share that news.

Coffee crossed the porch, opened the stout oak door, and stepped into the lodge's shadowy foyer. He started ahead, but stopped when a woman's voice, issuing from the kitchen on his left, stopped him.

"What is it, Jake?" Megan Donovan asked him. "What happened?"

The beautiful woman was setting plates down on the kitchen table, while a middle-aged, always somber Mexican maid, wearing a dark dress and stirring a steaming pot on the range, looked over her shoulder at him. Megan Donovan wore her customary blue jeans, wool shirt, suspenders, and riding boots. She always dressed like a man, but she was all woman—bosomy, chestnut-haired, and cameo-faced, with slate-gray eyes. She worked in the house, read books in her room, and played the piano.

But her real home was atop a fine thoroughbred.

Coffee was in love with her. But then, what man who'd ever met her was not in love with Megan Donovan? He'd once asked her to dance at her birthday party, here at the Double D, and was almost bullwhipped by her father.

"Jake," Megan said now, setting the last plate down and walking around the table toward him, her eyes wide with concern. "What happened?"

He removed his hat, held it in both hands.

"Tell me!" she commanded.

All Coffee could say was, "I . . . I . . . gotta talk to your pa."

Megan stopped before him, dug her fingers into his right forearm, and stared up at him with those mysterious gray eyes that contrasted almost bewitchingly with her hair. "Did he send men out after Logan Trent?"

"Ah, heck, I can't—"

"He knew he'd come. He sent men to cut him off, didn't he?"

"Miss Megan, please . . ."

She dug her fingers deeper into his forearm. "Coffee, you tell me!"

"Miss Megan . . ."

"Where's Pete?"

Coffee just looked at her, his mind in agony.

"Oh, God!" she said, raising her hands to her head. "It's all starting again!"

"I . . . I have to talk to your pa."

The cowhand continued through the foyer, then through a parlor where a fire snapped in a hearth, and then through an open doorway and into Big Ike Donovan's small but comfortable office, with its wooden shelves of books and the rancher's oak desk, behind which the big, regal man sat, lighting a stout cigar, turning it in his mouth, the match flame leaping and falling, the smoke thickly wreathing his weathered face.

A glass of Irish whiskey and a decanter sat on the desk to his right. The desk was cluttered with papers and account books and books about cattle and animal husbandry and even a few about Rocky Mountain elk.

Big Ike had been an avid hunter all his life.

Megan rarely saw him reading anymore, however. Like the rest of the man, his eyes were going.

He'd hired Coffee because Jake had once been a Texas gunfighter. He was fast, but now, working for a man like Big Ike, his confidence was low. No man could stack up to a man like Big Ike Donovan, even now in his later years. Not even Jake Coffee, who'd come here with a big shootist's reputation, having killed six men in saloons, bunkhouses, and brothels around the Texas Panhandle.

But then, Coffee wasn't as young as he used to be, either.

Squeezing his hat in his hand, kneading the brim, Coffee walked into Big Ike's office and stopped at the rancher's desk, behind which another fire popped and crackled, adding its fragrance of burning pine to that of the man's Cuban cigar.

The rancher blew out his match, set it in the ashtray before him, and sank into his high-backed leather chair. "Is he dead?"

Coffee hemmed and hawed, leaning forward on the toes of his boots, a little afraid he'd lose his balance and smash his head on Big Ike's desk.

"Oh, I don't mean Trent. I can tell by your expression he's fit as a fiddle. I mean my oldest boy. Pete." Big Ike pinned Coffee with a bright, hard gaze. "Is he dead?"

Coffee looked down at his hat, which he was mangling now. "Uh . . ."

"The others?"

"Uh . . ."

"They're dead, too," Donovan said darkly, and sipped his whiskey, which smelled like damp earth and peat. Suddenly a glimmer of emotion shone in his eyes. He sat in his chair, the fire crackling and popping behind him. "Pete . . . my oldest. Thought he could take him . . . Trent. But the man's savvy. He's been hunted. It makes a man savvy. . . . He knows how to ride . . . how to shoot from the saddle."

"Uh, Mr. Donovan . . . I sure am sorry."

Big Ike scowled severely, menacingly. "Why are you here?"

"What's that?"

"How did *you* make it?"

Coffee's hands were almost tearing the brim of his hat. "Well, uh . . . I, uh . . . see the . . . the others were dead . . . so quick. Trent . . . he's *fast*! An' he don't miss!"

"You ran."

"S-s-sir?"

"You ran."

"Well, I, uh . . . I didn't see . . . see no way that I—"

"You used to be a man, Coffee. What the hell happened to you?"

Coffee looked at his boss leaning back in his chair, cigar in one hand, drink in the other. Yes, what had happened? Working for a man like Big Ike was no small thing. A man who expected every ounce from him, sending him up against rustlers and nesters of every stripe. A man who harbored a rage ever since his youngest son had been killed by Logan Trent in Three Forks.

Now that rage would double in size.

Coffee had looked death in the eye.

And he'd run.

"I figured . . . best live . . . best live to fight another . . . day. I knew you'd want . . . you'd want to know what . . . what happened, Mr. Donovan."

"You ran."

"Wh-what's that?"

"You ran," came a woman's voice from the office's open doorway.

Both Coffee and Donovan turned to see Megan Donovan standing there. Her jaws were hard, her beautiful cheeks flushed, eyes wide with fury. Her long hair was pulled back behind her head. It hung straight down her slender back.

Coffee's heart thundered in his chest. "I didn't see . . . I didn't see no reason . . . Trent, he's . . ." He shook his head, unable to find the right word to describe the man who'd made hell out of Coffee's day.

"He's a man," Megan said. "And you're a mouse."

Her right hand rose. A Colt .44 bristled in it. She aimed it at Coffee, who had turned to her and stumbled backward, holding his hat against his chest.

"No! No! Now . . . you *wait*, Miss Meg—"

The .44 leaped in the young woman's hand, thundering, smoke and flames stabbing from the barrel. Coffee yelped and fell against an armchair behind him, knocking it over as he grimaced and grunted once more, then slid sideways to the floor, dead.

Megan Donovan glanced at her father. Big Ike stared up at her from his chair.

Megan lowered the smoking .44.

"Sorry to interrupt, Pa," she said.

She turned and walked away.

Upstairs, a baby cried.

"*Your brother's dead.*" echoed in Trent's head after his father had swung around and retreated into the three-story log lodge in which Trent had grown up with his brother, Devon.

His beloved brother, Devon.

Trent could hear his brother's wicked laughter in his head beneath the grim, harsh words of his father: "*Your brother's dead.*"

He swung out of the saddle and turned to the bunkhouse cook standing before him, tears running down the oldster's fleshy face.

Trent pulled his saddlebags and possibles sack off the roan's back, draped the bags over his shoulder, and shucked his rifle from its scabbard. "What happened, Morg?"

The cook just took Trent's reins, shook his head, then led the roan down the slope toward the stable on the other side of the yard.

Deeply frustrated, as well as heartbroken, Trent climbed the porch steps, crossed the porch, and pushed through the two double doors into the house. The doors opened onto a large great room, where a fire crackled in the hearth. He removed his hat—Trent's mother had taught him to remove his hat immediately upon entering the house from a very early age. She was deceased, as was his youngest brother, but sometimes he heard her soothing, motherly voice as though she were only a few feet away from him.

Trent walked across the great room and into the kitchen.

His father sat at the wooden table flanked by benches on each side. This is where the family had always eaten, leaving the dining room for special occasions with guests. They'd had many guests over the years, mostly wealthy men from the East who were in Trent's father's orbit. Trent could smell a roast in the oven.

Ben Trent, old and haggard, but still owning a Western mountain virility about him, was just then pouring from a bottle of Scotch into a big stone mug in which rich black coffee steamed. Another stone mug sat on the opposite side of the long table from him, steam curling into the air above it.

"Sit down," Ben said, and slid the bottle toward the steaming mug opposite him.

Logan crossed woodenly to the bench opposite his father. He set his hat down on the table and sank onto the bench.

He leaned forward, elbows on the table, his left hand closed over his right fist. "Pa, what happened?"

Ben nudged the bottle a little closer to Logan's coffee mug.

Anger blasted through Logan. "I don't want coffee! I don't want Scotch. I want—"

His father blinked once, slowly, and nudged the Scotch bottle even closer to his son's mug.

Logan gave a caustic grunt and closed his hand around the

bottle's neck. He froze when he heard the rasp of footsteps and saw Devon's wife, Rachel, clad in a robe, move up to the range and pour a cup of coffee. She came over to the table, looked at Logan blankly, her face drawn and pale and framed by her curly, shoulder-length brown hair, reached for the bottle, and added a good portion of Scotch to her own steaming brew. She set the bottle back down in front of Logan, gave him that blank, bleak look once more, then shuffled in her slippered feet out of the kitchen.

Seconds later, he heard the soft creak of his sister-in-law climbing the stairs.

He turned to his father. "Why's she here?"

"Doesn't like being alone." Ben Trent tapped his temple. "Nightmares."

Rachel and Devon had shared a cabin a hundred yards behind the main house of the Triple T. It had been Logan's grandfather's original cabin, when he'd settled here. When Devon had married Rachel, he had added onto the crude log shack and improved it with his own busy, capable hands.

Devon could do anything. He'd always been that way. Shoe horses, build tree houses. Logan had worshipped him.

He didn't even mind when Devon had beat him up just for fun, laughing.

Logan convulsed with a sob that just burst out of him. He splashed Scotch into his mug, then leaned over the table and asked, "What happened?"

Calmly, Ben said, "Just like with your grandfather, they shot him on Circle Double D range."

Logan sat back with his lower jaw hanging.

"There it is, boy."

"Did they hang him . . . like they did Grandpa?"

Ben shook his head. "That would've been too obvious—now, wouldn't it?"

Again, Logan leaned across the table. "*Who?* Was it him—Big Ike?"

Ben shook his head. He sipped his coffee, laced with Scotch, set the mug back down, and said, "I don't know. That's why I called you home. I want you to find out who did it and bring me their heads on a platter!"

Chapter 6

Logan sipped his hot, steaming, Scotch-laced brew. As he did, and took another and yet another sip, he realized why his father had been so insistent. It soothed him, however much he could be soothed in the wake of learning of his brother's passing.

No.

Of his brother's *murder*.

He took another sip and said, "What happened, Pa?"

"Spring branding. The herds were restless. The men got separated. Dev went off alone after a couple of cow-calf pairs. When he didn't return to the corral, Ed Ringo and a few others rode off looking for him."

Ben took a deep pull off his stone mug.

His voice quavered as he said, "They found him. Shot twice." Ben took another gulp from his whiskey-laced coffee.

"Front or back?"

"Back and belly."

"He died slow, then. Hard." Logan's shoulders slumped. "Those SOBs . . ."

After a time, fighting back sobs, rage burning in him like a wildfire, he looked up at his father, who was sitting stiff and ashen on the other side of the table.

"Ringo and I rode over there, powwowed with Big Ike."

"You don't think he did it or had it done."

Ben shook his head. "Big Ike knows the kind of trouble that would erupt, him killin' my boy."

"Like the one that almost erupted when he thought I killed his."

"It didn't. He knew better."

"I just shot another one of his."

Ben blinked, stared blankly at his son.

"Big Ike must have known you'd send for me. He sent out men to kill me . . . including his son, Pete."

"Go to hell!" Ben rumbled.

"That's what happened, Pa. Big Ike thinks I killed Buck. He knew you'd send for me to find out who killed Dev. Which means—"

"Donovan likely killed Dev to lure you home . . . for a bullet."

Logan said, "That old bastard probably hasn't slept in five and a half years, just lays there, wanting me dead. But now, his oldest boy is dead, so it came up to bite him in the—"

Ben rose from his bench, leaned forward, and planted his fists on the table. "Do you know what this means?"

"I knew what it meant when I kicked Pete over and saw his dead eyes staring up at me."

"There will be war."

"Uh-huh."

"I wish you hadn't had to kill Pete."

"If I hadn't, I wouldn't be sitting here."

"To think Big Ike and I once were friends," Ben said, and took another sip of his coffee. He looked at his son from beneath his shaggy, gray brows. "Think you can?"

"Think we can hold him off?"

The elder Trent nodded.

"We have to."

Ben nodded and sat back down on his bench. Collapsed into it, more like.

He looked much older than he did the last time Logan saw him five years ago. Older and worn out, Devon's death was the final stab. Logan wasn't sure Ben could outlast this—the death of his oldest boy. As well as the possibility of a war between the Triple T and Donovan's Circle Double D. It was too much for the thirty-four-year-old, much less a man in his early seventies, without a single easy year behind him.

How did he keep going, Logan wanted to know.

When he finished his coffee, he set his hat on his head and walked over to where he'd put his saddlebags, rifle, and possibles bag.

"Where you goin'?" his father asked.

He slid his saddlebags over his left shoulder. "Think I best stay in town. I'll just attract trouble here."

His father shook his head over the cup he held against his chin. "Trouble's already here." He slid his rheumy gaze to his son. "I need at least one boy at home. I'll be dead soon. You're going to inherit this ranch. You resolve the problem—find out who killed Buck—so we can live here in peace."

"Big Ike thinks I killed two of his boys. I can try to convince him otherwise about Buck, but I doubt it. I'll ride over there, see if we can resolve it. He sent Pete out to kill me. He knows I had to defend myself. All I can do is try. And try to find out who killed Buck."

A pipe dream, Logan thought.

The old man was mad. No point in pressing the issue, though.

"All right," Ben said.

"Lone Dog's cookin' steaks for supper. With beans. Simple cowboy meal," Ben added as Logan started up the creaky stairs.

Lone Dog lived in a shack east of the house and often sat up late and danced and sang and played his drums. He lived with the grief that the shining old times were gone. But, man, could that old Indian cook.

Logan climbed the stairs to his old room.

Everything appeared just as he'd left it.

He unpacked his saddlebags, then sat on the edge of the bed, holding his head in his hands. His mind was awhirl. Dev was dead. How could the earth keep spinning? How could he keep living? He thought about the man or men who'd shot his brother, and he dug his knuckles into his temples and tapped his booted feet on the floor.

A knock sounded on the door. "Logan?" Rachel said softly on the other side of the panel.

He lowered his hands and lifted his head. "Come in, Rachel."

The door opened. His brother's widow came in—*widow*, Jesus!—still dressed in her robe, her curly brown hair down. She looked as though she hadn't slept in days. A tall, quiet young woman, five years Devon's junior. She'd come to Three Forks to teach school. Devon had met her at a school board meeting, and two weeks later, they were married and living here in Ben's lodge until Devon could finish improving the outlying cabin.

They'd tried to have kids, but for whatever reason, Rachel couldn't get pregnant. Logan thought it was probably due to Devon having been a sickly child, though doctors had never figured out the culprit. In his teenage years, however, he'd blossomed into a strapping young man and held sway over Logan, who looked up to him as though he were a god. No one could ride or rope the way Devon had. Logan was the horse breaker—Devon had called him the "horse charmer"—so at least he had that. Most of the horses in the Trent remuda had been broken—gentled, rather—by Logan. He'd often slept in the stable with them. He far preferred horses over people.

Except his older brother, that was.

And now Devon was dead, and Logan felt wretched.

He'd never felt less spirit in his life.

He was probably the reason Devon was killed. They—whoever they were—hadn't been able to kill Logan before he'd fled the Wolf Mountains and Three Forks—so they'd killed Devon instead. He knew there was a good chance Big Ike had ordered Devon killed to avenge Buck.

He just needed proof.

He couldn't be wrong.

If Big Ike had killed Devon, Big Ike would die slowly, bellowing, begging for mercy.

Rachel closed the bedroom door. She had an unlabeled bottle in her hand. She crossed to a small table under a window to the left of the bed. She raised the bottle and said, "Your brother's favorite."

Logan smiled. "Lone Dog brews it behind his shack. He once told me he puts rattlesnake venom in it."

"Gives it a nice edge." Rachel took two glasses down from a short stack on the table and poured the home-brewed elixir into them. She corked the bottle and took one of the glasses to her brother-in-law, thrusting it into his hand.

"You and my dad are bound and determined to get me drunk."

Rachel smiled down at him, closed her upper lip over the top of her glass, and sipped. She lowered the glass. "I've been drunk since . . . since . . ."

Her face crumpled. She raised her arm to her eyes and sobbed. "Oh, God!"

Logan pulled her down beside him, wrapped his arm around her, squeezed her tightly against him.

"I couldn't even have a baby for him!" She was sobbing against his chest. He felt the wetness of her tears through his shirt.

"I know you wanted to. He knew you wanted to. It wasn't your fault, Rachel."

"I wanted to have his babies so bad!"

"Shh-shh, drink your busthead." He smiled down at her. "Make you feel better."

She sipped the rotgut, swallowed, and said, "Nothing really

makes me feel better. I watched his coffin being lowered into his grave and I wanted to jump into that grave with him!" She reached up and placed a hand on his face. "That's how much I loved him, Logan. I could never love another man like that. I will be alone for the rest of my life! Even if I did find a man I could love, I'm thirty-one. Too old to marry!"

"Nonsense, Rachel. You'll come out of this. We . . . get over things."

Do we really, though?

He was thinking of his mother's death. He'd wandered around for two years afterward, feeling as though he had a rusty knife in his heart. He lost himself in the breaking corral, performing more and more dangerous moves, half-consciously wanting one of the broncs to kill him.

One day his father walked past the circular corral where Logan was trying to break Wolf, and told his foreman, Ed Ringo, "Get him out of there. Don't let him back on one of those broncs until I say."

"You got it, Mr. Trent!"

Now, Rachel looked up at him, her jaw hard, her face red with fury. "Are you going to find them? The men who killed Dev. Are you going to kill them good an' slow, Logan? *Are you?*"

He ran his hand down her arm. "That's why I'm here, Rachel."

"I want to help."

"I have to do it myself."

"I want to put at least one bullet in one of them!"

"I know, but let me do it."

She glared up at him, her eyes bright with drink. "I am no hot-house flower, Logan!"

He drew her to him once more, his heart breaking for her. His heart breaking for both of them. "I know you're not. But I have to do it."

"That's not fair!"

He continued to caress her. "No, but that's how it's going to be."

She cried against his chest. “You think Big Ike did it.?”

“I don’t know. I think there’s a good possibility. He wanted me dead bad enough.”

After a time, when her cries had lessened, he tilted her chin up to gaze into her wet eyes. “Do you have any idea?” he asked. “Had he been crossways with anyone in the days leading up to his murder?”

She drew her mouth corners down, shook her head.

She looked out the window for a long time. “Not that I know of,” she said shakily. “He was just himself. You know, always laughing and joking. Just being Dev . . . the man I loved with all my heart.” She sobbed again and rested her quivering lips against his shoulder.

She looked up and pinned him with a hard look, narrowing her eyes, cheeks flushed with anger. “Whoever killed him . . . for whatever reason . . . kill him . . . or kill her!”

Logan frowned for a few seconds, curious. She was just out of her mind with anguish. He squeezed her again. “Like I said—that’s what I’m here for.”

Chapter 7

Trent woke early.

No. Waking early meant he'd slept. He hadn't caught a wink. He'd lain in his old bed, head on his old pillow, arms crossed behind him, listening, through the open window to his right, to the hunting owls and other night birds. His and Devon's first rifles, old-model Henrys, leaned against the wall beside the window. They appeared exactly as they had been left. On a nearby table were neatly stacked .44-40 shells for both long guns in yellowing boxes.

They'd replaced the Henrys for the more dependable Winchester Yellowboy repeaters, one of which Trent still carried now.

For a time, he heard Rachel sobbing in the room beside his—the room in which she and Dev had lived when they were first married. Even through the wall, her sorrow was palpable. Trent wished she'd had her way and that Dev had been able to give her a son or daughter.

At dawn, he rose, dressed, and went downstairs to find his father sitting alone at the dining room table. Lone Dog, dressed in his usual beaded buckskins, his hair in a braid threaded with rawhide, was refilling the elder Trent's plate with more ham and potatoes.

Ben was still in his bathrobe over striped pajamas. He looked old and haggard, his silver hair mussed, his eyes rheumy.

"I bring you plate," Lone Dog said as he passed Logan.

Logan nodded. "Thanks," he said in Lakota.

He watched the old man pour a good portion of brandy into his coffee and add two teaspoons of sugar and stir. He called them toddies; every man needed one to get his morning blood going. Ben's favorite drink was Scotch, but he preferred to start out the day with brandy and coffee. Logan sat down near his father's customary place at the end of the table, and when Lone Dog brought him a steaming platter and a mug of coffee, his father added brandy to the mug and stirred in two teaspoons of sugar without looking at his son.

He just said, "Every man needs to start off the day—"

"I know," Logan said, chuckling, "some damn way."

The elder Trent snorted a laugh, then dug into his fresh plate of vittles. "Where you headed today?"

"Circle Double D," Logan answered around the ham and potatoes in his mouth.

Ben looked at him for the first time. "Alone?"

"Isn't that why you called me here?"

"I'll send a few men to tag along . . . in case, you know, you need someone to watch your back."

Chewing, Logan shook his head. "You need them on the range."

"I don't need another son dead. That's what I *don't* need."

"You called me here to kill the man or men who killed Dev."

His father gave his head a single, fateful wag. "If there's a man who can do it, you can. I've seen you work with those Russians and the Yellowboy." He gave his son another direct, commanding look. "But I didn't call you here to get you killed. He has sixteen men riding for him, including Red Maclain."

"I've shot faster men than Red Maclain."

Ben gave another chuckle at his son's hubris. "Well, Big Ike'll likely be alone this time of the day, maybe just a few men to break broncs, his cook, and blacksmith. And that nasty daughter of his, of course." He laughed again. "Megan Donovan is a piece of work. Heard she has a child, though. Some say it's Basque. Who'd have thought!?"

"That's a ring-tailed polecat, for sure." Logan swabbed his plate with a scrap of grainy wheat bread, then polished off his flavored mud and slid his chair back. "I'd best be off."

"Logan?"

"What, Pa?" He pulled his hat off a wall hook.

His father poked his fork at him. He had an unlit stogie in his other hand. "You be careful. Don't make me regret callin' you back." He glanced around the nicely appointed dining room. "This place is all gonna be yours, maybe sooner than you think."

Logan frowned. "You sick, you old bull buff?"

"Hell, no—just old."

Logan smiled and headed out of the dining room toward the lodge's front door. "Tell Lone Dog to keep a plate warm for me!"

"Don't get cocky!" his father yelled at him as he left the house.

Trent paused to set his hat on his head and then went down to the bunkhouse to say hello to the boys. There was much laughing and slapping of backs and howdy-dos. Trent was a little surprised he still recognized so many of the men sitting on benches around the long eating table. Heck, even the cook's pet coyote—fittingly, if unimaginatively, named Coyote—was still alive.

They all talked for a while, and then Trent went to the stable, saddled Wolf, and rode out of the ranch headquarters fifteen minutes later, sliding his Winchester down snug in his saddle scabbard. He rode down the mountain the headquarters was perched on, crossed Arapaho Creek, and followed the trail up a steep incline through aromatic pines.

He spied movement on another ridge above his, on the other side of the creek, which ran through a canyon and into the valley below. He stared up at a figure sitting on a horse, both horse and rider silhouetted against the lightening morning sky above and behind him. The man held a rifle on his right shoulder.

He just sat there staring down at Trent.

Now, who in the hell is . . . ?

He cut off the silent question when the rifle quickly came down from the man's shoulder, was suddenly in the man's hands, and the mysterious rider was cheeked up to the rear stock.

Trent cursed and was about to spur Wolf ahead when smoke and flames lapped from the long gun's barrel. The bullet drilled into the trail just behind Wolf's rear hooves. The stallion pitched, whinnied, and ran up the trail, shaking his head angrily.

Like most men, most horses didn't like being shot at.

Crouching low in the saddle, Trent gave Wolf his head until they were nearly to the top of the ridge. Then he swung the roan off the left side of the trail and descended the steep ridge to the creek in the canyon above and to his right.

The shooter was no longer at the top of that ridge. Wolf crossed the stream, splashing, and then Trent put the horse up the incline on the other side, Trent staying low and sliding his Winchester from its scabbard. He leaned farther forward as the horse leaped and lunged up the steep ridge. He levered a round into the rifle's action just before he and Wolf gained the top of the ridge in case the shooter was waiting for him.

Wolf leaped up onto the ridge before Trent stopped him. Trent off-cocked the Yellowboy's hammer. The rider was just then galloping up the far side of a shallow coulee, glancing behind him, and then he booted his pinto into a dead run, heading north, away from Trent, who cursed and booted Wolf into a dead run of his own.

Who are you, you SOB? Trent wanted to know, his jaw taut with anger.

He pulled his hat down low over his eyes so the wind wouldn't blow it off his head.

He and Wolf galloped down into the shallow coulee and up the other side, Wolf gradually closing the gap between him and the shooter's black-and-white pinto, which was galloping a little awkwardly, as though it had thrown a shoe. Its rider glanced back over at his pursuer, then turned his head forward and whipped his reins against his horse's hip, trying to urge more speed.

Quickly Wolf closed the distance between him and the pinto, whose rider wore a green plaid work shirt and a gray Stetson, a neck-knotted red bandanna blowing behind him in the wind, as did the man's long brown hair. Anger at the bushwhacker burning in him, Trent put the roan up close against the pinto's left side. He leaped out of the saddle and into the pinto's rider, driving the man off the pinto's right side, Trent on top of him.

They both struck the ground with loud grunts, rolling, until the pinto's rider came up on top of Trent, straddling him, the man's face flushed, his hat no longer on his head.

No. Not a man.

Trent frowned, incredulous, as he stared up at the tanned, pretty face of a beautiful but tough-looking woman, a young lady of the outdoors.

"Megan?" Trent said in shock, wincing against the pain of his aching joints, shoulders, and hips.

Megan Donovan's gray eyes blazed, and then she went to work slapping Trent's face with both her gloved hands, making his cheeks sting, his eyes water.

"You killed another one of my brothers! Pete was the last one, an' now he's dead, just like Buck!"

Trent grabbed her hands, stopping the onslaught, and rolled her onto her back, straddling her and holding her hands above her head. "Pete dry-gulched me!" he shouted at the young woman. "And talk about a son of Satan. He's deserved that bullet since he was ten years old. I should have killed him when we were working roundup and he was trying to change the Trent brands to those of the Circle Double D. When Dev and I caught him at it, he came at us with an

Arkansas toothpick. Instead of dry-gulching me on my family's own land, you should be thanking me for keeping him alive as long as I did!"

She lifted her head and spat in his face.

Trent slapped her hard across her left cheek.

That seemed to daze her, eyes losing focus as she winced against the pain and rested her head back against the ground.

Trent brushed the spittle from his cheek.

"You ever try anything like that again, Megan," he warned, "I'll kill you just like any gutless, dry-gulching man. Just like I did Pete!"

"Thanks for the warning," she shot back at him, appearing to have recovered her senses, her rage.

"Did your pa have Dev killed?"

"What?" she spat out at him, her jaws hard once more. "Why would he? It's you he wanted dead for killin' Buck!" Suddenly she sobbed. "Now all my brothers are dead and it's only me an' Pa!"

She sobbed again.

"For the record," Trent said, "I didn't kill Buck."

She cussed him for a liar. "Hell, half the town saw you fighting in Senorita Ortiz's cantina that night! Before someone found him dead with his throat cut in a dark alley beside the place!"

"Do I really seem like a guy who would cut Buck's throat?"

"For Senorita Ortiz, I think you would. I think any man in town would."

Trent sat up. "Not me."

She sat up then, too, and leaned back against her hands. Her voice was still pitched in anger for his having killed her last brother, yet somehow it also owned a strange intimacy. "I know you would have . . . long ago . . . for me."

She looked away, both ashamed and embarrassed for having said something like that at a time like this.

Warm blood rose in Trent's face. "Like you said, that was a long time ago."

"If our fathers would have found out, they would have bullwhipped each of us," she said in a matter-of-fact tone.

"They would have—certain-sure."

"But that didn't hold you back, did it?"

"We were young, stupid."

He'd run into her out on the range. Because of their families, they were enemies. That had, ironically, added to the excitement of it. Not to mention Megan Donovan's maverick beauty, the fine-blooded horses she rode—a queen in blue jeans and work shirt, long chestnut hair tumbling down her back.

"Enough of this," Trent said, feeling uncomfortable in more ways than one. "Why did your father send Pete to kill me?"

"Who do you really think killed Buck?"

"You."

"Is that why he had Devon killed? To lure me back to Idaho so he could kill me?"

Megan shook her head and slid a lock of hair from her cheek, tucked it behind an ear. "Why should I tell you? You'll just want to kill my father, the way you killed my brothers."

"He did, didn't he?"

"Like I said . . ."

"Are you going to try to kill me again?"

She smiled. "Of course." She looked at the .44 thonged low on his right thigh. "Better kill me now, I reckon. If I had the upper hand and a six-shooter, I'd shoot you, get you onto your horse, take you back to the Circle Double D, an' let Pa kill you slow."

"When you talk like that, you drive me crazy."

She kept her expression hard, angry eyes narrowed. "What're you going to do about it?"

"Not a blamed thing."

"I didn't try to kill you back there." She jerked her chin to indicate the forested ridge on which she'd shot at him. "I just wanted to spook your horse—good old Wolf. Killing you then would have been too easy."

"I see. You'll wait till later. Take what you want first."

She shrugged her slender shoulders and gave her head a toss, shaking her hair back behind her again. The breeze kept blowing it forward.

Trent rose and set his hat on his head. "I'll fetch our horses."

"Don't do me any favors."

Megan rose and dusted off her pants and chaps, plucked her own dusty Stetson off a sage shrub. They started walking together, side by side, in the direction in which their horses had run.

"Tell me something," she said.

"Why should I give away anything to a girl who wants me dead?"

"Why did you come back? You knew what you'd be riding into."

"Oh, I knew, all right. I came back to find Devon's killer."

"You think it's my father."

"Yep."

She stopped and nudged his arm, turning him to make him face her. "It's not."

"Why don't you think so? That's how he killed my grandfather."

Again, she shrugged. "They were sworn enemies. Each wanted the other's land. That's how it worked then."

"Maybe it still does."

"Maybe."

When they'd run down their horses, tightened their saddle cinches, and mounted up, Trent turned Wolf to face Megan's pinto, Surly. "I'm going to ride over and talk to your father."

"Do you mean to kill him?"

"Not if he doesn't deserve killin'."

"He's dying," Megan said. "Big Ike has cancer."

Trent had conflicted feelings about that. If the old man was guilty of killing his brother, he wanted to kill him himself. But there was another aspect to the conflict of his feelings. Big Ike Donovan and Ben Trent had been enemies so long, it would seem strange to have their conflict resolved so blandly. Funny how a person can get so accustomed to conflicts, it was strange to see them resolved.

Trent hadn't thought about this till now, but the war between his father's and Big Ike's spreads had added depth, character, and a dark foreboding to the Wolf Mountains. How benign these mountains would seem with one of them dead—felled by something as common as cancer, the seemingly endless war over. Those two men and their sons, and their hired shooters, had given teeth and personality, indeed, to the Wolfs.

"What are you thinkin' about?" Megan asked.

"These mountains," Trent said, looking around at the high, forested ridges jutting around them. A golden eagle screeched as it circled a stony crag in the north. "How it was men like you and my father who gave them their names. I mean, I know the Sioux did, but maybe they foresaw the two crazy white men, as warlike as the Sioux themselves, who would move herds up here from Texas and compete for the same land, hate each other, try to kill one another, would kill each other's sons."

Megan stared at him for a time as they rode, side by side. "You know what, Logan? I've had those very same thoughts."

He gave a dry chuff. "Don't doubt it a bit."

"You know what I've also wondered?"

"I'm afraid to ask."

"If our fathers had been friends instead of bitter rivals, which they very well could have been, we might have been married."

Trent looked at her.

She kept her expression bland. It belied her words: "I know you're still in love with me."

Trent laughed. "Lady, you want me dead!"

"Yes. But we come from warring clans. Eventually one of us is going to bury the other." Megan shook her head wonderingly. "And, boy, will it be bloody. Can you imagine?"

Trent didn't know what to say to that.

"If it comes to that," she said, Surly giving an ominous whinny, "I'd like the honor of you killing me."

He just kept staring at her as she rode beside him, both jostling in their saddles. The wind blew her hair; the sun glistened in her gray eyes. "When Big Ike dies, you and all your men will take us out."

"Megan, you want to kill *me*!"

"You killed my brothers."

"Back to this again."

"Sure. Someday it will be an old, old story the other ranchers in these mountains and all throughout Three Forks will tell their children around fires at night, or while sitting outside as the stars die and others are born."

She'd always been a peculiar girl.

That, coupled with all her rough edges, had made him love her. At one time. Not now.

At least, he hoped not now. He didn't want to kill her, but if she stood between him and his brother's killer—a man he *needed* to kill—he would. It made him sad to think about. With her gone, the Wolf Mountains would lose another one of its sharpest teeth.

She drew back on Surly's reins and curveted the pinto, so she looked straight at him. He stopped Wolf and stared back at her. Their gazes held. His heart thudded.

"How deeply in love are you with Clarita Ortiz?"

"That train has left the station."

"After you killed my brother."

He sighed, and then left it at that. He hadn't killed Buck Donovan. Buck had been a pest that night. A foulmouthed one, and Trent had punched him when he'd taken Clarita's arm. But he hadn't killed him. To clear his own name, he wanted to find the man who had.

Megan looked at him from beneath her hat brim. "Kiss me."

It didn't surprise him. Nothing she said had ever surprised him. A curious turn of mind, this girl.

Staring at her, he shook his head.

"I have a secret," she said with a beguiling smile on her lips. "Want to know what it is?"

He did, but he didn't want to fall into this curious, dangerous vixen's trap. He said nothing.

She said, "I killed the man who ran from you when you killed Pete and the others."

Now, that surprised him. He remembered the hoof thuds of the fleeing rider.

"Want to know where I did it?"

Again, he said nothing. He knew it was coming.

She smiled, beaming as though at a man with whom she wanted to dance one late Saturday night in a barn.

"In my father's office while Pa drank Irish whiskey and smoked a cigar." A hardness came to her voice. "That's how bad I wanted you dead."

She booted Surly toward him. He saw the holstered revolver strapped near the horn of her saddle. She stopped her horse beside Wolf, and Trent closed his hand over the grips of one of his Russians. She gave his hat brim a playful tick with her index finger, nudging his hat up off his forehead. And then she was in his arms, her own arms wrapped around his neck, kissing him hungrily.

She repelled him as much as she attracted him, and he wrapped his arms around her, returning her kiss, which was every bit as hungry as hers. She must have realized he wanted to drag her off her saddle and lay her down in the pines, because just then she broke the kiss and, laughing, pulled his hat brim back down.

She pulled hers back down as well and said, "Now, then, should we visit Big Ike?"

"Why not?"

"I have to warn you, though," she said, narrowing one eye, her mysterious smile in place on her full mouth, "you might have to leave the headquarters shooting!"

Chapter 8

Trent smiled uneasily at Megan's humor, if it could be called "humor."

He might be following this woman, as though attracted by a siren song, into a trap.

Only a few riders from the Triple T had ever ridden into the Circle Double D headquarters, which was spread out in a broad, open valley between pine-carpeted ridges, and it hadn't gone well.

Years ago, Trent had been missing cattle, so he'd powwowed with his second-in-command, Mike Tracy, a dangerous former gunfighter who was wanted in Oklahoma for shooting a sheriff twenty years earlier. No lawmen or bounty hunters were going to mess with Ben to get to him, however.

Ben had ordered ten other good shooters on his payroll to ride with him and Tracy to the Circle Double D to demand his cattle back. Devon and Logan had wanted to join the pack, but their father had put the kibosh on that.

"If I don't come back, you're gonna have to take over and ready the other men for a raid. Fill Big Ike's men so full of lead they'll rattle when they walk!" Ben had reined his chestnut around, then shouted, "Let's split the wind, boy!" He galloped through the ranch portal, his foreman, Ringo, riding close at his side; Tracy and the other hands thundered along behind him.

Dev and Logan had shared skeptical glances, blinking against the dust the horses had kicked up, saying, without saying it aloud, *That old man is crazy as a tree full of owls.*

Apparently, there'd been a standoff in the Donovan yard that day. At first, the Triple T visit had nearly resulted in a bloodbath. But both sides had decided neither one wanted that powder keg to go off. The corral gate was swung open, the "stay beef," as Big Ike had called them, hazed out by riders from both spreads.

An hour later, the elder Trent rode back into the Triple T yard while Ringo, Tracy, and the ten other men hazed the stolen, mooing beeves into the yard behind him. Logan remembered seeing that smile on his father's face, a smile like no other he had ever seen on the man's face before.

He'd won the battle. The war was still on, of course. Several Triple T men had been found hanged or shot on Trent range. Thus, the war continued, several riders on both sides found dead here and there in the mountains and some in town. But that one battle that had meant so much to Ben Trent had been won.

He'd strutted for days.

He'd been an even bigger tyrant than he had been before that victory against his blood enemy, Big Ike Donovan.

And now here Logan Trent was, riding into that possible lead storm.

Trent felt sweat pop out under the band of his hat as he followed Megan Donovan through the Circle Double D portal and up to the long, low log cabin at the far end of the yard. Her father sat on the porch, drinking coffee with his foreman, Red Maclain. Maclain was a known lout. He was a tall, freckle-faced man with curly yellow hair—looking tougher, meaner, harder, and more leathery now than Trent remembered. Maclain wore a pinto vest over a red shirt, a green bandanna knotted around his neck. The two men held smoldering quirleys and heavy, clay-colored stone mugs in their sun-browned hands.

Big Ike and his foreman conferred, incredulous looks on their faces, and then Maclain dropped his cigarette, mashed it out with his boot toe, and said not so quietly that Trent couldn't hear, "What in God's name?"

Looking especially run-down, Big Ike just glanced without expression from his daughter to the man he so much wanted dead.

"I'll take care of this, boss."

Red Maclain rose from his chair—tall and lean, all muscle and sinew, with a severely chiseled face and dangerous eyes—and moved down the porch's three wooden steps, which creaked beneath his weight and made his spurs *ching*. His high-crowned cream-colored Stetson was badly sweat-stained around the base.

Two pistols were tied low on Maclain's thighs—matching silver-chased Colt .45s.

Maclain walked to Trent, his amber eyes glistening ironically, thin lips shaping an incredulous smile. His clean-shaven face was red from too much sun. He was an outdoorsman, but the high-country sun had always turned him campfire red.

"You're crazier'n your old man," he said.

"Some would say so."

"Done running from your responsibilities?"

Trent didn't respond to that.

To Trent's right, Megan said, "He came home to kill the man"—she gave the foreman a pointed look—"or *men* who killed his brother."

Red Maclain returned her look with a hard one of his own. "What are *you* doin' with him, Megan? He killed *your* brother!"

From the porch, the sallow-faced, gray-bearded Big Ike said, "Climb down from there, girl."

"He wants to know if you killed his brother, Pa."

Big Ike turned to Trent. "I did not. But I will kill *you*."

Maclain reached up to pull Trent out of his saddle, but stopped when the cold steel barrel of a Russian .44 was pressed against his belly; then there was the ominous *click* of a hammer being ratcheted back.

Maclain's eyes widened. He slowly lowered his hands to his sides.

Megan laughed.

She turned to her father. "Sure you don't need a new foreman, Pa?"

Maclain, who always carried himself on the range as though he were the cock of the walk, glared at her.

To the foreman, Trent said, "Remove that shell belt and toss it away. You're a known back-shooter, Red. I won't take one in the back if there's anything I can do about it. And this is what I'm doing about it."

The foreman glared at him.

Megan smiled in delight.

Big Ike said, "Oh, just suck it up and drop the belt, Red. Humor the man. He'll be dead soon enough."

Flushed with fury, glaring up at Trent, who smiled coldly down at him, Maclain unbuckled the gun belt and tossed it away.

Big Ike said, "Now get the hell out of here. You're fired."

The foreman turned to him in shock. "Wha—?"

"A Trent got the better of you at the Double D headquarters. That will get around and look bad. Ride out! You can return for your guns and your wages in a few days."

Weakly, cheeks flushed with the effort, Big Ike pushed to his feet. It was a warm morning, but he wore a mountain lion skin around his shoulders. Blue eyes bright with rage, he glared at his foreman. "I hate the smell of fear in any man, but especially in my foreman. Who *was* my foreman." He dismissed the man with a feeble, deeply insulting wave of his arm. "Go!"

Again, Megan laughed.

Maclain glared at her, then at Trent. "This ain't over," he said with quiet menace.

Trent holstered his Russian. "I wouldn't have it any other way."

Maclain swung around and marched off toward the bunkhouse like a scorned lover.

"Now, that is an angry man," Megan warned Trent.

"So am I."

Big Ike turned to the door of his worn, rustic lodge and beckoned to his daughter and Trent. "Come in. Let's palaver over a whiskey or two." He cast a dark, threatening glance over his shoulder at Trent. "Before I kill you over those two dead boys of mine, one of which I just planted this mornin'. With all this . . . craziness . . . this oldster needs fortification!"

"You know, I didn't know I was killin' Pete," Trent called to him. "I was just killin' a man with a rifle who was tryin' to kill me!"

Big Ike said nothing. He disappeared inside his large, crude cabin.

Trent and Megan shared skeptical looks, then swung down from their saddles. They tied their mounts to the hitchrack and then Trent followed Megan inside, feeling even more certain that if he stayed too long he was probably going to have to shoot his way off the ranch, and that he probably wouldn't make it. Even though Maclain would soon be gone and there were few other ranch hands working around headquarters this time of day, when they returned, Big Ike would send them after him.

That would likely detonate the shooting war that had been building since both families had moved to this country.

Still, Trent needed to know who killed his brother.

He needed to know who killed Buck Donovan, too, but that looked like an even longer shot than getting off Circle Double D range alive.

Trent followed Megan past a parlor in which a middle-aged Mexican woman in a dark dress, her nearly black hair in a tight bun atop her head, held a small child wrapped in blankets in her arms. The baby's face was a tea-brown shade. Trent glanced at Megan, one brow arched.

She shook her head. "I know the rumors going around, but she's not mine. It's a long story."

"None of my business."

Megan shrugged. She said that the child had belonged to a local ranch couple, the Olsons. The husband had been killed by rustlers just after he and his wife had adopted the child from an itinerant sheepherding Basque couple. The shepherds moved all the time. It was hard on the child. They'd wanted her to have a better home. The ranch woman had died from a fever, soon after her husband had taken that bullet.

Megan and Big Ike had adopted the baby, who just couldn't seem to find a home, though it was mostly their housekeeper and cook, Rosa, who minded her. The quiet Mexican woman had raised a large family of her own in southern New Mexico.

"Ah," Trent said, then followed Megan into Big Ike's rustic but well-appointed office, where trophy heads gazed down at them from log walls. Old rifles and animal traps lined the walls as well. The rich smell of old cigar smoke hung heavy in the air.

Big Ike sat in a leather chair near a fire that crackled in the small room's fieldstone hearth, which made the office as hot as a sauna. Instantly Trent began sweating. Big Ike still wore his mountain lion skin and was just then lighting a fat stogie. Sure enough, Trent thought, the man was dying.

Big Ike pointed to a crude table on which several bottles stood—some labeled, some unlabeled. They were of all shapes and sizes. The most prominent on the table was Irish whiskey. A box of fat cigars lay on the table as well. Trent saw a large, crusty bloodstain on the floor, near where Big Ike sat.

The rancher pointed to the table and, after hacking while still drawing on the stogie, said, "Help yourself. Nothing like hooch to help bring out the truth in a man. Of course, the Irish is best. I drink that so I'll never be killed by a Scot."

Big Ike gave a wolfish grin. "Megan's a chip off the old block. Doesn't mind a nip to get the day off to a good start, though what she does with her days I have no idea. Rides horses, mostly. Don't think she does a lick of work around here. Takes a turn now an' then with the child." Smoke wreathing his pale, gaunt face, with its sunken cheeks, he glanced at the bloodstain on the floor. "Doesn't balk at killin' a man she deems worthy of killin', though."

He sat back and laughed at that. A grating, sickly hack. The blood left his patch-bearded face—what little blood was in it, that was.

Megan filled two water glasses, nearly brim full, and thrust one at Trent, looking at him from beneath her brows. Trent saw that Big Ike had an old-model Colt conversion revolver on a table beside him, the same one on which his drink sat, also nearly full.

Megan sat on a leather sofa near her father. Trent sat awkwardly on the other end of it and rested his Irish whiskey on his knee.

"Now, then," Big Ike said, "let's get down to brass tacks." He shuttled his gaze between his daughter and Logan Trent, the man who, he believed, had killed his son, Buck, in Three Forks. "What on earth are you two doin', ridin' in here together? In *front* of my *men*!"

"Don't get your bloomers in a twist, Pa," Megan said in her customarily bold, ironic style. "I was out ridin' an' felt like shootin' somebody. Turned out it was Logan. I missed. He told me he was headin' here to palaver with you about his brother."

Trent said dryly, but with genuine indignation, "She took a shot at me, all right."

Megan shrugged. "You know how unpredictable girls can be. Couldn't help myself."

To Big Ike, Trent said, "My brother was killed as my grandfather was killed—on Double D range."

"Was he hanged, too?"

"No."

"But the killin' leads you to me, though you have no concrete proof. He was just found on my range."

"Yes."

"Why would I do that? On my own range?"

It was Trent's turn to shrug. "Old family history of two warring clans. I'm thinkin' you killed Dev on your own range to draw me back here so you could kill me, because you think I killed Buck in Three Forks."

"You still maintain you didn't?"

"I sure do."

"Why did you run, then?"

"I didn't run. After the trial, I left to stop the scrutiny and harassment of my family. I figured things would settle down after I was gone. But then, Devon was murdered."

"Everybody gets murdered around here, sooner or later." Big Ike took a big sip of his drink, choked on it, and coughed, making his icy blue eyes water, then added, "I didn't kill your brother. I understand why you think I did, but I didn't."

"My grandfather was killed here."

"We're warring clans. Those old bull buffs were always going head-to-head." Ike picked up the old Colt from the table, aimed it at Trent, and clicked the hammer back. His hand shook.

Trent winced, knowing the dying, weak old man could shoot him without even meaning to.

"Really, Pa," Megan said. "Here?"

Big Ike gave a phlegmy chuckle. "You're one to talk."

"I shot a coward. You know how I hate cowards. Trent here rode in, knowing he could very easily be killed, but he did it, anyway. He just wants to know who killed his brother." She looked at Trent. "Who, I know, he worshipped."

Big Ike scowled at his daughter, incredulous. "How do *you* know so much about it?"

Again, she shrugged. "You often get to know your enemies better than your friends."

Big Ike returned his rheumy gaze to Trent, keeping the shaking pistol aimed at the son of his rival rancher. "I'm still convinced you killed my boy over that purty Mexican gal."

"Give me time to prove I didn't."

Big Ike scowled.

Trent said, "Give me time to find your son's real killer."

Big Ike turned his head to one side, his scowl growing more severe. "What's your play?"

"No play. I'll find your son's killer. I'll find my brother's killer, too, even though I think there's a good chance you did it. On the other hand, it would take a cork-headed fool to kill my brother after you hanged my grandfather."

"And I'm no cork-headed fool," Big Ike said, his voice low, eyes hard and slightly narrowed. He glanced at Megan. "What do you think about this? You wanted this man as dead as I did. *Do!*"

She leaned forward, holding her glass in both hands between her knees. "I still might. But he rode in here knowing there was a good chance he wouldn't ride out. At least, not upright." Megan glanced at Trent with a crooked smile. "Maybe we oughta give him a chance. If not, we'll never know if he really did kill Buck. I mean, a jury didn't convict him."

"That's because of his name."

"I think we should give him a shot." Megan glanced quickly at Trent, blushing a little. "Pardon the pun."

"Not funny," Trent said.

Big Ike said, "He might run again."

Trent snorted a caustic laugh. "You think I rode all the way over here to run again?"

"I never have figured out what a Trent would do." Big Ike narrowed one eye. He depressed the Colt's hammer and returned the piece to the table. "But you ain't stupid, are you? You Trents are killers an' cattle thieves, and here I always thought you were stupid, to boot."

Trent laughed. "That's what we always thought about you. Rustlers and killers. But we also thought you were stupid."

Megan had just taken the last sip of her whiskey. It spewed out from between her lips as she laughed.

She turned to her father. "Give him a chance, Pa. If he can't do what he says, we'll kill him. Hell, *I'll* kill him. But if we kill him here, you know there's gonna be war. Our ranches will burn, our men will die, and our cattle will be scattered to the four winds!"

Chapter 9

Big Ike scowled at his daughter.

In the distance, a baby cried.

Megan rose from the couch, then said, "I have to help Rosa with the baby," and left the room.

Big Ike turned to Trent. "You have two weeks. If you can find his killer—if it's not *you*, I mean—we'll bury the hatchet, as well as a hatchet can be buried between our two clans."

"I'll be looking for my brother's killer, too. That's part of the bargain."

Big Ike threw back the rest of his drink and set the glass on the table near his gun. A phlegmy cough rose from deep in his chest. He pressed the end of his fist against his chest and, canting his head to indicate where his daughter had gone, said, "Did she tell you I'll probably die within the year?"

"Yes."

Big Ike poked an admonishing finger at his guest. "Don't be getting any ideas. Megs will be in charge, an' she's even more uncompromising than I am."

"You ain't tootin'."

"And we have some of the most gun-handy men, mostly outlaws, anywhere in the West."

"They probably came from the same places ours came from—Texas, Oklahoma, Kansas . . . a few from Dakota. Ex-Indian fighters turned regulators, shotgun messengers when they weren't robbing the stagecoaches, and cowpunchers." Trent chuckled, polished off his own drink, set it on the table, and rose, donning his hat, which he'd set on the sofa beside him. "I'll be getting back to you, Donovan."

"It's *Mr.* Donovan to you, Trent," the old man said, his face coloring with the ancient feud between their families.

Trent didn't respond to that. He just left the room and made his way through the house, pausing in the parlor where Megan held the baby in her arms, rocking her gently in a frayed brocade wooden rocker. She was lovingly cooing to her. Trent stared, incredulous.

She looked up at him and flushed. "I can ride a horse and wield a rifle, but I can still get a little one to sleep, too, Trent."

He pinched his hat brim to her and left the house, untying Wolf from the hitchrack, mounting up, and riding across the yard toward the Circle Double D portal. Several of Donovan's men, who were taking a break, smoking and resting after tending chores about the place, watched him with stony animosity in their eyes.

One man sat on a bench fronting the bunkhouse, running an oily rag down the barrel of a Spencer repeating rifle. When he saw Trent, he smiled, tossed the rag on the bench beside him, cocked the large-caliber rifle, raised it to his shoulder, and aimed it at Trent, his menacing grin in place.

Anger rising in Trent, he stopped his horse, stared back at the man, who kept the old rifle aimed at him, and booted Wolf over to him. Trent rested his arms on his saddle horn, leaning forward. "When you aim a rifle at a man, you better use it. Or . . ."

He swung down from the saddle and walked over to the man. Fear darkening his eyes, the man slowly lowered the rifle. Quick as lightning, Trent jerked the Spencer out of the man's hands, turned it around, and smashed the rear butt plate against his face. He heard the crunch of the man's nose breaking. The man yelped and fell back against the front of the bunkhouse behind him. His hat tumbled off his shoulder to the ground.

Trent tossed the rifle away, leaned toward the man now clutching his bloody nose, and said, "Or, with that busted beak, it'll take you a long time to get a partner at a barn dance."

The other men around the yard, few as there were, just stared at him.

On his way back to the Triple T, Trent stopped Wolf abruptly atop a high, windy ridge. Along the relatively flat ridge crest, he could see the prints of about ten cattle. Mixed in with the cow prints were the tracks of three shod horses.

Warning bells tolled in his head.

He'd dealt with rustlers most of his life here in the Wolf Mountains. He knew instinctively when he crossed the trail of rustlers, and not those of his father's own men. Now, as he swung down from Wolf's back and ground-reined the roan, he dropped to a knee to inspect the tracks more closely. In the summer, which it was now, his father had his men, who'd once included Trent and Devon themselves, keep the herds in the high country. A few men were left behind to stay in the line shack at the base of Bear Ridge.

These tracks of cattle and horses seemed to be heading away from the Bear Ridge shack.

Why?

Bear Ridge was on Triple T range. But these tracks were heading for the open range and into a valley below to the west.

Apprehension tickled the back of Trent's neck.

He peered to the east, where another forested ridge rose.

He rubbed the back of his neck, grabbed Wolf's reins, mounted up, and headed east along the current ridge he was on and then climbed through the thick pines of the higher ridge, backtracking the trails of the cattle and horses. When he was halfway up, he swung off into a canyon he knew well.

It led up into a rather treeless stretch. He crossed the stretch into the high country, which flattened out in even thinner forest. He crossed a creek, along which the grass and sage grew thick, and entered a broad valley at the bottom of which the old, age-silvered line shack sat hunched all alone without a tree in sight. The creek curled around the south side of the shack, offering plenty of water for the summer herds and the men who tended them.

When Trent was roughly a hundred yards from the shake-shingled shack, which Trent's grandfather had built with an old mountain man friend, "Lonely" Bill Weathers, he stopped Wolf abruptly.

What appeared to be three bodies lay twisted in the sage fronting the place. A saddled horse lay dead beside one of the men, off the cabin's right front corner. The tracks he'd been following curved around the south side of the shack. Beyond were short horns and red angus, some mixed with the blood of the original longhorns that had made the trip up here from Texas.

Smoke curled from the shack's rusty stovepipe.

Someone, likely the men who'd shot the men manning the shack and the herds, was holed up in the cabin. Quickly Trent reined Wolf around and, hoping he hadn't already been seen, rode halfway up the ridge. He swung right and rode another hundred yards before dropping back down the ridge and into a ravine he knew well, having manned the shack a few times over the years with Dev.

They'd had a good time up here, away from the old man's watchful eye. They kept close watch over the herds, of course, but they'd also hunted deer and elk, cooked at night over an open fire, joked and laughed—mostly about girls from other ranches they'd fancied—and played poker and drank whiskey they'd pilfered from their father's liquor cabinet.

A few times, they'd run into men messing with the herds—rustlers—and shot them out of their saddles and left them to the wolves and grizzly bears. They'd been good shots at even sixteen and eighteen years old, respectively. One of the ranch hands, on the run from the law in Minnesota and a known pistoleer, had taught them both how to shoot animals, as well as men.

At first, shooting men had been hard for them, but the men they'd shot had been as much animal as men. Once they realized that, it got easier. So easy, they'd almost become afraid of themselves.

Now Trent rode Wolf along the ravine. Once he was behind the stable, privy, and woodshed flanking the main cabin, Trent dismounted and ground-reined Wolf. Carrying his Yellowboy low in his right hand, he ran, crouching, to the rear of the woodshed, hoping that none of the horses in the stable would wind him, whinny, and give him away. The best way to do that, he knew from experience, was to go into the stable and give them each—there were four—a bait of oats.

When he left the stable minutes later, they were switching their tails contentedly.

He eased the doors closed and racked a round into the Winchester's action; then, running at a crouch once more, he moved around the cabin's east side, ready for business.

Chapter 10

Moving quickly but quietly, Trent crossed the porch, heading for the door of the rustlers' lair.

He could hear the voices of men inside. The voices of the *vipers* inside, more like. He stopped in front of the door, raised the Yellowboy, took one step back, then bounded forward, planting the bottom of his right foot against the door, just left of the latch.

Bang!

The door broke open, the latch flying across the room.

Trent took one step inside to catch the door with his left foot after it ricocheted off the wall.

Four men leaped up from the chairs around a square table littered with cards, coins, and shot glasses. Three reached for the pistols holstered on their hips and thighs. One jerked up a carbine resting across the table on his right. Trent knew from long years of experience how to handle rustlers. He aimed the Yellowboy straight out from his right hip, fired and cocked, fired and cocked—the spent cartridges flying back behind him to clink together on the porch.

Bang! Bang! Bang! Bang!

All four went flying backward, screaming as the .44 rounds shredded their hearts. Only one of the four—the man with the carbine—got off a shot, which chunked into the herringbone-patterned ceiling above his head. Trent shot him again as he fell, just for good measure. The man—big and bearded and wearing a wool-lined cowhide vest—groaned, ground his bootheels into the floor, arching his back, and then collapsed and turned his head to one side, dead.

One of the others lay groaning, clutching his chest as though to stem the blood flow.

Trent lowered the smoking repeater and crossed to him, recognizing him. Randall Hagen had once punched cattle for Big Ike. Cowboy turned rustler. Much more lucrative—if you knew where to sell stolen beef.

Using one hand, Trent lowered the Winchester's barrel to the man's forehead.

"Where are they taking them?"

The man groaned.

"Where are they taking them?"

Hagen glared up at him, dung-brown eyes bright with pain. Blood oozed from his lips to stain his gray-brown beard. "You . . . go to . . . *hell*! You kilt me, you son of a—"

Trent finished him. He wasn't going to get anything out of him, anyway.

"You're right on that count," Trent said, staring down at the dead men as he reloaded the Yellowboy. He'd seen all four, but could remember only Hagen's name. He was pretty sure they'd all ridden for one outfit or another in either the Wolf Mountains or the Bitterroots.

Cowmen turned rustlers.

A hanging offense, but they'd taken their chances. Their eyes, glassy in death, stared up at the man who'd pronounced their death sentences.

Now, for the others.

He swung around and whistled for Wolf, who climbed up out of the ravine and came running, reins bouncing along the ground beside him. The roan stallion stopped before his rider, smelled the blood stench issuing from the cabin, and twitched his ears and shook his head.

Trent sheathed his rifle. "An ugly job, but someone's gotta do it, boy."

He and Devon had been killing rustlers since they were teenagers. It had gotten easier as the years flicked past, because their father had drilled it into them that the only good rustler was a dead rustler. Neither boy had taken pleasure in it, but it was a job that had to be done lest the range be overrun, and they'd lose their herds and then their ranch.

That's all a rancher had—his herds and his ranch. He had his family, of course, but without his herds and his ranch, he didn't even have them.

When Trent had gone wild, his father had forced him to take the deputy sheriff's position for Dan True in Three Forks. That hadn't tamed him much. After Buck Donovan had been killed, and even after Trent had been cleared by a jury of the killing, he'd ended up heading for a life of anonymity in Montana.

It was best for his family that way. Maybe with him gone, the town would more quickly forget.

But Dev had stayed on the ranch, punching and branding cattle, turning young bulls into steers, brush popping those that had gotten lost in thickets, and shooting or hanging "long-loopers," the ranching term for cow thieves.

Now Trent had returned to the job by necessity.

He mounted Wolf and rode off to follow the tracks of the rustlers hazing the Triple T beef through the mountains to the west. He followed the tracks to the windy ridge crest where he'd first come upon them and continued following along the top of the ridge and then down into a valley, then up the opposite side.

He dropped down into another broad, treeless valley and continued following the tracks, where they swung south along a shaggy, ancient, two-track mining trail. A mile ahead, the valley became a bottleneck of sorts, produced by thick pine forest closing down around it. When he arrived there, he reined Wolf to a halt.

Wolf pricked his ears and turned his head to one side.

Trent could hear the distant lowing of cattle.

He knew where it was coming from. A little ghost town called Tin Cup lay ahead, built up when a European country had established a gold and silver mine there. The Wolf River angled around it, long before it dropped down out of the mountains to break off into three tributaries that cradled Three Forks.

The town had been established a good twenty years earlier. It was choked with little log hovels in which the miners had lived. The ridges around it were pocked with the bleak, black mine portals and the slag that had been blasted out of them. There was a crude wooden mine office and a tall wooden tipple and a stamping mill near a long log saloon and brothel, which had kept the miners entertained when they weren't a quarter mile deep in the surrounding ridges.

A dismal, remote place, it closed down during the winter with its hip-deep snows. But there were several corrals there in which the mine's mules and the miners' horses were housed. A perfect place for storing and rebranding stolen beef, until the rustlers had gathered enough to haze them up into the Bitterroots and to the crooked ranchers, who would then buy and sell them to equally crooked stockyards in Bozeman and Missoula.

The ghost town was about a quarter mile away, just around the trail that curved through the pines. He could smell the smoke from a fire, as it was chilly up here at eleven thousand feet, even in the summer. The fire meant someone was here. There was usually someone here, occupying one of the cabins. Trent pulled into the trees to his left, dismounted, tied the roan to a pine branch, and shucked his Yellowboy from its scabbard.

He ran his hand along the roan's sleek neck.

"You wait here, boy. I have to check it out. I should fetch help, but by the time I got back, those cows and long-loopers might already be gone." He grimaced, shook his head. He turned to one side and saw Dev sitting his white-socked black, grinning down at him, ready for the challenge.

Trent blinked his eyes, trying to clear the obvious mirage.

Still, Devon Trent remained.

Logan's heart thundered. Devon was alive!

His older brother, clad in his customary black Stetson and denim jacket, with a thin, sand-colored mustache mantling his broad, expressive mouth, swung down from the leather. Devon Trent shucked his Henry from its scabbard, racked a round into the action, and, keeping his voice low, though the glee of yet another challenge was keen in his whisper, said, "How do you think we should play this one, little brother?"

Logan drew a deep breath, let it out slow, returned his brother's bright-eyed grin. He cleared his throat, but it took him several seconds to speak above the emotion making his heart thud, his knees weak. "Like always . . . your way, big brother."

"All right, then," Devon said with a dimple-cheeked smile.

But then, he faded slowly, growing dimmer and dimmer, as though the universe were swallowing him up, as though death were reclaiming its hold on him. Logan reached for him, wanting to grab him and keep him here. But Devon and his fine black were gone, dispersed like smoke on the wind, until there was only the sunshine filtering through the trees and the breeze-swept pines around him.

"Wait!" Logan heard himself say, the tremor of grief and longing in his voice. "Dev!"

Bereavement swept through him. His knees buckled, taking him to the ground. He swept his hat off his head, pressed his forehead against the ground, and wept.

For nearly a minute, he couldn't control the heaving of his grief-stricken heart.

"Dev," he said, grinding his forehead into the pine needles. "Dev . . ."

Finally, he told himself no, grinding his molars against the unexpected emotional onslaught. He lifted his head and used his rifle to hoist himself to his feet, his hands shaking as they gripped the barrel.

"You're a Trent, gallblastit," he told himself. "And you have a job to do!"

Wolf had turned his head to regard his rider with concern. He put his snout up close to Trent's face, rubbed his nose against his cheek.

Trent choked back another sob, blinked his eyes to clear them, and ran a loving hand under the horse's snout, caressing him gently, reassuringly. "I'll be all right, boy. Sorry for the display. Ain't like me—you know that." He gave a dry chuckle. "But I guess it is now, ain't it?"

He drew a deep breath, felt the burn of rage once more. He gritted his teeth. "When I find who killed my brother, they're gonna die hard. Hell, it could be one of those men over there."

He turned to peer toward the old ghost town of Tin Cup. He hoped the killer was there. A rustler Dev had become crossways with. Trent would kill them all, just to make sure he got the one who needed killing the most.

For Dev.

Of course, there was no real way to find out for sure that Dev's killer or killers were over there, but his mind was not working logically.

Just fiercely.

Sometimes fierceness was the best way.

Chapter 11

He racked a round into the Yellowboy's action, off-cocked the hammer, moved back to the trail, and began following the bend in the trail to the moldering ghost town. The lowing of the cattle grew louder before him. He continued to the edge of what was left of Tin Cup.

The small, gray log cabins, some with their roofs collapsed, spread out before him. Sage and prickly blond grass, and a few gnarled cedars as high as some roofs, had grown up around them. A shack that had been shorn up on stone pylons listed severely, the rocks having crumbled beneath it. On many, the porches—the ones that had *had* porches, that was—had turned to sticks.

Smoke issued from the chimney pipe of the old saloon that sat on the far side of the mine company office, whose roof was Ireland-green with moss. Keeping the Yellowboy aimed straight out from his right hip, Trent moved toward the long, low saloon, whose batwing doors were still intact, though the one on the right had lost its upper hinge and sagged to the wooden boardwalk below. Moss had turned the saloon's roof green as well.

Trent rested his rifle on his shoulder—a casual pose. He marched toward the saloon, crossed the boardwalk, whose splintered boards sagged beneath his feet, and pushed through the batwings.

He grinned affably and chuckled at the six men sitting at the only two tables remaining in the place. Two rose quickly from their chairs, dropping their playing cards and closing their hands around the grips of their holstered six-shooters. Trent chuckled again with feigned good humor to set them at ease and said, "Hell, I didn't know anybody was keepin' this place open anymore. Used to stop here for a beer when I was fishin' up at Mirror Lake!"

He doubted any of these men recognized him, for he didn't recognize them. Many rustlers had once cowboyed on the ranges they now rustled. Knowing a country made a man more efficient at moving cattle through it. These men weren't locals, though. Trent knew most people from around here. These six, likely, all had reputations elsewhere.

He glanced at the swaybacked old cowboy, with his thinning gray hair, a sweeping gray mustache, and a thin gray-brown beard, who stood behind the bar. Several bottles were lined up on the shelves behind him, fronting a badly time-stained and cracked bar mirror.

"Sully?" Trent said, scowling incredulously. "Sully McIntyre—is that you, you old reprobate?"

McIntyre had once ridden for Trent's father and grandfather—more than twenty years ago now. He and the Trents had held off the Sioux together. Trent hadn't expected anyone he knew to be here, certainly not as old a man as Sully McIntyre, whom he couldn't help being friendly with. He no longer cared about the others. They'd be dead soon enough.

His father's admonition echoed in his head: "*Don't get cocky!*"

"Uh . . ." The oldster in a denim shirt and suspenders was drying a beer mug with a dirty towel. "Uh, well . . . yeah, it is me." He frowned and canted his head to one side. "Logan . . . Logan . . . *Trent*?"

Trent shaped a stiff smile.

Well, now the others knew who he was. He felt six targets drawn on his back. He winced at the sensation. He also saw that Sully McIntyre had a double-barrel shotgun leaning against the long line of shelves behind him, beneath the backbar mirror.

"Sure enough." The stiff smile in place, Trent walked between the two tables occupied by the unfamiliar men, who had hazed the recent herd here. Trent set his hat and rifle on the bar. "I was just passin' through, keepin' an eye on the range, you know. Rustlers will clear the range if you let 'em, till you don't have more than five or six to gather in the fall." He laughed. "Glad to see you're open again, Sully."

To cover his guilty look, the old barman and former cowboy flushed and quickly looked down at the glass he was drying. He'd opened the bar for the rustlers, which made him one of their ilk. He knew it. He likely knew Trent knew it, too, and was seeing the slack being taken fast out of a hanging rope coiled around his neck.

Trent scrutinized the bottles on the shelf behind the bar. "Say, what do you have that's good?"

McIntyre glanced at the six men with Trent, then turned back to Trent, gave a dry chuckle, and said, "Nothin'." He chuckled again. His face, which resembled an old coffee tin that had been used for target practice, was thoroughly flushed with unease. He said, "I brew it myself, don't ya know. In an old waterin' trough. It ain't much good, but it'll get you high . . . especially at this altitude."

Trent chuckled and, keeping an eye on the six men flanking him, said, "Don't doubt it a bit. My old man once said you gave him a hangover so bad he wanted to hang himself. Ah, hell, just pick a bottle and pour me a shot. Ridden a long way an' I'm ready to circle back home before dark."

With a hand gnarled from handling ropes over many decades, as well as from arthritis, McIntyre filled a shot glass and slid it across the plank bar to Trent. Trent lifted it up against the outside light reflected in the mirror, then said, "Well, I don't see nothin' movin' in it, so."

He threw back the entire shot. He thought it would burn a hole clear through to his loins, but he set the glass back down on the bar and said with a sigh, "That wasn't so bad. I think I'll have another!"

McIntyre shook his head, glanced again at the men with Trent, and said, "It's *your* innards!"

He refilled the shot glass, his hand shaking so badly now that he spilled some of the rotgut down over the side.

Before Trent could raise the glass, a man behind him said, "I thought you left these mountains, Trent."

Holding the glass in one hand—the whiskey, if you could call it that, felt as though it were burning through the glove—Trent turned and looked at the man who'd spoken. He was bearded and round-faced, with a badly sunburned, peeling nose.

"I did leave," Trent said, keeping his voice even. "I came back to help my father out on the range." His voice dropped an octave. "And to find the son of Satan who murdered my brother."

All six men shared dubious glances, shifting in their creaking chairs.

Trent said, "Do any of you men know who that might be?"

Looking away from him, they gave little shrugs.

A willowy man in a feathered bowler hat, who was looking toward the front of the saloon, murmured, "Might wanna look a little closer to home."

Trent's brows ridged. "What's that supposed to mean?"

The man, clad in a collarless shirt and suspenders under a threadbare elk-hide jacket, shrugged his shoulders. "Ah, hell . . . I don't know."

"Sure, you do."

"Ah, hell, no. I just been drinkin' too much of Sully's poison. That snake venom goes to a man's head, fries his brains."

The others chuckled.

Trent found none of it funny. He pulled the Yellowboy down

off the bar, thumbed the hammer back, and walked over to the bowler-hatted man who'd made the comment.

"Mister," he said, aiming at the man's right ear, "I want to know what you meant by that. Better speak up or you're gonna get a canyon drilled between your ears!"

"Now, now . . ." The willowy man held up his hands.

One of the three men at the opposite table jerked to his feet, unpouching a Schofield .44. Trent swung the rifle at him and drilled him a third eye in the dead center of his forehead. He fell to the floor like a fifty-pound bag of cracked corn. The man positioned before Trent leaped to his feet and ran to the batwings.

When he heard Trent recock the Yellowboy, heard the spent cartridge clatter onto the floor, and knew a fresh round was seated, he whipped around in front of the doors and held up his hands, palms out. Trent aimed the barrel down at him, right gloved index finger drawn taut against the trigger.

He said, "You vermin are nothin' but that—vermin cattle thieves. I'm gonna shoot you and hang you. I'll be a little merciful on *you*, stringbean, if you tell me what you meant."

"I can't! I can't!"

Bang! Bang!

The man screamed and flew backward through the batwings, making the one with only a single hinge clatter to the boardwalk. The other four rose quickly, jerking their six-shooters out of their holsters. Trent shot the one nearest him, then threw himself forward and rolled as guns thundered around him, bullets chewing into the floor just inches away from him.

He jacked and fired, jacked and fired, until the other four were down, howling.

Trent gained his feet, walked to a man who'd fallen before him, blood oozing from a shoulder wound. He aimed the rifle down at the man.

"What'd he mean?"

"Just what he said. Best look closer to home."

Trent finished him.

He turned to the batwings and the sunlight beyond, heart thudding, deeply pensive.

What in the hell did the man mean?

Closer to home . . .

He heard a heavy hammer ratchet behind him and swung around to see the old barman raise a double-barrel shotgun to his shoulder. Trent snapped his Winchester to his shoulder and dispatched McIntyre, shooting three times through his scrawny chest.

"Sure am sorry, Sully!" Trent yelled, meaning it. A hard way to end an old life, much less a longtime friendship.

The barman discharged both barrels into the ceiling over his head and, howling, flew back against the shelves behind him, knocking off nearly all the bottles of tarantula juice, which shattered on the floor at the base of the backbar.

Immediately the stench of strong, poison-like who-hit-John filled the saloon.

Trent reloaded the Yellowboy, then pushed out through the batwings and stared down at the man out there, now dead, arms and legs spread wide in the street.

"What did you mean, you son of Satan?"

Silence, save the thuds of horse hooves on his left.

He turned just as a man on a tall gray horse glanced toward Trent, then swung the gray around and put the spurs to it, galloping away. The shadows of the forest partly concealed him, but Trent thought he glimpsed a green bandanna, a pinto vest, and a high-crowned cream Stetson just before horse and rider galloped around the bend in the trail, shaded by pines, and was gone.

Trent glowered with incredulity.

Red Maclain?

* * *

Trent rode over to the south end of town, where three connected corrals housed nearly a dozen upset cattle. All wore the Triple T brand.

He opened the gates and hazed them out of the corral, then got behind them and herded them back up the trail that they'd been herded down by the six long-loopers. It was a job of work for one man to herd that many cattle, and he didn't have a whole lot of light left. They kept him busy, but fortunately he had a plug pony that could turn on a dime and was not only good at herding cattle, but Wolf enjoyed it.

Trent pretty much gave Wolf his head; the roan kept the cattle all in a tight gather, and when any of them decided to quit the herd, he turned sharply and without command and soon got them back with the others. It was a long, hard, up-and-down trek through the forested mountains.

Meanwhile, the light was dying, but Trent and his loyal ride got 'er done, as they say, though it was good and dark before they rode down into the valley where the line shack sat. It helped that the cattle knew their summer graze and wanted to get back to it. Like humans and horses, cattle liked familiar surroundings.

When Trent and Wolf got them back on their range, he halted the roan abruptly. He'd been so intent on the herd that he hadn't realized that lamplight shone behind the flour sack–made curtains hanging over the two front windows. He sniffed the mountain's chilly night air.

Woodsmoke.

He cursed.

Had more rustlers moved in when he'd been gone?

He reached down, shucked his Winchester from its boot, quietly levered a round into the chamber, and stepped down from the saddle. He lightly slapped Wolf's back, sending the horse toward the stable flanking the shack.

Surprised he hadn't been shot at yet, Trent moved slowly toward the cabin's open doorway. He held the Yellowboy in both hands and walked toward the cabin, crouching, trying to make himself as small a target as possible.

He winced as he stepped onto the cabin's rickety porch, the rotting boards creaking beneath his boots. He moved up to the door's right side, pressed his shoulder against the wall, listening.

Silence.

Drawing a deep breath, steeling himself against a likely hail of gunfire, he swung around quickly, taking one step into the shack and raising the Yellowboy to his shoulder.

A deep, shocked scowl stitched his brows.

Sitting at the cabin's lone table was a chestnut-haired young woman in a gray Stetson and a wool shirt, with a red bandanna knotted around her neck. An uncorked brown bottle sat on the table before her.

Megan Donovan held up a half-empty shot glass. "Sit a spell? A girl hates drinkin' alone!"

took a sip from her shot glass. “What—are you going to play cat’s cradle with my head because I trespassed on Trent range?”

Trent closed the damaged door, as best he could, walked into the cabin, dragged a chair out from the table, and sat down to Megan’s left, facing the cabin’s north wall. He wasn’t going to give his back to the door. He doubted any more rustlers would want to rendezvous here tonight, but he hadn’t lived most of his years in outlaw country to start being stupid now.

He set the Yellowboy on the corner of the table and looked at the extra shot glass sitting by the bottle.

He arched a brow at her. “Expecting someone?”

“I knew it could only be you who’d laid out those men. I recognized them. They’re fast and crafty, known rustlers. I should say they *were* fast and crafty.” She filled the extra shot glass and slid it toward him. She raised hers and smiled.

He raised his.

“Here’s to killin’ vipers,” she said. “Cheers!”

They clinked glasses together. She threw back what was left of her whiskey. He threw back his entire shot. It had been a long day. The tarantula juice filed the edges off his nerves. He set his glass down and she refilled both his and hers.

“Did you get your elk?”

She shook her head. “I got distracted. Not much excitement for a girl this deep in the mountains. When she hears shootin’, she has to investigate.”

Trent raised his glass. “Here’s to excitement.”

“Cheers!”

They sipped their whiskey and then she regarded him with a curious frown.

“What’s on your mind, Logan? You always look so proud and confident. Tonight you look like you’ve seen a ghost.”

A slight flush rose in his cheeks. He crossed his arms on the table, slowly turning his shot glass between the thumb and index finger of his left hand. Habit had taught him to always keep one hand for his guns. He thought a while, then, feeling embarrassed, and said, "Nah. It was just a stupid thing."

"Tell me."

When he just stared down at the table, badly scarred with overlaid carved initials and infantile dirty pictures, she kicked him, connecting with his right shin. "Tell me," she prodded, more forcefully this time.

He looked up at her, frowning. It took him nearly a minute to find the words and the courage to say them, but then he said, "When I was off tyin' Wolf in the trees near Tin Cup, where I knew the rustlers had taken the beef, a crazy thing happened. I heard a horse ride up and turned to see Devon, on his white-socked black, with that old devilish grin I remember so well on his face. It was so *real*. I could smell his horse and the cowhide leather of the old vest he always wore—the cracked one that had belonged to our grandfather."

"Ah," Megan said, slowly nodding and probing Trent with her deep slate gaze. "Just like he was there."

"You know, for a few minutes, I thought he *was* there. I thought he'd come back to help me. Hell, him bein' two years older, he always called the shots, an' I *wanted* him to be there. I wanted him to lead the way."

"That's what older brothers are for."

Trent's cheeks warmed with guilt. He looked at the table. "Sorry about Pete," he muttered.

"I know," she said. "What happened?"

"He was just about to swing down from his saddle, but he started to fade away. I called to him, pleaded with him to stay. But then, grinning down at me, he disappeared and it was just me there again—me an' Wolf."

Trent took a deep pull from his shot glass. When the whiskey was finished, he said, "My knees buckled as though they'd just turned to mud. Swept my hat off and leaned forward, grinding my forehead against the ground."

Megan reached over and placed her hand over his. She gently asked, "Did you cry?"

Trent's chest heaved with emotion. Embarrassment burned in his cheeks. He felt a sheen of tears in his eyes, and he choked back a sob. He drew several deep breaths, not wanting to cry in front of this tough girl.

"Let go, Logan," she said softly, squeezing his hand in hers. "It's all right. It's just us here."

"Yes!" He blurted it as though to purge himself of it. He looked at her, a mix of humiliation and anger burning in him. "Are you happy now?"

She smiled at him gently, slowly nodding her head. She held his gaze for a long time.

Finally she said, "It's no sin to love your brother. I cry for Buck . . . for Pete. I know most people saw him as a drunken thug, but he was gentle with me. He was my big brother. Yes, Logan, it's all right to cry. It's all right to admit you cried for your dead brother . . . your dead big brother I know you loved very much."

She squeezed his hand still tighter. Tears glazed her eyes.

"Oh, hell," Trent said, holding her emotional gaze. "We're gonna make damn fools of ourselves."

He threw back the last of his shot and was about to refill both their glasses, but the bottle was empty.

"Any more of this hooch?"

"Your men kept the place well stocked." Megan rose and walked to shelves at the back of the room, over a dry sink and near where some elk sausages hung from the ceiling. She brought back a bottle, uncorked it with her teeth, and refilled their shot glasses.

She held up her glass, smiling, tears still glinting in her eyes. "What shall we drink to, this time?"

He gave a dry chuckle. "To you not tellin' anyone about this embarrassing display."

"Oh, I know," she said. "Folks might get the idea you actually have a heart. That the tough Logan Trent loved his brother and misses him terribly." More tears shone in her eyes. A few dribbled down her cheeks. "Wouldn't that be awful?"

"Oh, shut up!" Trent clinked his glass to hers, threw back his entire shot, as she did hers, and then refilled their glasses once more. He looked at her. "If we ain't careful, we're gonna get drunk."

She snorted, laughed. "*If* we ain't careful."

He took a sip from his glass and looked at her once more. "Looks like we'll be spendin' the night here. What if Big Ike finds out?"

"I won't tell him, if you won't."

"Agreed. How 'bout if we drink to you not stabbin' me in the back in my sleep?"

She smiled at him tenderly, then slowly shook her head. "Not a chance, Logan Trent."

"I bet you say that to all the men you want to kill."

She rose from her chair, tossed her hat on the table, and came over and sat on his lap. She swept his hat off his head, wrapped her arms around him, and kissed him.

Despite the fatigue he felt down deep in his bones, Trent rose before dawn and set a ring of elk sausage in a hot pan. After it had browned on one side, he broke six eggs into the same skillet.

As the food started to cook, he turned the sausage over to brown the other side. He scrambled the eggs in the bubbling juice of the sausage. When the eggs were done, he shoveled the food onto two tin plates, set three-tined, wooden-handled forks on the plates, and went over to where Megan still slept, curled in a ball under two heavy blankets.

He leaned down to whisper in her ear, which was covered by her thick, mussed hair. "Have some sausage and eggs. Coffee's on the way."

She lifted her head with a start, turned, and gazed into his eyes, looking as though she wasn't quite sure who he was, where she was, or what she was doing here. Then it must have come to her. She looked down at the steaming plate in his hand, smiled, and took the plate as she sat up, wrapping a blanket around her bare shoulders.

In a sleep-froggy voice, she said, "Logan Trent, you are a caution."

"So I've been told."

He set his plate down beside her, then went over to the range and filled two cups from the big pot on the warming rack. He gave her one, then sat down beside her, leaning back against the log wall, his feet on the floor. He set his cup down to let the coffee cool while he went to work on his sausage and eggs. It didn't take him long to finish his meal. He set the empty plate aside, picked up his cup, held it in both hands, and sipped the still-hot mud at his leisure.

When Megan had finished her plate, she picked up her own cup, sipped the coffee, and leaned her head against his shoulder. "Thank you."

He took another sip of his coffee. "Least I could do when I woke up without a knife in my back."

"The least you could do."

He sipped his coffee again and stared pensively across the shabby cabin.

She watched him, her cup steaming in her hands. "What is it this time?"

"The varmints in Tin Cup were holed up in a saloon I think they must have reopened because they spent so much time there in that ghost town, changing the brands on the cattle they rustled. I asked them if they knew who killed my brother. Most shrugged and turned away, but one man—a string bean in a feathered bowler hat—murmured something about I should look closer to home."

Megan canted her head to peer into his eyes, frowning deeply and with incredulity. "That's what he said? You should look closer to home?"

Trent nodded and sipped his coffee.

Megan started to speak again, but before she could get the first full word out, a bullet blasted through the door, ripping it open before drilling into the wall in the kitchen end of the cabin.

"*Down!*" Trent yelled, tossing his cup away, rising, and lunging for his Winchester.

Chapter 13

Just as Trent wrapped his hand around the Yellowboy's neck, another bullet whistled through the air inches from his head to drill into the cabin's rear wall. He pulled the Yellowboy off the table and turned to see Megan running to fetch her own Winchester carbine from where she'd leaned it against the wall to the right of the ruined door.

"Dammit, Megan—stay down!"

She pressed her back up against the log wall—or what was left of it—and yelled, "You stay down. I'm gonna show those guttersnipes what happens when you mess with a Donovan!"

She turned and darted out the door.

"Oh, hell!"

Trent ran toward the door, crouching as another bullet slammed into the frame on his left. He ran out the door to find Megan on one knee, sending bullet after bullet into pines roughly seventy yards from the cabin, where pale powder smoke now wafted. Trent dropped to a knee, fronting the open doorway, and sent his own hail of hot lead into the trees.

Amid the cacophony of barking rifles, he heard a man yelp,

followed by the crackling of brush as whoever had taken a bullet had dropped. There was more snapping of brush and then the rataplan of several sets of running horses. He emptied his Yellowboy just as Megan emptied her carbine.

They both reloaded quickly.

Trent said, "They're on the run, those cowardly, dry-gulching bast—"

He stopped abruptly when between pine boughs, and in the pearl light of dawn, he caught a brief glimpse of a green neckerchief and what appeared to be a pinto vest. A second later, that horse and rider were out of sight. He could tell by the hoof thuds there was more than one rider—two, possibly three more. The hoof thuds dwindled to silence.

Trent racked a fresh round into the Yellowboy's action, off-cocked the hammer—obviously, the dry-gulchers hadn't expected such a quick, violent response to their bullets—and said, "By God, it *is* him!"

Megan looked at him. "It *is* who?"

"Your old man's former ramrod—Red Maclain!"

She frowned, deeply curious. "How do you know?"

"Yesterday, in Tin Cup, I saw that green neckerchief and pinto vest—a big man with a cream Stetson sitting a tall gray horse. He was just riding into town after I'd dispatched six rustlers drinking in that ancient saloon. He saw me, turned on a dime, and galloped off down the trail and around a bend, concealed by shadows."

"Are you *sure*?"

"Pretty sure. I mean, I didn't see his face, but . . ."

"Other men wear pinto vests, you know, Logan. And they ride gray horses, too."

"Are you tryin' to tell me you don't think Maclain is in with the rustlers?"

Megan drew a deep breath and stared into the forest from which the shooters had been shooting. "No. It's just hard to believe he'd pulled the wool over my father's eyes—likely for a long time. He was probably stealing our own beef, as well as yours, since our ranches sit next to each other. It also means my father is getting old, an' he's sick, an' . . . well, he's dying."

Her jaws hardening, she said, "Red Maclain is taking advantage of that. The younger wolf going after the older wolf . . . and me."

"You."

Megan drew her mouth corners down and nodded grimly. "He's got it in his head I'll marry him, and we'll run the ranch together. He's delusional."

"Don't worry," Trent said. "He can't marry you if he gets his head blown off. I'll see to it."

She gave him a crooked smile. "You're just sparking me because you don't want that knife in your back."

"Guilty as charged, Your Honor." Trent straightened. "Come on. Let's see who we laid out in the brush." He dropped into the yard and said, "Be careful. He might still be alive."

Striding up beside him, Megan said, "This ain't this girl's first rodeo, Trent."

"That's *Mr.* Trent to you." He winked at her.

She smiled again, this time devilishly. "Not after last night, it's not."

He chuckled.

They slowed when they gained the brush at the edge of the woods. Slowly they moved into it, looking around carefully. When they'd walked twenty feet, Trent heard a gurgling sigh and wheeled to his left, where a man lay on his side, aiming a cocked pistol at him. Blood and viscera oozed from his belly. He was pasty and sweating; his beard was wet. His hand shook.

The Yellowboy leaped and roared in Trent's hand.

The bullet took the ambusher in the neck, and he flopped onto his back, the revolver still in his quivering hand. Trent kicked the gun out of it.

"Chauncey Pace," Megan said. "He once worked for my father. Ike fired him because he was drunk all the time."

"I have a feelin' quite a few of these rustling rattlesnakes worked for ranches in these parts one time or another. That way, they learn the range and the best routes for taking the cattle out. A good many prob'ly aren't from here, because they'd be recognized, but whoever's the main snake, he knows what he's doin'. Mixin' men from here with men from *not* here."

Still staring down at the dead man, Megan shook her head. "Times have always been hard up here. Now they're gettin' harder."

Trent kept his eyes on the dead man as well. "I wonder who they're workin' for."

"I wonder."

"There has to be a leader, someone pullin' the strings. One who's smarter than these men, who just throw ropes and haze cattle to Tin Cup. None of the ones I've met so far have seemed smart enough to be in charge, to negotiate with the crooked ranchers buyin' the stolen beef."

"This one especially." Megan gave Pace's left leg a fierce kick. "Dumber than a barn door!"

"Let's head back to the cabin." Trent turned and started out of the woods. "I'm gonna bury the men who worked for my father, leave the others for the predators, and head for town."

"What're you going to do in town?" Megan asked, walking beside him.

"I think it's time to send for the U.S. Marshals. A bunch of 'em."

When Trent, with the help of Megan, had buried his dead and had erected crude markers at the heads of their rock-mounded graves, bound with rawhide, he and Megan strode to the stable. They freed the dead men's horses, saddled their own, and headed west across Triple T range.

At the border of their ranges, they stopped and looked at each other in awkward silence.

"You be careful on the way to Three Forks," Megan warned

Trent. "Maclain could be lying in wait for you, figuring your intention to call in the authorities."

"Don't worry," Trent said. "I always keep one finger on the trigger and one eye on my back trail."

She smiled. "Who said I was worried? Last night doesn't mean I might not still have to kill you."

"You're a hard lady."

"First time I've ever been called a 'lady.'"

"Oh, but you are." Trent pinched his hat brim to her, reined Wolf around, and started down out of the mountains in the direction of Three Forks.

Behind him, Megan yelled, "You stay away from that Senorita Ortiz. She's no good for you. You should know that by now!"

He smiled over his shoulder at her and put Wolf into a gallop.

He didn't know what to make of Megan Donovan.

Yes, he did, but he didn't want to think about that now. His life was complicated enough. And he didn't want Big Ike to shoot him in the guts.

He chuckled at that and continued down out of the mountains, surrounded by green meadows and water, and into Three Forks. He pulled up at Sheriff Dan True's office, Trent's own place of employment for a few years long ago—until that fateful night that he'd found himself occupying one of the cells—and swung down from Wolf's back. He gave the reins a cursory toss over one of the two hitchracks fronting the place, crossed the porch, rapped twice on the sheriff's door, then opened it and stepped in.

The portly True, face puffy from alcoholism, was sitting at his desk, to Trent's left. The big man swung around in his swivel chair and leaned back in it, crossing his arms behind his head of thinning silver hair. "Well, well—look what the cat dragged in!"

Trent hiked a hip on a corner of the desk, which had at one time been his.

"Dan, we got trouble."

"I knew we had trouble the minute I seen you ride into town."

"There's a rustling syndicate operating in the Wolfs."

True frowned. "You think so?"

"I know some of the men involved had at one time worked at various ranches up there. But there's a head honcho. Someone who organizes it all and stays out of sight. We need marshals to go up and do a thorough investigation. I can't do it. I got too many irons in the fire, already."

True nodded grimly, his double chins jouncing. "You want to find the real killer of Buck Donovan."

"That's right."

Again, that skeptical nod.

"Look, I know you think, along with everyone else in this town, that I did it. I need to prove I didn't. And I need to find Dev's killer, too."

"Rustlers, most like."

"Let's call in some marshals. Bona fides. Men with federal badges who can make arrests and bring men to trial."

True shook his jowly head. "I've been tryin' to bring marshals in for weeks. Coupla government surveyors were killed here weeks ago. That's a federal offense! I got prisoners down in the basement lockup"—he stomped a booted foot on the wooden floor—"that need to be taken to the Montana Territory for trial on a federal charge. But there's not a one to be had. They're all off tracking men selling whiskey to the Indians, and a bunch of bank robbers in the Bitterroots, and stage robbers, who shot a federal ridin' a Concord, in the Crazies. It's a big coupla territories out here, and there just ain't enough law to cover it all. The chief marshal would see your problem as small potatoes, relatively speaking."

"They'll wipe us out," Trent warned.

True sighed and drew his mouth corners down. "I'm sorry, Logan. You're gonna have to go it alone, I think."

I'll go it alone, Trent thought as he swung up onto Wolf's back. *Well, I reckon I've done it before. I can do it again.*

An angry obstinance was a hot stone inside him.

It was late in the day, and he could smell the smoke of supper fires. He wasn't so much hungry as thirsty, however. His sharp nerves needed filing. He rode two blocks east, along the main drag, Bitterroot Avenue, still choked with ranch supply wagons, mining and logging drays, a stagecoach just then rolling into town, pulling a thick, tan dust cloud behind it, and range riders in town. They were just as in need as he was of a strong belt or two before riding back to their home ranches for beans and steak in the bunkhouse.

He pulled in at the hitchrack of his favorite watering hole in Three Forks—Fred McGillicuddy's Elk's Head Saloon.

Actually, it was his second-favorite watering hole. For obvious reasons, his favorite was Clarita Ortiz's the Yellow Flower, with its spruce-green wooden sign stretched between its second and third stories, the profiles of naked, curvaceous women holding large, gaudy yellow flowers painted at each end.

The sign lay in stark contrast to the building's crude adobe-brick frame. It had been one of the first establishments in Three Forks, back when mainly prospectors, miners, and freighters passed through here between the Bitterroots and the Wolf Mountains, bisected by tributaries of the Three Forks River, made passable here and there by rickety wooden bridges. Back in those days, gold panners peppered those streams, their wood and canvas tent shacks lining the verdant banks. The panners' Indian wives might be out hanging wash on rope lines, copper kettles steaming on nearby fires.

Trent swung down from Wolf's back and tied the roan to one of the three hitchracks, already crowded at three in the afternoon, by other saddled horses, most with their latigos hanging free. He'd just mounted the boardwalk fronting the Elk's Head, from which thick, rich aromas of heavy ales emanated, along with an earthy blend of cigarette and cigar smoke, when movement caught his eyes.

A beautiful senorita, in a white blouse and a long black skirt, her thick, dark-brown hair piled high above her head, stepped out through the batwings of the Yellow Flower. Her slender legs were bare. She wore high-heeled black shoes, which glistened in the high-country sunshine.

Clarita Ortiz turned to him and dipped her chin, inky-black eyes glinting with remonstration.

"What?" Clarita said in her lilting Spanish accent, which sounded like clear water sliding slowly over barely submerged rocks. "Are you too good for the Flower these days, Logan?" She glanced up at a window above her—a window of her own suite. "I saw you ride in. I thought you were coming here. My heart grew light."

A frilly black choker, trimmed with a single diamond, adorned her neck. Her legs and her bare shoulders were the deep, rich, nut-brown hue of finely polished cherry.

"Prob'ly not a good idea," he said.

"*Por qué no?*"

"Folks will talk."

Clarita Ortiz threw back her head and gave a throaty laugh. "Silly gringo, do you think they have ever stopped talking? Did you think running away would make them stop? You are badly mistaken. They talked even more after you left than when you were here!" She tilted her head toward the batwings, one door of which she held open with a delicate, perfectly proportioned, beringed hand.

"Come. Let a girl buy you a drink."

Trent sighed. He thought of Megan. But they didn't mean anything more to each other than last night. Why not let Clarita buy him a drink? He'd wanted to talk to her, but had resisted. She might have important information that could lead him not only to Buck Donovan's killer, but to Dev's killer as well.

He took another deep breath and walked to her, indicating for her to go in ahead of him. As soon as they'd both stepped into the opulently appointed saloon and hurdy-gurdy house, with a sizeable clientele of well-dressed businessmen and beautiful, scantily clad women in corsets and silk skirts, with feathers dancing in their hair, the low roar of previous conversation almost fell silent.

All eyes turned to the lovely Mexican madam and the man who'd been accused of murdering his rival.

To detract the attention from her and Trent, she raised an arm and swirled it, smiling enchantingly. She looked at the two bartenders scurrying around behind the bar on the room's left end and yelled, "Drinks on the house!"

That did the trick, all right.

The crowd roared and clapped, and the two barmen, finely dressed in Spanish-cut white shirts and red foulard ties, their hair and mustaches impeccably groomed, grinned and set to work. They filled shot glasses and set them on the trays of the Mexican serving girls, who were all dressed nearly as scantily as the doves. Clarita walked around behind the bar and turned to Trent, who bellied up to the bar's left end, facing her. He tossed his hat down on the polished mahogany and smoothed his hair down with his hand.

She leaned toward him, elbows on the bar, her face only inches from his. "You are more handsome than the last time I saw you . . . though that is not what I want to remember. Name your poison."

That was her old line. She loved her gringo impression of saying it. She could say it in almost impeccable country English.

"Same," he said, not wanting himself to get lured in by her. There would be trouble there. She might not think so, but there would be, and he didn't want her to get into it.

He'd tried to forget her, but he knew now he never had.

He knew he still loved her as much as the first night he'd fallen in love with her.

She drew him a beer in a stout, dimpled schooner, filled a glass with fine bourbon whiskey, and dropped the shot glass into the beer. She smiled as the amber whiskey blended with the ale. The mixture of beer and bourbon foamed as she slid the schooner across the bar to him.

"Just how you like it."

He stared down at it. *Easy*, he thought. *Go easy.* Everyone in town—hell, everyone in the Wolf Mountains and the Bitterroots—

thought he murdered a man for her. He didn't want to reinforce their beliefs.

She pulled a labeled bottle of *bacanora* down from a high shelf and half-filled a small, delicate goblet with it. He winced. That had been what she'd been drinking when he'd had the "altercation" with Buck Donovan.

Easy, he told himself once more. *Go easy. Just one drink and then you're back on the trail.*

Chapter 14

Clarita sipped the *bacanora* from her elegant glass, leaving a clear sheen of the potent brew on her full red lips.

The liquor, a mezcal, was a delicacy from the Mexican state of northern Sonora, from where she hailed. It tasted vaguely of milk and grapefruit juice, laced with the astringency of the fermented agave. Holding her glass in both hands, Clarita leaned across the bar toward Trent, who just then turned to look around the room behind him.

"Don't worry about them," she said. "They are enjoying their free drinks."

"It's you I'm worried about. They think I killed a man over you."

"That's not important. I know you didn't."

Trent sipped his drink and licked the foam from his lips. "Do you have any idea who did? I mean, I know we talked about this before, but I thought maybe over the years something had come to you."

She shook her head. "No. I've thought about it over and over. It must've been someone who saw an opportunity to get back at you. To see you hang, maybe."

Trent leaned on his elbows and rubbed his chin. "It ain't like I don't have any enemies. I was a deputy here for five years, arrested a lot of men, shot a few, too."

"*Sí.*" She took another sip of her Sonoran mezcal, the *bacanora*, and looked up at him from beneath her dark-brown brows. "First and foremost, you are here to investigate your brother's murder."

"First and foremost, though, I'd like to clear my name as well."

She glanced at the dimpled schooner Trent held in both hands atop the bar. "Drink. You will feel better. You will be calmer, think more clearly."

Trent gave a lopsided grin and raised the heavy mug. "Never doubt the advice of an expert."

He took a deep sip of the potent beer and whiskey. She was right. It made him feel better. At least, it calmed his nerves a little so he could think more clearly.

"It was probably rustlers who killed Dev." He pursed his lips, rage burning in him once more. "They're thick as mice in a haystack up there." He lifted his chin to indicate the Wolf Mountains, humping up darkly in the northwest, a long, low, forested ridge connecting them to the Bitterroots. He scowled, deeply perplexed. "Why do I feel the two murders are connected?"

She frowned. "How could they be? They took place nearly five years apart."

"Maybe Devon discovered who killed Buck Donovan."

"Ah, *sí.*" Clarita sipped her drink, holding the glass in both her delicate, bejeweled hands. She thought about it, shook her head. "It will be an impossible thing to find out."

"Maybe. But I'm not gonna stop until I do." Trent took another pensive sip of the boilermaker, then looked at the beautiful Mexican woman leaning toward him from the other side of the bar. "How've you been?"

She arched her brows, then looked around the nicely furnished saloon and brothel filled with moneyed men and beautiful doves. The polished tables, chandeliers, attractive women, and the glistening mahogany bar stood out in sharp but pleasing contrast to the adobe brick of the walls, the ancient oak beams of the herringbone ceiling. Trent could hear the clatter of the roulette wheel in the gambling parlor, opening off the main drinking hall, near the staircase, which rose to the second and third floors.

The girls worked on the second floor. They and Clarita lived on the third floor.

Trent looked at her. "It's as fine a place as I've ever seen, but I wasn't asking about your business."

Clarita pursed her lips, nodded. "I get lonely."

"No man?"

"No time."

Trent nodded, sipped his drink.

"How is it at home?"

"Empty now, with Devon gone. The old man's sad and stares into his own grave most of the time. Rachel is a ghost, stays drunk on cheap whiskey. Rustlers have run amok. I tried to get True to bring in the U.S. Marshals, but he claims they're all tied up."

Clarita looked at him darkly, nodded slowly.

"What is it?" Trent asked her.

She held his gaze for another second, then shook her head. "Nothing. There are rumors, but they are only rumors. I won't spread them."

"You hear everything."

"*Sí.*"

"Tell me."

She ridged her brows, and her dark eyes glinted with annoyance. "Logan, no! It could be . . . dangerous. You're in enough danger already."

"But—"

"No!" she said quietly so no one near would hear, but she spoke in a hard, commanding voice.

Trent knew her well enough to know the conversation was over. A deep frustration nettled him.

She glanced at the beer and whiskey he'd nearly finished. "Another drink? A steak with a side of beans?" She smiled enticingly. "I have a Norwegian cook, who is a master; he has a sheep's haunch roasting on the spit out back. He keeps a shotgun near, so he won't be overwhelmed by the passing citizens made famished by the smell alone."

Her smiles always reminded him of Christmas morning.

Trent shook his head. "I have to get back to the ranch, warn my old man about the rustlers I ran into. They killed three of our men in a line shack."

"Will you stop again?"

Trent glanced around the room, then nodded. "Why not? I haven't been shot yet." He gave her a hard look. "I don't want you to run into any trouble—any *more* trouble—on account of me."

She smiled. "Don't worry. I have a sawed-off twelve gauge under the bar."

He returned her smile, pinched his hat brim to her. He crossed the room, feeling eyes on him once more, and pushed out through the batwings. He stopped on the boardwalk to look around and ponder. As he did, he saw a man in a pinto vest over a green wool shirt, with a high-crowned cream Stetson and a knotted green silk neckerchief, emerge from a side street on a fine gray stallion.

Trent's heartbeat quickened. His right hand instinctively dropped to the .44 thonged low on his right thigh.

Red Maclain rode west along Bitterroot Avenue, negotiating the still-heavy traffic and drifting slowly toward the street's right side before pulling up at the sheriff's office, two blocks away from the Yellow Flower.

Trent's hands grew sweaty inside his gloves.

He whistled softly.

"It's him, isn't it? It's True!"

* * *

Red Maclain pulled his gray gelding up to the hitchrack fronting the jail office in Three Forks and swung down from the saddle. He tossed the reins over the rack and grumbled, "Stay, Devil, stay."

Scowling his dismay at the dismal turn of events in the Wolf Mountains, where he and so many others thought they had a lucrative business going, he mounted the porch. He could see the lumpy, balding sheriff, Dan True, kicked back in his chair, tallowy arms crossed on his chest, head tilted back, eyes closed. Asleep as usual . . . probably after a big bowl of late-afternoon chili over at Ma Weatherford's diner.

An uncorked bottle and a half-filled water glass sat on the desk before him.

Annoyed at the sheriff's sloth, when Maclain and so many others were doing the man's dirty work in the mountains, the former Double D foreman hammered the age-silvered door three times loudly with the end of his right fist.

Through the window, he saw True wake with a start, sitting up in his chair, and then scowl toward the door, flushing with annoyance. He didn't appreciate his naps being interrupted. Maclain shaped a devilish grin on his bony, flat-eyed face.

"Come in, come in, fer cryin' in the queen's ale," True yelled, deep wrinkles ringing his fleshy forehead.

Maclain tripped the latch, walked in, cocked one foot forward, leaned on the opposite hip, and crossed his arms on his chest. His big Colt .45 jutted from the tooled leather holster on his right hip.

True's gray-brown brows furled with anger. "What in the hell are you doin' here? I told you to stay away from here, Red!"

Maclain pegged his hat on the wall to the right of the door, then walked over to the stove in the corner and poured himself a cup of coffee. "Yeah, well, we got trouble. Sorry to disturb your busy day." He moved over to True's desk, picked up the bottle of expensive Scotch the lawman had come to prefer it when the money started pouring in like rain in a barrel, and dumped a heavy load of it into his coffee.

"Hey!" True objected. "I didn't invite you to—"

"Logan Trent's causin' havoc in the Wolfs. He killed a number of our men and freed the fresh herd of Triple T beef from the pens in Tin Cup."

"Tin Cup?" True said, suddenly worried.

"Tin Cup."

True chewed on that for a time, scowling at the window beyond which the late-afternoon traffic was still heavy, large clouds of tan dust rising from horse hooves and wagon wheels. "So he knows what you boys are up to in Tin Cup." He massaged the line of his jaw, which had been slightly more pronounced before he'd started making money.

Maclain sipped his laced mud. "He saw the doin's in Tin Cup. Shot six of our men in the saloon, includin' that old man you brought in to open it back up."

The sheriff cursed and rubbed his chin between one pudgy thumb and index finger, keeping his gaze on the window, though he wasn't seeing the passing ranch supply wagons and drovers entering town for a night of frolic. He was seeing himself living with men he himself had put away in the federal lockup in Boise. He muttered, "He was here—persistent Trent that he is—wantin' me to call in the marshals."

"The what?"

True shuttled his worried gaze to the rangy, hawk-faced, blond Maclain. "He was just here an hour ago, wanting me to summon the marshals." He glowered at the younger, straighter man, with the .45 on his hip. "How in the hell did he find out about Tin Cup? No one goes there anymore! Weren't you boys watchin' your back trail?"

"Sure we were!"

"Well, kill him!"

"Done tried. Several times. But he's savvy."

"*You're* supposed to be savvy, Maclain! That's why I hired you to ramrod this operation!"

Maclain lifted his steaming cup to his mouth to cover his humiliated flush. He lowered the mug, swallowed the potent brew, and muttered a frustrated curse.

"Does Big Ike know you're in town?"

His humiliation growing, Maclain muttered into his cup, "I don't work for Big Ike anymore."

True slammed his hand down on his desk in fury. "What the hell happened? That was your cover!"

"We, uh . . . had us a fallin'-out, me an' Ike."

He wasn't about to tell True that the falling-out had been caused by Logan Trent and the fear he'd evoked in Red's eyes. If Big Ike saw fear in a man's eyes, that man became an old wolf who needed to be driven out by the younger pack.

Rage burned in the humiliated former Donovan foreman. He wanted Trent dead in the worst way, but somehow the man kept slipping out of his fingers. And to think it was not only Trent, but Big Ike's daughter, Megan, who'd foiled his last attempt to turn Trent toe down.

How many men had Trent taken down now, anyway? Four in the line shack, six—*six!*—in the saloon. Well, seven, if you included the old man. Maclain had found the guts to circle around and check out the old saloon, though he had to admit, if only to himself, that his guts had turned to jelly after his shameful encounter with Trent at the Double D headquarters in front of Big Ike and Big Ike's pretty daughter, whom he'd hoped to convince to marry him one day, after the old man had succumbed to his cancer. He'd have gotten Big Ike's blessing after the old lion had seen the worth of a tough, hard man like Red Maclain running the Double D . . . the strong brood of offspring he and Megan could drop and keep the ranch running for generations to come. Eventually they'd overtake Ben Trent and would fold that man's holdings into the Double D . . . that narrow strip of open range between them, too.

That would make Big Ike an even prouder man than he already was, even in death.

Now, after Red's encounter with Trent—and after the debacle at the line shack—all was lost.

The thought made Maclain's face swell up in fury, made him feel like his head would explode. Not only had he messed up at the Double D headquarters, showing himself to be a coward, he'd messed up on the range as well. Trent had tracked the stolen herd to Tin Cup.

The man had to die. Was Maclain the man to do it?

A few days ago, doubt never would have crossed his mind.

Now . . .

Now he couldn't get beyond his frustration and humiliation.

True rose heavily from his chair, breathing hard against the weight of his big, soft gut. He strode up to Maclain and grabbed the cup out of the hands of the former ramrod of Big Ike Donovan and, with his face six inches from Maclain's, said, "I don't know what happened to you up there." He tossed his chin to indicate the dark humps of the Wolf Mountains. "But you get your cowardly behind back up there and you kill Logan Trent. You understand? Find him an' kill him, or I'll find a capable man."

True chuckled jeeringly. "I once thought there was no one as good as you. No one as available as you. You were livin' right in the heart of all that beef—all that cattle just ready to be hazed off to Tin Cup and to the ranchers willin' to buy the long-looped stuff . . . and to the stockyard that don't ask questions. You prove to me you are still that man. If Logan Trent isn't dead by this time tomorrow, I'll get you a job you can handle. Plenty of saloons here in Three Forks that need swampers—men to mop and empty spittoons!"

Flushed with degradation, a bone-deep shame, Maclain glared at the fleshy-faced, gone-to-seed lawman, who, despite his growing disabilities, had managed to keep thriving over the years. Some men, even the most unlikely men, were born survivors.

The world was not a fair place. Not by a long shot.

"Don't give me that look," True demanded. "I've made you too much money for you to do anything but lick my boots." He thrust an arm out, pointing at the door. "You get your raggedy behind up there, kill Trent, and resume the operations. I have men waiting on that beef, an' they are not patient!"

Giving a ragged sigh, feeling like a schoolboy who'd been taken to the woodshed, Maclain hiked his gun and shell belt a little higher on his hips, grabbed his hat, and slumped out onto the porch. He peered up the street to his left. Senorita Ortiz's Yellow Flower hurdy-gurdy house lay two blocks away. If anyone knew where Red could find Trent, he knew one pretty, little senorita who would.

He mounted up and booted the gray toward the seedy little den, an oasis of knowledge in an otherwise-parched desert of secrets.

Chapter 15

So, then, Trent wanted True to call in federals.

As Maclain pulled up to a hitchrack fronting the Yellow Flower, he gave a grim smile. True calling in federals was like the mouse calling in a wild tomcat. It did, however, mean that Trent had uncovered the rustlers' ploy, and that, if he was left unchecked—left alive, that was—there would be hell to pay. Either Logan Trent had to die, or Maclain and his cohorts would have to vamoose and reestablish themselves elsewhere.

Without True. The man might be squattin' in high cotton at the moment, but that couldn't last forever. Not even for a man as lucky as True.

The local lawman was probably the only one who would get off scot-free.

Neither Maclain nor any of the other members of his cattle-rustling syndicate would rat the man out. Ratting anyone out was not a good business practice. It did not make for a good reputation. Not a good way of staying alive, either.

True knew regulators, had used them in the past, and with just a quick telegram, he could have one of the baddest of the bad men in here to clean the mice right out of the mountains. Then, after a year or two, he could start operations again, with the intention of wiping out the two largest ranches, buy both outfits for cheap, and run them himself. True wasn't getting any younger, however, and Maclain knew he wanted to make a name for himself.

A *business* name. Not a tin star name.

A tin star who mostly slept, kicked back in his swivel chair, drinking coffee and whiskey and taking long naps, snoring so loudly he could be heard on the busy street at midday. At the moment, he had no deputy. That didn't bother him. Deputies would just arrest folks and that would mean work for Dan True, a man for whom the word "work" was the foulest one in the language.

Maclain looked around carefully.

He doubted he'd see Trent inside, for the man's horse wasn't here. But in here, the former Donovan foreman thought, he had a good chance of learning the man's whereabouts and how much anyone in town might have overheard about what he'd discovered in Tin Cup. That right there could make a world of difference in the futures of Maclain and his cohorts.

He stepped under the roofed boardwalk fronting the three-story, adobe-brick structure with its large, gaudy sign, which stretched the width of the building between its second and third stories and peered over the batwings. Even in the late afternoon, between lunch and supper, there were a good dozen customers in the place, ensconced in a fog of cigar and cigarette smoke, as well as the mixed aromas of good beer and labeled whiskey.

Maclain scrutinized each man quickly, some with a bar girl on his knee or giggling in his lap. An old man in a green eyeshade and sleeve garters was playing the piano abutting the wall to Maclain's right, under the carpeted staircase rising to the second and third stories, with a hand-scrolled wooden rail on the staircase's left side. That was relatively new, of course. When Maclain had first patronized the place, it had been a mere hole-in-the-wall, with dusty spiderwebs hanging like nets from the rafters and from the candle chandeliers, mouse droppings on the tables.

All the liquor sold by the former German prospector who'd run the place had been brewed in horse troughs out back.

No one knew where the pretty senorita, who'd taken over the place when the German had died, had come from. She'd been tight-lipped about her past, so the rumors had flown. They were still flying. Her mystery only seemed to accentuate her beauty. Some thought she'd escaped the dangers of a Mexican revolution; others believed she was on the run from the law, maybe having plunged a stiletto into her wealthy gringo husband down in New Mexico or Arizona.

But in the end, no one really cared about her story. She was a feast for the eyes, and she served the most beautiful and talented doves, as well as the best liquor in Three Forks.

Her taste in piano men had much to be desired, however. The little man in the green eyeshade was banging around on the keys until Red Maclain thought he'd grind his molars to powder. The man was likely practicing now for the evening crowd.

Good luck, Maclain thought as he made his way to the bar, behind which the *hermosa* Mexican herself was pulling bottles out of wood crates and setting them on the shelves behind the bar and underneath it. Clarita Ortiz was beautifully flushed from her toil, wisps of dark-brown hair, having come loose from the thick double bun atop her head, slid across her smooth red-brown cheeks.

She glanced at Maclain as she stooped to set two more bottles on a shelf beneath the bar. She stopped and glanced at him again, and her eyes grew wider and apprehensive. She froze, then straightened and set the two bottles atop the bar rather than beneath it, and looked at him once more, trying to appear casual.

"Name your poison," she said woodenly.

"You."

She didn't respond to that.

"You heard me," Maclain said, feeling powerful now, when he'd been feeling as worthless as a bent penny only a few minutes ago.

He smiled, enjoying the fear in her eyes.

He tipped his head back. "Let's go upstairs, you an' me. Let's have us a palaver about a, uh, mutual *friend*."

"You know I don't work upstairs. Downstairs, only. If you want a girl, there are several—"

"No, no, no, no," Maclain said, annoyed. "I just want to talk."

"Go to hell, Red!"

Maclain pushed through the swing door at the end of the bar on his left. He walked along the bar, stepped around her so that his chest was very close to her back, and pulled a bowie knife from a sheath on his cartridge belt. He touched the razor-edged tip of it to her back, just above her right hip.

"Get the idea? Upstairs."

She winced at the prick of the knife against her back. "What the hell do you want, you pig?"

"Upstairs."

"Ouch! That hurts!"

"Shh! Upstairs," he said into her ear with quiet menace.

She moved forward stiffly. She pushed through the swing door and began walking toward the stairs at the far end of the room. The old man was still banging away on the piano, appearing to be intent on giving everyone in the room a headache. A few of the male customers looked at Senorita Clarita and the infamous Red Maclain, then frowned curiously. Most of the others were too involved in their own drunken ramblings to notice.

Clarita, flanked by Maclain, slowly climbed the stairs. Maclain smiled down at the few men staring up at him, trying to put them at ease.

Was the pretty little senorita really going upstairs with the rakish, thuggish foreman of the Circle Double D?

The senorita led Maclain to her room, unlocked the door, and stepped into her finely furnished sanctuary. Brightly colored paintings trimmed the walls. There were several brocade armchairs and a long leather sofa fronting a cold fireplace. There was a head of a helmeted conquistador mounted on a masonry pedestal. The carpet was red, black, and thick. Probably Oriental, though Red wasn't sure what that was.

"Where's the bedroom?" Maclain asked, keeping the point of the savage knife pressed against her back, just above her hip.

"No!" she said.

"Ah, here it is."

He'd opened a door to his left, then grabbed her arm and shoved her into a room that had more paintings on the walls, an ancient Spanish bayonet leaning in a corner, and, importantly, a large bed with an ornate spread and bright-red cases over the pillows.

She turned to him, her jaws hard. "*No!*"

He smacked her left cheek with the back of his right hand. She flew onto the bed with a scream and sat up, glaring at him and rubbing the blossoming welt on her cheek. He grabbed her arm and tossed her up higher on the bed, near the curtained window in the wall to the right.

He walked up to the head of the bed and grinned down at her as he started to unbuckle his cartridge belt.

"Now," he said with a goatish grin, "we're gonna have us some fun. When you wanna stop, you'll tell me everything Trent told you about what he knows about the doin's in the Wolf Mountains. Oh, I know he's been here." He grinned lasciviously as his gaze undressed her. "How could he not have been?"

Maclain wanted to know everything she could tell anyone about his doings, because everyone in town talked to Senorita Ortiz sooner or later. He could threaten her with slow death if she told a soul, but that wouldn't do him much good. She had Logan Trent on her side, and that would embolden her.

Besides, she had plenty of powerful friends in town, including the mayor. They would embolden her, too. She probably thought she could go to Dan True for help, not knowing he was on the side of the rustlers. But being young and beautiful, as well as a powerful businesswoman in Three Forks, she had plenty of other powerful friends, who could throw one hell of a wrench in Maclain's life.

He shucked his knife and his .45 from its holster, set them on the bedside table, and let his cartridge belt drop to the floor. He grinned down at her.

"Ready to be with a *real* man?"

"That sure as hell isn't you, Maclain!" came a man's voice from the bedroom's open door.

The man's voice nearly made Red leap out of his boots. He turned to see Logan Trent enter the room, his thumbs hooked behind his shell belt. He removed his left hand from the belt, tossed a key in the air, and caught it. He grinned.

He still had a key to the senorita's suite. Of course!

Maclain cursed. His heart raced in panic.

He swung around to grab his .45 off the bedside table.

He'd just turned toward Trent, clicking the .45's hammer back, when Trent's bullet took him through the dead center of his forehead. Everything instantly went black.

His wick snuffed, he was not aware that he was blown out the window behind him to land with a thud and a final gush of air from his lungs on the street below.

Chapter 16

Trent lowered the smoking Colt and stared at the broken window through which Red Maclain had flown two seconds before like an awkward bird, losing his hat in the process, his eyes rolling back in his head as he expired.

Trent had heard the thud of the man's landing and the *whoosh* of the man's last exhalation.

Clarita rose to her knees and twisted around to stare at the broken window, eyes round with shock.

Holding the Colt low in his right hand, Trent moved to the window.

Clarita rose from the bed.

"You best stay there," he said.

"He is a savage," she said, not heeding the warning.

She moved up to stand beside him and to stare through the broken window at the street below, where Red Maclain lay in a twisted heap just beyond the boardwalk fronting the saloon/brothel. Folks from across the street and from both sides of the Yellow Flower were rushing toward him, one man staring down at the dead man, exclaiming, "Why, that's Red Maclain, Big Ike's foreman!"

There were a good half-dozen men gathered around the dead man.

They all looked up at the broken window through which Maclain had flown.

They saw Logan Trent and Clarita Ortiz staring down through the broken glass.

"Good God!" cried one man, whom Trent recognized as one of the town's two barbers. "He's killed another one!"

"Over *her . . . again*!" exclaimed a mule skinner, who still held a beer in his hand. He must have emerged from the hurdy-gurdy house when he'd heard the shot, the breaking glass, and the thud of the dead man landing in the street.

"What did he want?" Trent asked Clarita. "Just to—"

"He wanted to know what you told me. He wanted to know how much I knew about his and True's operations. He knows that eventually everyone in town talks to me." She looked at Trent. "I never would have told anyone anything about that. I know *you* will handle it." She crossed her arms on her chest. "I just wish your brother were here to give you a better chance."

"Believe me . . ." Trent put an arm around her, drew her to him, and squeezed her affectionately. He didn't need to say anything more.

Clarita looked up at him gravely. "It's starting all over again."

"Don't worry," Trent said. "I'm going to end it once an' for all, if I have to cable the federals myself. I know the chief marshal in Boise."

He swung around, left the bedroom, and exited the hall door he'd left open. "Lock this behind me," he called to her, then closed the door behind him.

As he started walking down the hall, Clarita opened the door and said, "Logan, they need to know you had a good reason for killing that *animal*!"

"I'll take care of it." Trent kept walking toward the stairs. "You stay there. I don't want you a part of this mess."

He moved down the stairs. Several men stood in front of the batwing doors. More stood or sat at tables, staring at him.

He moved toward the batwings. The men standing there didn't make way for him. A tall, bearded mule skinner, whom Trent knew as Shelby Leonard, said with a jeering smile, "We had a bet goin', the boys an' me, on how long it would take you to start trouble again." He glanced around proudly at the others, puffing out his chest.

Leonard turned back to Trent. "Guess who won?"

"Get out of my way."

"Everybody in the room seen her go up with Maclain. Couldn't stand it, could you? So you killed another'n."

"I'm gonna give you one second to get out of my way and then you'll wish you'd done it yourself."

"Go to hell, Trent! You Trents ain't nearly as big as you thi—

"*Uhhffff!*" the mule skinner said as Trent buried his right fist in the man's soft paunch.

Leonard lowered his chin to his chest and dropped to his knees, gasping like a landed fish.

"What do you think about that now?" Trent asked the mule skinner, who was trying desperately to draw a breath.

As Leonard's friends moved toward Trent, Trent drew his six-shooter and, holding it half out from his side, said nothing except with his eyes. Leonard's friends got the message. They backed away, hands halfway raised. Trent stepped backward through the batwings, keeping the Colt aimed at the small gathering of tough nuts behind him.

He swung around to face the dozen or so men and a few women staring down at the twisted body of Red Maclain.

"Big Ike ain't gonna like this," commented one of the men, down on one knee regarding the dead man. He shook his head. "He ain't gonna like it a bit. If I was you, Trent, I'd run like hell . . . again. That's who you are. You're a man who needs to keep runnin'."

Apparently, word that Big Ike had fired Maclain had not yet reached town.

Trent said, "Go to hell."

"What happened, Logan? Someone said you shot Red Maclain!"

Trent turned to see the thickset, fleshy-faced Dan True half-walking, half-jogging toward him. His face was puffy and red with exertion. He didn't walk, much less jog, if you could call what he was doing jogging.

"He was in the wrong girl's room, and he was about to assault her."

True walked over to the body and barked, "Everybody, clear out! Get the hell out of here!" He turned to one of the men clad in miner's denims and hobnailed boots, a dirty straw sombrero on his head. "Clancy, fetch the undertaker. Tell him to bring his wagon. One of you others best ride up to the Double D and tell Big Ike."

"That won't be necessary," Trent told True. "They had a fallin'-out an' Big Ike gave Maclain his wages."

"Pshaw! That true?!" said True in feigned disbelief.

Trent now knew everything about Dan True was fake. He didn't want him to know he knew, though. Not yet. He'd tell him when he had his gun barrel in True's mouth, just before he pulled the trigger. Right now, he had other plans for the local lawman and the rest of the rustlers in the Wolf Mountains. He didn't want to scare them off. He wanted to kill them. That was the punishment . . . and a warning to others with similar ideas.

"It's true. Must've gotten drunk, started pestering Senorita Clarita, forced himself upstairs with her." Trent hardened his voice. "I blew him to hell, and only wish I could do it again."

He stepped forward and gave the dead man a savage kick to the ribs.

Maclain's body jostled.

His lips were still stretched back from his teeth in the grimace he'd shaped when he'd realized he was about to be the dead man he was now.

"Easy, Logan—he ain't gonna get no deader!" True placed a hand on Trent's shoulder and canted his head toward the Yellow Flower's batwings. "Let's go in an' have us a drink. I'll buy."

"I'm not really in the mood for a drink," Trent lied. He wanted to probe True, but he didn't want True to know that he was being probed.

"That's why I think ya need one." The outlaw sheriff squeezed Trent's shoulder.

Trent gave a feigned reluctant shrug. "Since you're buyin'."

True chuckled and pushed through the batwings, Trent right behind him. Clarita was behind the bar now, serving drinks. She and Trent locked brief, dark glances, and then he and True bellied up to the bar.

True set his hat on the bar top and arranged the few last strands of hair he had left on his head. "Sure am sorry he pestered you like that, Clarita. Big Ike's firin' him must have knocked somethin' loose in his thinker box. Prob'ly drunk as a gandy dancer on a Saturday night!"

Clarita glanced quickly at Trent again. "*Sí*. That must be what happened." She rose from where she'd been shelving bottles beneath the bar and, without her usual aplomb, placing both brown hands atop the bar, said, "Name your poison."

"The usual," True said.

"For me, too," Trent said.

When she went to work throwing their drinks together, Dan True, leaning toward her across the bar, said, "Did he say anything to you?" He flushed and added quickly, "You know—about what had made him so upset?"

Another quick glance at Trent, who thought, *Smooth, Dan. Real smooth.*

Drawing Trent's beer, Clarita rolled her eyes and shrugged. "Not really. He just taunted me, told me what he wanted to do to me." She gave a revolted shiver.

She set Trent's schooner in front of him and dropped the shot glass of whiskey into it. True glanced at the fizzing drink and smiled. "Old habits die hard—don't they, Logan?"

"Sure do." Trent gave Clarita a fleeting glance.

She did likewise to him.

True raised his glass of Scotch. "*Salute!*"

"*Salute*," Trent said, and sipped his drink.

True sipped his hooch and turned to Clarita. "Sure hope he didn't hurt you."

"He didn't have time. Logan came in just when he was about to . . ." She let her voice trail off and glanced down at the bar.

True took another sip of his Scotch and turned to Trent, frowning curiously. "How did you know what was going on up there?"

"I was starting back to the mountains, then remembered I'd forgotten to get my old man his bottle. So I came back, didn't see Clarita behind the bar. I asked if anyone knew where she was and someone told me she'd gone upstairs with Red."

That, of course, was a lie.

He'd been watching True's office since Red had ridden over there. Trent had been sitting astride Wolf on the corner of a side street. He saw Maclain ride his gray over to the Yellow Flower. The man had a dark scowl on his face, brows hooding his eyes. Trent waited, not wanting to go inside right away, not wanting the man to know that he was on to the former Double D foreman, not wanting him to know he, Trent, knew whom he was working for.

Who the head honcho was.

A dark voice inside him told him it was all related—Buck Donovan's murder and Dev's murder. Those two killings were somehow tied to the rustling in the Wolf Mountains. He just needed to know *how*.

He needed to know whom he needed to kill and *why*.

He'd just picked up his drink again but froze with it halfway to his mouth. He stared into the backbar mirror behind Clarita. Five men filed into the Yellow Flower, pushing through the batwings. They were a hard-looking lot in dusty trail garb, including chaps, wool shirts, suspenders, battered hats, and prominently displayed pistols on their hips or tied down on their thighs.

One wore a fox-fur coat.

Trent recognized him but had trouble remembering his name until "Missouri River" Ralph Benton came to mind.

Missouri River had worked for one of the outfits in the Wolfs at one time or another.

The other men looked familiar as well. They'd all worked for outfits in the Wolfs.

Trent's gut tightened when a couple of the men glanced at True, who made eye contact with them in the backbar mirror before quickly looking down at the whiskey glass he turned nervously in his hand. Clarita, just then pouring a whiskey for another man standing at the bar, ten feet down from True, gave Trent another fleeting, dark glance.

In the backbar mirror, Trent watched the five hardtails sit down at a table on the far side of the room, sighing and muttering among themselves. Their eyes kept darting toward Trent.

True had called in support staff. They'd likely been drinking in a dive more suited to their kind beyond the jail office.

True must have learned from Maclain, or suspected from all the events adding up, that Trent knew he, True, was likely the head honcho.

True needed him gone.

What about Clarita?

Damn, Trent wished he hadn't accepted her invitation to have that drink with her! She needed no part of this. She'd been part of enough.

Since she'd first shown up in town, Trent had always had a weakness for her. He couldn't let his weakness get her killed.

He just had to hope that True didn't know he'd informed her of the nefarious doings in the Wolfs. Maybe True would think, incorrectly, that he wouldn't have said anything to her to jeopardize her life.

But he had!

He needed to arm Clarita against True, who was old and fat. And he had to get these obvious rustling killers out of town. And kill them deader than dead and dump them into a ravine for the wild-cats and wolves to clean and scatter.

Five of them, one of him.

Doable.

Chapter 17

The afternoon wore on. More customers came in. Clarita delivered drinks to several tables.

As she did, Trent finished his drink and said, "I'd best be off before it gets dark."

"Headin' for the ranch?" True asked him.

Trent looked at him. He knew suspicion touched his eyes, and he didn't care. He was tired of True's charade. If those five men turned out to be after Trent, which he fully expected they were, Trent would come after True and shoot him down his throat.

"Where else would I go, Dan?"

True hiked a heavy shoulder. "Just wonderin', Logan. Just curious. A long ride for so late in the day!"

"Might have to find a place to camp. That's all right. I like building a fire and watching the stars."

True threw back the rest of his Scotch, tossed some coins on the bar, rose, set his hat on his head, and moseyed in his slightly bow-legged fashion toward the batwings. When he was gone, Clarita came back to the bar with her empty tray. Trent grabbed her arm.

"You have a gun in your room?"

She gave him a lopsided smile. "I have two .38s, two derringers, and three stilettos!"

Trent gave an ironic chuckle. "Good fer a fella to know!" He turned serious. "Keep them handy." He paused. "When are you finished for the day?"

"Behind the bar? At five. Then I go to work upstairs overseeing the girls."

"If you see True up there, shoot him."

Holding his gaze, she nodded slowly. She glanced at the five hard cases playing poker and drinking whiskey. "What about them?"

"I 'spect they'll leave right after I do."

"Ah, *sí*." She glanced at them again. "They are five. You might be Logan Trent, but you are one."

He grinned. "Doable."

She gave him a sidelong look. "Don't get overconfident, *mi amor*."

Trent set his hat on his head. "Never." But he did wish Devon were here. He'd always felt invincible in the company of his big brother, though Devon had been an inch shorter than Trent. In his younger brother's mind, Devon would always be taller. He pushed away from the bar. "I'll ride back to town tomorrow to check on you."

"We will be seen together again," she warned.

"Tomorrow's not gonna do any more damage than today did. It's me they want dead. If anyone touched a hair on your head, the whole town—at least, every *man* in the town—will tear them apart like a pack of wolves after an old elk."

She flushed, smiled, and kept her voice low as she said, "I am in love with you." Tears glazed her eyes. "But I don't think you are going to be alive much longer." She brushed a tear from her cheek with the back of her hand. "I've seen enough of everything in this world except you."

He swung around and headed for the batwings, hating himself for having fallen for two women in the past twenty-four hours. What in the hell kind of man was he, anyway?

He knew exactly what kind of man he was.

He was a Trent.

He pushed through the batwings. Wolf whinnied, shook his head, and pawed the ground. The roan was ready to ride back to the high country, where he, like his rider, had been born and bred. Where they felt at home.

"I know, fella," Trent said, swinging up onto the roan's back. "It's hard standing around bein' a horse."

He turned the roan away from the hitchrack, trotted down a side street opening kitty-corner from the Yellow Flower, crossed one of the many rustic board bridges spanning the forks in the Wolf River, rode ahead to another fork, and put Wolf into the narrow stream.

He followed the fork upstream and began climbing a forested ridge. At the top of the ridge, he dismounted, hauled his spyglass out of his saddlebags, and climbed atop an oval-shaped granite rock.

He focused the glass until he could see the settlement's western edge.

No sign of the hard cases yet.

Three minutes later, still no sign.

Then they rode out of the town and onto the main trail that traversed the forks in the river leading to the main trail that led up into the Wolfs. They traveled each of the three forks and disappeared to Trent's right as they followed the trail into a stone-floored canyon, a torrent during the spring runoff and sheathed in pine forest.

In that rugged terrain, they disappeared.

They weren't tracking Trent because the trail was hard and rocky and wouldn't hold a print. They just assumed he was heading back to his home ranch and that they'd catch up to him eventually, ride around him, get ahead of him, and shoot him out of the saddle.

He chuckled and collapsed his spyglass, then reprimanded himself, remembering Clarita's admonishment for him not to get overconfident.

That was another Trent habit.

He hoped it hadn't gotten Dev killed.

As he dropped the spyglass into a saddlebag pouch, his brows stitched. He wondered if any of those five men, who obviously intended to follow him into the mountains, had killed Devon. The only way he could find out was if he left at least one of them alive and somehow got him to admit to the killing or to point out who'd killed his brother.

Probably, more than one.

No one man could kill Devon Trent. Dev was handier and faster with a six-shooter than his younger brother was and—not to be pompous or overconfident—that was saying something.

Trent stepped into the leather and angled Wolf down the mountain to the south, picking up the main trail that rose into the sierra to the southwest, and held the roan to a trot, though he knew the stallion wanted to give his lungs, heart, muscles, and sinew a workout. But he had to hold back. Those five hardtails of Dan True needed to believe he was ahead of them, not behind them. He knew a good place, a side canyon, where he could ride up a ridge and down the other side, getting ahead of them.

That's where he would take them.

That's where he would scour them from his trail.

A mile or so after he'd left his perch, where he'd watched the men leave town and take to the main trail into the mountains, he crested a ridge and saw the five riders just then ascending the next ridge beyond him, a quarter mile away. Five man-and-horse-shaped silhouettes were for a few seconds outlined against the dimming sky before dropping down the ridge's other side, disappearing from sight.

Trent rode down the ridge he was on. Halfway up the other

side, the canyon he'd been watching for opened off the main trail's left side.

He swung Wolf into it, the roan balking at first because the entrance was cramped; rocks and pines were pushing up close on either side. It widened about thirty feet farther in and started to climb, the floor of the canyon littered with old driftwood and sand scalloped by the previous spring's violent floods.

He rode for a half hour up the side canyon, climbing gradually between banks of nearly solid rock, from the cracks in which roots and a few dwarf cedars protruded. Faded paintings of the ancient Indians who'd once traveled the canyon shone here and there on the rock walls—stick figures of hunters with spears and yellow suns and blue stars and what Trent figured were leaping orange campfires.

All were badly faded, of course, but, amazingly, still recognizable. The human race was savage. But it could be beautiful, too, he reminded himself.

Wolf picked his way up the stone-floored canyon. They climbed for nearly a mile and had just crossed a bend in the canyon, angling right around a hump protruding from the canyon's right wall, when Wolf stopped abruptly. Suddenly the roan pricked his ears, shook his head, and loosed a shrill whinny.

He took one quick, frightened step forward. The move saved Trent's life, for just then a bullet whistled mere inches from his right ear.

The shooter lay prone atop the stone bank ahead and to the right.

Trent recognized one of the five hard cases from the Yellow Flower.

Automatically, his movements honed from frequent practice, Trent jerked his Russian .44 from its holster and triggered three quick rounds. The man dropped his rifle, lost his hat, and fell back out of sight.

Another bullet plowed into Trent's upper left arm. It was like a hard jab by a glowing branding iron.

Wolf whinnied shrilly and bucked. Trent reached for the horn, but with his .44 in his right hand, he couldn't grab it. Instead, he kicked out of his stirrups to keep from being dragged and hit the ground hard on his left shoulder and hip. Wolf whinnied again and galloped on up the canyon, buck-kicking angrily.

The only one who hated getting outsmarted and dry-gulched more than Trent was Wolf.

Despite the pain in his arm and hip, and how badly the ground was pitching around him, Trent rose and hurried back around the bend in the canyon wall. He ran fifty yards, hearing the roar of gunfire behind him and the shouts of angry men, and found a break in the canyon wall on his right. Holding his right hand, in which he still clutched his Russian, over the bloody wound in his upper left arm, he ran through it and up a rise filled with firs and pines.

He lost blood and energy.

Hearing his pursuers behind him—they were shouting and on foot now—he fell, as much as threw himself, behind the roots of an uprooted spruce. He sat back against the ball, ripped off his neck-knotted bandanna, and wrapped it tightly around the wound in his arm, biting his tongue to keep from screaming from the pain.

Moving as quickly as he could, his hands shaking from the burning misery in his arm and the blood he was losing, he broke open the top-break Russian, plucked out the spent shells, and replaced them with fresh ones from his cartridge belt. He closed the pistol and unsheathed the other one, which he wore in the cross-draw position on his left hip.

Footsteps sounded on the slope below him.

"Where'd he go?" a man said softly.

Trent recognized the voice of Missouri River, who wore the fox-fur coat. He'd been rustling cattle for years, and should have been hanged years ago, but no one had actually caught him at it. When he'd been fired off several consecutive ranches for fighting, drunkenness, and general sloth, he went to work as a market hunter for some of the merchants down in Three Forks and neighboring settlements.

Everyone knew that was just a cover for long-looping Wolf Mountain beef, however.

Trent removed his hat, set it down beside him, turned his head to his left, and edged a look around the root-webbed ball of dirt behind him. The four remaining hard cases were slowly climbing the slope, tracking with their rifles, spreading out, and weaving through the trees. Benton was nearest Trent, roughly twenty feet away and moving toward the root ball.

Trent pulled his head back, lips stretched from his teeth in misery. His arm was on fire and he felt himself weakening fast. He listened to the crunching footsteps of the approaching killer from Missouri. The footsteps grew louder. After a long, slow minute, the man came into Trent's view, moving wide around the root ball to Trent's left as he sat facing up the ridge.

Benton aimed his Henry repeater straight out from his right shoulder.

The man's eyes widened under his floppy, brimmed leather hat when he saw Trent, whose Russians bucked and roared, both bullets taking Benton in the chest, making the fox fur jounce and immediately spout bright-red blood. The man discharged his Henry wide as he stumbled backward, dropping the rifle and falling to his knees, cursing, crossing his arms on his chest to cover the wounds with his hands.

"Dammit!" he yelled, lifting his head to glare at Trent.

He fell back on an elbow. He glared at Trent. "Do you know who I *am*?"

"Were," Trent said calmly. "I know who you were. Now you ain't worth a turd in a bucket."

Benton smiled through a grimace. A jeering humor flashed in his brown eyes. "Figured you outsmarted us, didn't you? I had a sense, though. Comes from long experience rustling Trent beef.

I knew you'd sneak around behind us. No shoe scrapes on rock, no fresh horse apples. Hell, you ain't no smarter than me!"

The other men had scurried for cover, yelling and shooting at the root ball, their bullets plunking into the ball's far side and into the tree trunk lying parallel to the forest floor.

"No, but I'm still alive," Trent said.

He ratcheted the Russian's hammers back, took aim, and drilled two more rounds into Benton's chest. The man grunted and fell back against the ground, boots quivering.

"And you're dead!"

A man's raspy voice yelled from down the grade over Trent's right shoulder. "You're dead, too, Trent! You just don't know it yet!"

A bullet thunked into the spruce trunk to Trent's right.

Chapter 18

As more guns thundered and more bullets hammered the spruce's trunk and the root ball, sending dirt and snakelike bits of root flying in all directions, Trent peered up and over the trunk on his left. The man who'd yelled the ominous warning was running, crouching, from tree to tree, trying to make his way up and around Trent.

Trent's right-hand Russian bucked and roared.

The bullet thumped into the trunk of the aspen the man had just taken cover behind, causing white bark to fly. As bullets caromed around him—to both sides and over his head and into the rear side of the root ball—Trent aimed his Russian once more.

The man who'd taken cover behind the aspen edged a look around the left side of it.

Trent aimed, held his breath, and pulled the trigger.

The Russian roared.

The bullet turned the man's eyes the color of a smashed tomato. It knocked him on his back. He rolled wildly down the steep grade toward the canyon below.

Trent pulled the Russian down and pressed his back against the uprooted ball of the spruce.

The shooting from below was tapering off.

The remaining two men knew they were only wasting bullets. They were probably getting damn low.

Trent pressed his back against the root ball and drew deep, even breaths, fighting to remain conscious. If he passed out, he would die. That much was obvious. He set his Russian on his thigh and used that hand to tighten the neckerchief he'd wrapped around the wound. He had to hold more blood in, or he'd pass out, and that would be the end of him.

Clarita had been right.

He'd gotten overconfident.

He should have known those five would figure out his ploy. But they hadn't *looked* that smart! When they'd seen the narrow canyon angling off from the main one, they'd gambled he'd take it. He'd been too damn predictable, because he was too damn confident. These men knew this country as well as he did. They'd probably been in this range for as long as he'd been, although following differing pursuits.

He'd been raising cattle with his father and brother.

These men had been stealing them, somehow avoiding hanging ropes for years.

The joke was on Trent.

The shooting dwindled, then died altogether.

The two remaining men were talking in low tones before one of them said clearly, "Let's get outta here!"

Trent peered out around the right side of the root ball. The two remaining men were running downhill, heading for the break in the canyon wall—one tall and bearded, the other short and stocky, with a mustache and goatee, and wearing a low-crowned black hat. They'd both just gained the base of the ridge and were ten feet from the break. Trent snaked his right-hand Russian out from around the ball, closed one eye, aiming, clicked the Russian's hammer back, and fired.

The short, stocky man cursed shrilly and grabbed the back of his buckskin-clad right thigh. He took two hopping steps forward, then dropped to his knees. The other man leaped over him and disappeared through the break in the canyon wall.

"Pageant, you wait for me, damn you!" the stocky man shouted in a voice shrill with pain.

But Pageant was gone.

The short, stocky man turned toward Trent, cursing like a mule skinner. He fired his rifle toward Trent, then, cursing in agony, crawled through the break, and was gone in an eye blink after Trent had tried to finish him, but his .44 slug merely plowed into a rock inches away from the stocky man's right foot.

Trent sank back against the root ball once more.

Hands shaking, his strength waning still further, he broke open the Russians and managed to pluck the spent casings out of his six-shooters and replace them with fresh. He wasn't going anywhere without two loaded pistols. He doubted those two would be back. He'd scared the holy hell out of them both and put a chunk of hot lead into the short, stocky gent. He wouldn't be using that leg for a while. Trent grinned at the thought of the man dragging himself up the canyon toward the taller man, who was likely running, with the fear of God in him, for his horse.

Trent would have gone down and finished the short, stocky gent after getting what information he could from him, but he didn't have the energy. He had to seek shelter, build a fire, if he had any strength in him at all, and cauterize the wound. If not, he'd be dead in an hour, maybe two.

But those would be two long, agonizing hours.

He peered up the ridge ahead of him. A stone escarpment rose roughly seventy yards away. Boulders littered its base. Could he make it that far, and, once there, would he have the energy to gather wood and build a fire?

He'd kill for a shot of whiskey.

That might get him there.

Wolf.

He might be around here somewhere, intending to remain with his rider. He was as loyal as a dog that way. Trent managed to pull the glove off his right hand with his teeth, stick two fingers in his mouth, and whistle. He didn't have the wind for much of a whistle. He doubted the horse heard it. He tried once more, then gave up.

He had no energy to spare.

He pulled his glove back on, then pushed off the root ball behind him to help lever himself to his feet. He groaned deeply against the pain the maneuver kicked up in his arm. He was dizzy, off balance. He pushed off the root ball and stepped forward slowly. He took another step, another . . . and then he was moving steadily. Not certainly for sure, but at least he was climbing the grade toward the scarp.

His heart pounded. His pulse screamed in his ears. His lungs felt the size of raisins, and he had to gasp for every breath. He kept his right hand clamped tightly around the wound in his left arm.

He stopped frequently, shouldering up against a tree, for a breather.

It would have been so easy for him to just slide down the tree to the ground and go to sleep. But that would be certain death. He'd never wake up.

With a fierce will, fighting the weakness growing inside him by leaps and bounds, he pushed off the trees and, putting one leaden foot in front of the other, continued climbing. By the time he reached the scarp, his head was spinning, his vision blurred. He made his way into a pocket of the wagon-sized boulders and fell, as much as sank, down to his knees, then maneuvered himself around until he had his back against the rough wall of the stone scarp.

He meant only to take a breather, to gather enough energy to forage for dead branches for a fire, but then his heavy lids shut, darkness swept over him, and he slid down across the scarp to lie with his shoulder on the gravelly ground. A horse whinnied in the distance, the sound barely reaching his ears. Still, he slept, unable to stir. Not even wanting to. He just wanted to lie here and sleep, even if it meant he might never wake up.

He vaguely felt a vibration in the ground beneath him.

A horse snorted, blew.

A young woman's voice: "My God!"

Trent gurgled, grunted, tried to heave himself up out of unconsciousness. Something touched his cheek, snorted in his ears. He smiled.

Wolf.

"Logan!" Even in his one-quarter state of consciousness, he recognized Megan Donovan's voice. Then her hands were on his shoulders, shaking him desperately. "Wake up! Wake up, Logan! Sit up!"

She grunted as she pulled up on his shoulders.

The pain in his arm bit him deep. The only way to stop it was to rummage around at the bottom of himself to find just enough strength to assist her in lifting him against the escarpment wall. Her face was six inches from his.

"You stay there!" she demanded. "Wolf, keep him there!"

Wolf pawed the ground before his downed rider and nodded, pressing his nose against Trent's cheek. "You're mixin' with the wrong crowd, boy," Trent grumbled. "That girl's a ring-tailed nag!"

"You stay right there, Wolf!" Megan demanded as she reached into one of her saddlebag pouches. Her pinto stood just off Wolf's right hip.

Megan came back with her canteen hanging from a shoulder and pulling a bottle out of a tightly wrapped burlap bag. She dropped the bag, handed Trent the canteen, and said, "Have a big drink of that. You need to make more blood."

When he'd had several deep pulls from the canteen—he hadn't

realized how thirsty he was—she uncorked the bottle and dropped to a knee beside Trent.

"Have a sip of this. Just a sip."

She touched the bottle to his lips, poured some into his mouth. He swallowed, but choked on it.

"More," she said. "It's a bracer, and believe you me, you need a bracer!"

She poured a little more into his mouth. That went down better. Soothing, taking some of the bite out of the sharp teeth of the arm wound. He reached for the bottle. She slapped his hand. "That's enough for now. I don't want you passin' out again."

"How'd you find me?" he asked.

"Later," she said.

She corked the bottle, set it on the ground beyond his reach, then moved down into the pines flanking the boulders, gathering wood. It was dusk. Shadows from the trees, rocks, and the tall, flame-shaped escarpment grew long around her. She dropped the wood near Trent's extended feet, quickly formed a ring of rocks, broke some of the smaller branches into tinder, adding some crushed pinecones, and reached into her shirt pocket for a box of lucifers.

She had the fire blazing just as dark settled in like a giant black-gloved hand closing over the world. She set Trent's own iron claw in the fire, made coffee, poured him a cup, and added a liberal splash of whiskey. Then she set his bowie knife in the flames, resting the handle on one of the rocks comprising the ring.

"Ohh . . ." he groaned, dreading the anticipation of that soon-to-be-red blade pressed against the bloody hole in his arm.

"Go easy on that," she ordered, glancing at the smoking cup in his hands.

She rose and unsaddled both horses, hobbling them to keep them near. She gave them a quick rubdown with the burlap from the bottle, then returned to the fire and removed the bloody neckerchief he'd wrapped around the wound. She cut a large hole in the sleeve of his shirt around the wound, cleaned it with whiskey and water, making him want to howl like a gut-shot coyote, then plucked his knife out of the fire.

The blade glowed brightly.

"Look away," she said. "You don't want to see this."

"If you're going to kill me, just kill me. Don't torture me!"

Without further ado, she touched the glowing blade to the ragged hole in his arm. He dug his heels into the ground and moaned. He would have screamed, but he was a Trent, and she was a Donovan. They were warring clans, after all. They could show only courage.

Might start a land war, otherwise.

"You stay conscious, dammit," she ordered, wrapping a fresh bandanna from her saddlebags around his arm and tying it tightly.

Again, his head was spinning from the agony. His vision was blurry. He felt the searing pain of that glowing blade all the way to his toes.

Badly slurring his words from the misery extending through his entire being, he said, "I feel sorry for your husband."

"I don't have a husband."

"Ever wonder why?"

"Been waitin' on a Trent!" She leaned down and kissed his cheek. She sat back against the wall of the stone escarpment, right beside him, and crossed her ankles. She blew a wisp of hair from her cheek.

"Do you know who shot you?"

Trent shook his head.

"A well-known pack of long-loopers who started haunting these mountains the year after you left. My father hanged three of them two years ago, but the others are still around, seen from time to time. Slippery as spring ice."

"How'd you find me?"

She tossed that pesky wisp of hair from her face. "I was out riding to get some air. You won't believe this, but Pa can be a little stifling."

Trent grunted out a chuckle.

"I came upon Wolf grazing a ways off the trail. I led him down the trail, knowing he'd eventually lead me to you. A rider came galloping hell for leather, nearly ran into me as he rode past. His eyes were wide as silver dollars. Ernie Pageant. A killer from Arkansas. I rode farther down the trail and found a man crawling, cursing and grunting and clutching his leg. I asked him who shot him and he said, 'The killer Logan Trent!'

"I shucked my carbine from the boot an' said, 'Let me finish the job.'"

"You killed him?"

Megan smiled and tossed another branch on the fire.

"What happened?" she asked him.

"Long story." Trent didn't want her involved. He was already endangering one young lady because of her involvement in his investigation. He wasn't about to do that to another.

She placed a hand on his thigh. "Tell me."

"No."

"Why?"

"You know enough. Guns have been fired, bullets have flown."

She turned to him, tilting her head forward a little. "You don't need to worry about me. I can take care of myself."

"That fella who galloped past you might have gone for help. Likely won't come till morning, but we're gonna have to pull out early."

"How many do you think there are?"

Trent shrugged. "It's a syndicate. I'm guessing at least twenty or more. Quite a few are dead. I know where they were holing up and doctoring brands, but now they know I know, so they'll look for another place. A remote canyon somewhere, an abandoned ranch at the northern edge of the mountains. Maybe even the Bitterroots. They have a lucrative business going. They won't want to give it up. They're not afraid of one man, but they don't want more men coming in and hunting them down."

"Who's the leader?"

"Can't tell you that."

"Oh, come on!"

"In the morning, you get your purty behind home, and you stay there. Your old man and his cold-steel crew can protect you."

"I told you—"

"I know, I know. You can protect yourself. But you can't." Trent glanced at the bandage wrapped tightly around his arm. "Hell, I can't even protect myself. In the morning, I'm gonna ride back to Three Forks and send a telegram to the chief marshal in Boise, have him send U.S. deputy marshals to help me track these vermin down before they clean out every beef in these mountains. If he can send between ten an' fifteen men to buoy my ranks—"

"This isn't just your fight, Logan. They're loopin' our beef, too."

Trent nodded. "We haven't lost many yet. I'm bettin' your old man hasn't, either, because not every man on both of our rolls is out scouring the mountains for the rustlers. But there's gonna be a bloody war soon. Not between our two outfits, but between us and the rustlers. We have to stay together. Your outfit an' mine. They'll try to pit us against each other, clean each other out so they won't have to."

Trent shook his head. "We can't fall for it." He gave Megan a direct look. "We can't fall for it," he repeated.

She studied him with a frown cutting deep lines across her forehead over which light and shadows from the fire danced.

"Why are *you* sending for the federals? Why isn't . . . ?"

Uh-oh, he thought.

"Forget it," he said, and rested his head back against the scarp's stone wall.

"Dan True!" she exclaimed.

Trent cursed.

Chapter 19

"Forget about that—understand me?" Trent said, giving Megan a hard, commanding look.

She snorted. "Don't try to order me around, Trent. I mean, you were fun, but you weren't that much fun!"

Trent sighed. "Lordy . . ."

She got up and used a swatch of leather to remove the coffeepot from the rock she'd set it on to keep it hot. She refilled Trent's coffee cup and then her own. She returned the pot to the rock, then picked up the bottle, which was on the other side of where she'd been sitting, just out of Trent's reach.

Trent reached for the bottle. She slapped his hand, gave him a schoolmarmish frown, then uncorked the bottle and added a conservative jigger to his steaming mud. She added two conservative jiggers to her own, giving him a jeering look, then corked the bottle, sat beside him again, and set the bottle down beside her right thigh.

"Why do you get more than I do?"

"You need to get your strength, not drunk."

She pulled a rawhide pouch out of her pocket, opened it, and set it down between them. "Have some jerky."

"Ain't hungry."

Another commanding look. "Have some jerky."

He scowled. "Don't go thinkin' I'm gonna marry you. I won't marry a harpy."

Megan smiled, chewing. "You'll marry me. You've wanted to for years. You just got that little saloon gal stuck in your craw, with her sexy accent and those purty . . . well, you know. But you need a mountain girl who won't take your crap."

Trent sighed, plucked a strip of jerky from the bag, and chomped into it. She took one, too, bit into it, and, chewing, said, "Dan True is one useless lawman. I'll send Pa and his new foreman—when he gets a new foreman—into town to bullwhip him. I bet that will put an end to the rustling in these mountains."

"Don't count on it."

"Why not?"

"For a syndicate the size of the one he's running, he's likely got hired killers up there." Trent jerked his chin to indicate the higher reaches. "I'm sure one or two or three of 'em are just waiting to take over, take True's cut of the profits."

"There is no honor among thieves."

"Somethin' like that."

"Why don't we just send our best gunmen out, round them all up, and throw necktie parties in their honor?"

"They'd never find them. You send that many men after them, they'll scatter like church mice on Sunday morning. They'll be back at it again in a month."

Megan sipped her whiskey-laced coffee and turned to him, frowning curiously. "So, what do you propose?"

"I don't know." Trent drew a deep breath, glanced at his bandaged arm, which, despite the painkiller, still felt like a badger was sinking its teeth into it. "I wish Dev were here."

"What would Dev do?"

"I think he'd scout around until he found their main hideout. They herded the beeves to Tin Cup, where they drank while using running irons to change the brands and turn them over to buyers from the outlaw ranches in the Bitterroots. They might return there, believin' I . . . er, we . . . would think they wouldn't. That's what Dev would think. He was a good teacher, that brother of mine." Trent cleared his throat, choked back emotion. "That was the rustlers' permanent camp. It'd be a job of work findin' another one. Besides, they likely think they're tough an' mean enough . . . an' there's enough of 'em . . . to hold us off."

Megan gave him a crooked smile. "You'd make a good rustler."

He chuckled dryly. "Makes my neck hurt just thinkin' about it." He flexed his neck. "When this heals up"—Trent glanced at his arm, wishing like hell he hadn't taken that bullet—"I'm gonna scout Tin Cup again . . . from a distance."

"And then what?"

"Then we'll employ a variation on your idea. I'll talk to your old man and my old man, and we'll send the cream of their crops out to *shoot* them all down, like ducks on a millpond." Again, Trent shook his head. "They're gonna rue the day they messed with the Triple T and led me to Tin Cup."

"How many do you think there are?"

"Fifteen or maybe twenty left. I know True. He may be old and obsolete, but he thinks big. He wants to retire soon, and, knowing the town council as well as I do, he doesn't have much of a pension. No, he's headed for a rockin' chair in the Ladies for Abstinence House of Christian Charity. He doesn't want to go out that way, bein' browbeat by harpies. He fought in the War Between the States and the Indian Wars. He was one of the men who shot the Sioux out of these mountains. He was a shotgun rancher for a few years, never makin' much of a livin' at it, before a bad back, a big gut, and generally unhealthy living put him in that shabby jail office in Three Forks."

He sipped his smoking brew and turned to Megan. "I think this rustling scheme has been on his mind for years. Lots of ranches up here. Small ones, big ones. None bigger than yours an' mine. He can make a lot of money just siphoning off a few cows at a time, probably at night when all our hands are sawing logs in our bunkhouses."

"You think one of them killed your brother." It wasn't a question.

Trent nodded, took another sip of the soothing elixir of coffee laced with a good brand of whiskey. No bottom-shelf stuff for a Donovan.

"I don't think I'll know which one. There was definitely more than one. Just one man couldn't take Dev down. Hell, they sent five after me and only two—er, *one*—survived." Trent chuckled at the image of Megan feeding the fourth one to the wildcats, who were probably fighting over him right now.

He chuckled again as he stared off, pensive.

"What's funny?"

"Us. Throwing in together. Two warring parties."

"We were at war. You an' me, I mean."

"We're damn lucky our folks never found out."

"Our behinds would still be mighty sore."

Trent laughed, then held his cup out to her, one brow arched plaintively. "I'm in a lot of pain here."

She gave him a disapproving grimace, reached for the bottle, and uncorked it. He still had a little old stuff left in his cup. She gave him several liberal splashes.

He arched both brows at her.

"Ah, hell," she said, "I have another bottle in my saddlebags. It was Pa's an' he'll roar, but . . . let's get drunk." She rose and replenished their tin cups with the steaming coffee from the dented, white-speckled black pot. "Trouble lies in both our futures," she said, returning the pot to its rock, adding a stout, forked branch to the fire, and sitting back down beside him.

They said nothing for a while, just studied the flames. They didn't need to worry about compromising their vision in the dark. The horses, hobbled near, would warn them of possible trouble, giving them time to kick dirt on their fire and reach for their rifles. At a dangerous time like this, they shouldn't be drinking. They knew better. But like Megan had said, trouble lay in their futures, and they might as well enjoy a night away from the world.

Devon would admonish the hell out of them. Trent, half-drunk, smiled at the thought. God, how he missed that boy!

The smile faded. His eyes glazed.

He and Megan were silent for a long time. From a far-distant ridge, a wolf howled. From another ridge, also far in the distance, came another wolf's answering howl.

Megan turned to him. "Did you see her?"

Trent nodded.

She turned her head away and nodded then, too. After a minute, she turned to him again. "Anything happen?"

"I killed Red."

She turned to him quickly, eyes wide in shock. "Why?"

"He forced her upstairs to her suite . . . was about to . . . before I walked in. Shot him out her window. He died in the street like a dog."

Megan sighed. "At least, another long-looper is dead."

"A few more to go."

Again, Megan looked at him. "You're in no condition to ride back to town tomorrow, you know."

He nodded. "I know."

"Besides, you'd shoot True, and it's not time yet. They'd flee from this town, like rats from a sinking ship."

Trent finished his brew, set his cup down, and pulled his hat down over his eyes. He folded his arms across his chest, crossed his ankles. "One step at a time," he said. "I'll save the best for last."

"True?"

"True."

* * *

Trent felt something pressing against his right shoulder.

Or his right shoulder was pressing against something.

The painful wound in his left arm and the hooch still swimming around in his blood served to make him badly disoriented. Where was he and what was he doing here?

He opened his eyes.

A soft pearl morning light enveloped him. Cold mountain air slithered into his nose to touch his lungs with its chill and freshness, the smell of damp pine duff. A head rested against his shoulder. Chestnut hair tightly pulled back from her temples to tumble down her back in a long, sleek queue.

Megan's nose was buried against his neck. He could feel her soft, steady, warm breath against his chin, just inside his shirt collar and the collar of the denim jacket he'd donned last night as the sun had sunk and the high-country chill had come down, increasing in strength just as the stars had intensified their flickering light. Megan had draped her soogan over them both, but he could vaguely feel her shivering as she slept.

There was no frost on the ground, as there often could be at these climes, even in the summer, but as Trent lifted his head, straightening his back a little, he could see his breath in the near-dark, still morning air.

Megan stirred, groaned softly, and tightened her shoulders, but kept her head on his shoulder.

Quietly she said, "Is it morning?"

"Not yet. You can sleep a little longer. I'll build up the fire and make coffee."

She lifted her head quickly. "I'll do that. You're the one who needs his beauty sleep."

"I can't get any purtier." He tossed his part of the blanket off him and onto her, planted his hands on the ground, and heaved himself to his feet. "You babied me plenty. I have to start doin' for myself." He winced and clutched his arm. "Even though that badger chompin' my arm don't seem to have lessened his dander much."

She started to rise, but he pushed her back down with a hand on her shoulder. "I have to get back to it sooner or later. Go to sleep. I'll wake you with a fresh cup."

"You're such a Trent," she complained, and leaned her head back against the escarpment's cold wall, drawing the soogan up tighter around her shoulders.

It wasn't easy, but he poked and prodded a few of the fire's flames back to life, gradually adding small branches, then larger ones. He filled his coffeepot from both their canteens and set it on the iron claw in the building flames. He saw the empty bottle on the ground beside Megan's right hip, the cork nearby, then tiptoed over to where she'd piled her gear, found the fresh bottle, and, keeping an eye on her, brought it over to where the pot was gurgling to life, then set it on the ground.

"I saw that," she muttered.

Trent grunted like a cowed schoolboy. She didn't miss much.

But then, she was a Wolf Mountain girl. What did he expect?

That's why he'd tumbled for her years ago when they'd both been much younger. When they'd both known anything between them was impossible, because of who they were, each being from a separate clan at war against the other.

He unhobbled the horses to let them graze in the forest down the slope. He returned to the fire to fill his and Megan's cups with the rich, steaming black brew, added a little whiskey to each—yes, a little. He had to get back on the trail, so to speak. The rustlers' trail and the vengeance trail and the trail to find out who had killed Buck Donovan, thus clearing his own name. He couldn't sit on the corral—literally and figuratively—until he'd accomplished those tasks.

Then he'd be right here, back in the Wolf Mountains. Home again. He'd enjoyed Montana, but he'd only return to sell the saloon. Then he'd come back home, and, in the wake of Devon's death, he'd help his father run the ranch, then take over for him once the old man had lived out his days.

Megan had been right. He was a Trent.

But he was getting ahead of himself.

He set his cup down beside him, then grabbed his rifle from where it leaned against the rock wall between him and Megan and rested it across his thighs. He looked at Wolf watching him from where the horse stood down the slope, with Megan's pinto at the edge of the trees. The roan would warn him of danger. The one dry-gulcher he'd left alive might bring others. He had to be mindful of that.

But if they came, they wouldn't come till later.

Wherever they all were gathered was a long way away. Either holed up in a temporary camp, a remote canyon, say, that would be damned hard to find, even by the men who resided in these mountains, hazing herds around every day of the spring, fall, and summer.

Still, Trent looked at Wolf once more. The stallion grazed contentedly with Megan's mount. But then, the horse jerked its head up suddenly and craned his neck to peer behind him, ears pricked, tail switching anxiously.

Trent pumped a live round into the Yellowboy's action and rose.

"Stay here," he whispered to Megan, and began moving slowly out from behind the boulders toward the forest below.

As he walked, he heard the metallic rasp of Megan racking a round into her Winchester's breech.

Chapter 20

Trent stopped where Wolf was still gazing anxiously down the forested mountain toward the canyon a hundred yards below.

The horse turned to face downslope, kicking a rock, and whickered.

Trent ran a soothing hand down his neck.

"Easy, easy. Quiet, now, boy."

Megan's pinto was facing the same direction, apprehension in his eyes, his tail slightly arched.

Something or *someone* was down there.

Trent was betting on the latter.

That's all right. He was Trent enough to think it was as good a morning as any to resume the killing against those trying to overtake the mountains.

He glanced at Wolf again. The horse turned his head to stare farther down the slope through the pines, firs, and aspens silhouetted against the growing dawn light, toward the right. Someone was trying to circle around him. Did that mean someone was coming up on his left, too?

Low, furtive voices sounded straight down the slope ahead of him.

Pulling his Winchester's hammer back to full cock, and holding the rifle straight before him, he continued striding slowly, quietly, down the slope toward the canyon, pausing to hole up behind trees and taking a careful look around. He'd walked maybe fifty yards, when a deep, guttural snort rose not far down the slope on his right.

Hooves thudded behind Trent then.

He stopped and glanced over his shoulder. Wolf and Megan's pinto were running up toward the boulders where they'd spent the night. Megan stood now in a gap between them, with her rifle held in her hands, her feet spread, and her shoulders stiff. She, too, had her head turned to gaze down the slope on Trent's right.

Another guttural grunt and then a bugling cry rose, vaulting up out of the forest like the throaty voice of some enraged god. A man screamed. Another man screamed. Rifles thundered and men yelled. Another bugling cry, even louder than the first, and then the sounds of men running beneath the heavy thunder of some four-legged creature chasing them.

Brush crackled, branches snapped.

Men downslope, and on Trent's left, yelled and started running toward the growing cacophony of men and the pursuing beast.

"What the hell is *that*?" one of them shouted straight down the slope before Trent now.

More screaming. More shouting. More cursing.

More savage grunting and bugling and guttural growls.

The sounds of ripping cloth and tearing flesh.

A few more rifle shots. Trent could see the stabs of flames from rifle barrels seventy or eighty yards below.

The growls continued, but grew quieter.

The men's screams dropped to whimpers before they died and there was only the plodding of four heavy feet and rumbling grunts issuing up from near the base of the ridge. Trent stood frozen, staring down the declivity, squeezing his Winchester in his hands, his heart hammering against his breastbone.

Silence.

Trent pricked his ears, listening.

After a minute, he smelled the sickly sweet stench of something wild growing more and more intense on the chill dawn air. Something moved on the slope below him, weaving through the trees. A branch cracked beneath a heavy foot and then the bear appeared, coming around from the far side of a large spruce, roughly fifty feet away from Trent, who was in such shock that he couldn't move his feet.

Suddenly the bear came running at him, dark-brown fur rippling, its hump swelling, its dark eyes growing wide as it approached, its mouth opening and showing long, savagely curved white teeth. That enraged, bugling cry sounded once more, echoing loudly and making Trent's ears ring.

The bear was thirty-five . . . thirty feet away.

Blood glistened on its chest, where it had been shot, enraging it further.

Heart hammering, his pulse throbbing in his ears, Trent dropped to a knee, raised the Winchester to his shoulder, and fired once . . . twice . . . three times, watching the bruin's fur part, where his bullets plowed into its thick hide. A rifle roared behind Trent, on the upslope, causing the bear's fur to part further, in more places.

The bear was twenty feet from Trent, roaring, shaking its head, making biting and slashing motions with its huge mouth, an ancient savagery glinting in its eyes.

Trent emptied the Yellowboy into the grizzly, while Megan fired from behind and above him.

The beast rose, roaring, showing its teeth, raising its front paws above its head; its curved, bowie knife–like claws were extended, ready for the kill.

Suddenly it stopped.

It shook its head, as if to ward off a swarm of wasps. It brushed its claws across its cheeks. Eyes pinned on its intended quarry—Trent—its head went up, its eyes rolled back, and it fell straight forward and down, like a tree that had been sawed off at the base.

Trent cursed, rose, and stumbled backward.

He got his feet entangled and fell hard on his back with a grunt, dropping the Yellowboy.

The big bruin blotted out the lightening sky above and behind it for just a second or two. Its vast body, with a massive hump, landed ten feet away from Trent. The bear's big, square head hammered down between his legs, making dirt and pine needles plume.

The beast turned its head from right to left, gave a last, low grunt, slashing once more with its teeth, then lay still. Trent had felt the reverberations of its massive heart beating in the ground beneath him. Suddenly the reverberations died. All that was left was the cloying odor of the wild bruin of the Wolf Mountains.

"P.U.—that thing stinks!"

Trent looked up to see Megan staring down at him, her smoking Winchester aiming out and down at a slant from her right hip.

Trent looked down at the massive head at rest between his legs. "Like my old man—prob'ly just takes a bath once a year whether it needs it or not."

"You all right?"

"My nerves are dust."

"Join the club. I thought you were gonna be that big bruin's breakfast . . . me, its dessert."

She extended a gloved hand to him. He took his rifle in his right hand and accepted her hand with his left. She rocked back on her heels, hardened her jaws, and heaved him to his feet. He rose with a grunt, glancing down at the beast once more.

"He nearly killed us, but I reckon we have him to thank for saving our lives."

Megan glanced down the slope through the forest, the pines and firs standing out darkly against the lightening sky above. "How many you think are down there?"

"Prob'ly kinda hard to count 'em now, there likely not bein' much left but human porridge. I'd say four, maybe five."

Megan wagged her head. She moved up to him, leaned down a little to inspect his arm. She swiped her thumb across the bandage. "That wound's opened. I see blood."

Again, Trent glanced at the arm. "There was about to be a whole lot more."

"Let's get you back to the Triple T. I'll need to rewrap that arm, put you to bed."

Trent took his rifle in one hand, easing the pressure in his left arm, and began striding back up the mountain toward their dying fire. "Let's saddle the horses . . . if we can find 'em."

"I never did see horses with eyes that big," Megan said, following him up the steep grade.

Trent chuckled, despite the fire in his arm. "Nothin' a horse fears more than a griz. Second only to a mountain lion."

When they managed to run down the horses, standing frozen now in the forest to the east, withers rippling apprehensively, Trent and Megan bridled each and led them back to the camp. They rigged up both mounts, stowed away their gear, kicked out their fire, and mounted up. They reloaded their empty rifles and slid them into their saddle sheaths.

Anywhere, there could be more surprises.

They did not descend the mountain in case more death-intending rustlers were headed their way. Instead, both knowing these mountains like the backs of their proverbial hands, they rode around the west edge of the scarp, rose even higher on the mountain, descended into a deep valley, and rode south. When they came to a fork in the trail, the tine to the left leading toward Triple T range, the right tine leading to Circle Double D range, Trent reined up and curveted his mount, facing Megan.

"Well, I reckon we'd both be gettin' on. Thanks, uh . . . fer savin' this Trent's bacon, though my pride ain't gonna be the same again."

"Oh, stow your pride! I'm going with you. I'm going to make sure that wound gets the tending it needs and you get into bed and that you stay there a good two, three days. Get lots of food and coffee in you. That's the only way you'll heal. If you keep goin' like you been goin', you'll keel over for the last time."

"Oh, no," Trent said, shaking his head. "You best not face my pa an' Rachel. Your family and mine are blood enemies. You should know that by now."

"Have you felt that knife in your back yet?"

"No, but I ain't takin' no more chances. I think you're still sizin' me up for the kill."

Megan gave a wry snort. "You know me too well." She sidled her pinto up to his roan, gave a tug on Wolf's bridle, and trotted her mount onto the tine in the fork that led to the Triple T.

"Megan!" Trent yelled behind her, and booted Wolf into a fast trot, wincing at the pain in his arm. "This ain't a good idea. You an' me—we're gonna ignite a land war. A *holy* land war!"

She only laughed and kept riding, her mare's tail of chestnut hair glistening in the sunshine as it jostled across her back.

"What in blazes?" exclaimed Ben Trent as he rose from his wicker chair on the broad porch of the Triple T's sprawling lodge. Rachel sat beside him in a day dress, still looking sad. But now, astonishment flickered in her eyes and parted her lips.

"Easy, Pa," Logan said as he and Megan reined up at one of the two wrought-iron hitchracks—each with three connected wrought-iron *T*'s adorning each end. "She's agreed to be on her best manners."

"No dang Donovan has such a thing as manners!"

"He's not dead *yet*—is he, Mr. Trent?" Megan retorted.

"You mighta given him some poison that'll kick in later. That's the only way I figure he'd be bringin' a Donovan onto *my* headquarters!" The old man had ambled out to stand atop the steps. "What happened to your arm? She shoot you? You can tell me, boy!"

"Five tough nuts followed me out from town, outsmarted me . . . bushwhacked me." He glanced at the Donovan girl. "She came along and saved my hide."

Rachel scowled and shook her head as she rose from her chair and crossed her arms beneath the knit shawl draped over her shoulders. She gave Megan the woolly eyeball. She was certain a Donovan had murdered her husband.

"No Donovan saves a Trent hide. They *kill* Trents!"

One of the hostlers was striding up from the stables. He also looked at least incredulous, if not flabbergasted, at seeing the daughter of the Triple T's blood enemy riding alongside a Trent.

"No Donovan killed your husband, Mrs. Trent," Megan said as she and Logan stepped down from their saddles. "I would know. I know all the doin's about the Circle Double D."

"You probably do, but you would also lie," Rachel said in a deep, angry voice.

She glanced at Ben, then swung around and strode to the lodge's front door. Over her shoulder, Rachel said, "Mr. Trent, don't believe a word she says, and don't let her into your house . . . and Dev's house. Order her off the property!"

She went into the lodge and slammed the heavy oak door behind her.

"Well, this has been a nice introduction," Logan dryly quipped, slinging his saddlebags over his shoulder and sliding his Yellowboy out of its scabbard. He glanced at Megan. "Wish you would have gone home now?"

"Not in the least," she said with typical Donovan stubbornness. She looked at the leonine-headed Ben Trent, face partially shaded by his high-crowned black Stetson, glaring down at her. "We have to get a few things straight—your father and I." She glanced at

Logan's wounded arm. "Just as soon as we get that wound rewrapped and have a few shots of whiskey to dull your pain."

"By God!" exclaimed Ben, staring dumbfounded at his blood enemy's daughter, viewing her as though she were a sleek, dangerous jaguar who had just wandered onto his ranch headquarters, fresh blood staining her teeth while she yearned for more. "You got a lot o' gall, girl!"

"Yeah, well, I'm my father's daughter." While the hostler led the horses toward the stables, looking over his shoulder in awe at the two newcomers, Megan shifted the saddlebags draped over her shoulder, glanced at Logan, and pointed her Winchester barrel commandingly at the front door.

Chapter 21

Logan climbed the porch steps behind Megan.

His father stopped him and leaned in close to say into his ear, "You didn't get drunk in town and marry this girl, did you? We can have the paperwork burned. It ain't too late. Word has it she's a *witch*!"

"We haven't exchanged vows yet."

"Praise Jehovah." The frown lines across Ben's forehead deepened. "Does her father know she's here?"

Logan shook his head.

He went into the lodge and found Megan in the kitchen with its heavy-beamed ceiling, pumping water at the wet sink into a cast-iron pot. Her saddlebags lay at the far end of the table. She set the pan on the range, chucked a split log into the firebox, then walked over to the table, fished her whiskey bottle out of her saddlebags, set it down, and hauled three glasses down from a shelf over the sink.

She half-filled each with her father's whiskey.

"Range war for sure," Logan said, sitting down at the end of the table nearest the door to the foyer.

His father had come in to stand in the doorway, looking at the bottle. He looked at Megan with a wolfish grin. "Is that Big Ike's who-hit-John?"

Logan nodded.

"Mine now."

Ben, who wore a wool-lined denim jacket against the mountains' customary chill, chuckled, rubbed his hands together delightedly, then came over and sat down at the far end of the table from his son. Megan had just set a half-filled glass there. Now she fished cloths out of a saddlebag pouch, set them on the table, then placed the saddlebags on the floor, near where Logan had set his own. He'd leaned his rifle in a corner near the door to the foyer.

Megan produced a porcelain bowl from a separate cabinet at the kitchen's far end, opposite the snapping, warming range. She set the bowl on a pine counter near the range, then leaned back against the wet sink and crossed her arms on her chest. Her pretty features were expressionless, save for a calm resolve.

Ben Trent sipped his hooch, made a pleased expression, then shuttled his gaze back to Megan Donovan. "What's your ploy here, missy?"

Megan said, "To get you drunk, steal your money, rustle your herds, and drive them to the Circle Double D, just as Big Ike ordered me to do." She tapped a toe of her boot on the floor. "Even though they're of a lesser blood than ours, and we'd just as soon they didn't mix. Any more questions, Mr. Trent?"

The elder Trent looked at his son. "You know—she grows on a fella."

"Especially when she hasn't slid a knife in your back."

Ben took another sip of the whiskey and pointed a warning finger at Logan, holding the glass, narrowing one eye. "You watch out for this one."

"Slept all night with one eye open."

Ben scowled. "You two . . . you didn't . . ."

"Oh, yeah," Megan said. "Who do you think so neatly wrapped his arm for him? This Donovan witch."

Ben said, "You two've had eyes for each other for a long time."

Logan scowled at his father, incredulous.

"Oh, I knew. Hell, all the men on my roll knew. We all saw you makin' goo-goo eyes at each other during spring roundup and the fall gather."

It was Megan's turn for an incredulous scowl. "'Goo-goo eyes,' Mr. Trent?"

"I didn't just fall off the manure wagon yesterday." Ben took another sip of his whiskey, swallowed, shook his head, and stared down at his glass. "Dang, that's good." His glass was not empty, but he reached for the bottle to replenish it.

Megan grabbed it before he could and set the bottle out of his reach. She canted her head at the man's son.

"That's for his arm."

"Didn't he shoot your brother?"

Megan sighed and glanced at Logan, who frowned. "Didn't have much choice, and I didn't know it was Pete I was shooting."

"That was on my father," Megan admitted.

Logan sipped his own whiskey, set the glass down on the table, and looked at his arm. He glanced at his father seated at the table's opposite end. "It opened up a little when the grizzly bear attacked us."

Ben had just taken a sip of his own hooch. He choked on it then, face crumpled with exasperation; his blue eyes wide with disbelief, he shifted his gaze from Logan to Megan and back again. "*Grizzly bear . . . attacked . . . ?*"

"It saved our lives," Megan said.

"You two are right complicated!"

Logan said, "Glad you weren't there to see it, Pa. You woulda keeled over and"—he spread his hands to indicate the massive holdings surrounding the headquarters—"all this woulda been mine all too soon. Not sure I'm done sowin' my wild oats yet."

Megan laughed.

"What the heck have you two been up to?" Ben said, dipping his chin and regarding them both suspiciously from beneath his heavy gray brows.

"Fightin' rustlers, mostly," Logan said. "At the same time, I've been tryin' to sniff out Devon's killer. I think his killin' an' that of her brother, Buck"—he glanced at Megan—"are somehow tied together."

"How?"

"I don't know. But I will tell you who's at the head of it."

"*Who?*"

"Dan True," Logan and Megan said at the same time.

Ben looked at each as though both had gone even more addle-pated than he'd suspected. His cheeks bunched above his patchy beard. "That fat old slob who can barely ride a horse anymore?!"

"One an' the same," Logan said as Megan poured warm water into the pan and went to work cutting yesterday's bandage off his arm with small shears from her saddlebags.

"Who'd you learn this from?"

"I saw Red Maclain ride over to the jailhouse. He was there for quite a while before he rode over to the Yellow Flower to find out how much Clarita Ortiz, who knows pretty much everything that's goin' on around Three Forks, knows about the rustling syndicate that's invaded these mountains."

Logan winced as Megan removed the bandage that had been stuck to the crusted blood and ooze that had seeped out of the cauterized wound.

"Maclain's dead, by the way," Megan said. "Here, I thought Logan's gun prowess was overblown."

Logan said, "I found the men from our line shack dead in the yard. Also found the tracks of about fifteen beeves and six horses angling up into the mountains. Followed the herd and the long-loopers to Tin Cup."

"Way the hell out there?"

"They were corralling them there, switching the brands, and

apparently, they were then selling the beeves from there to crooked ranchers either here in the Wolf Mountains or the Bitterroots. I think it's quite an operation, Pa. I turned a number of them toe-down yesterday."

"Nope, it ain't overblown, all right," Megan said.

Logan continued, saying, "Some men came huntin' for us today and ended up gettin' crossways with that bruin."

Logan winced, shook his head. "Winchesters don't do much good against a griz that size. Wish I'd had Dev's Sharps .56."

The elder Trent shifted his scowl from Megan to his son. "Have you two tumbled for each other again?"

"What does that have to do with anything?" Megan wanted to know as she cleaned the ooze from Logan's wound with a damp cloth and whiskey. Logan winced against the sting of the liquor, as well as the young woman's ministrations, gentle as they were. Having a goose feather brushed against that blazing arm would have made him weep. The girl was aghast. "Have you not heard a word we've told you?"

"Not sure what's more dangerous." Ben rose from his chair, limped arthritically along the side of the table, dumped some whiskey from her bottle into his glass, gave her a defiant look, set the bottle down, and returned to his chair. "You an' my son throwin' in together or me gettin' wiped out by a syndicate of long-loopers I didn't even know was here an' led by a dried-up old lawman I lost respect for fifteen years ago!"

"The long-loopers," Logan and Megan said at the same time.

Arms on the table as though to protect his whiskey, Ben leaned forward and, brows knit, voice coarse as gravel, said, "How in the hell did you kill Maclain?" He looked at Megan again, who was wrapping a fresh white cotton cloth tightly around his son's upper left arm.

The elder Trent shook his head, cheeks bunched with bewilderment. "This world is getting all too complicated for me." He turned to his son. "I do believe I'm ready to sprout wings and fly above this earthly plain of crooked men and stolen cattle. Especially when there's a lawman I once considered a friend at the head of it."

"Not so fast, Pa," Logan said as Megan finished wrapping the wound and was cutting off the cloth with the shears. She returned the cloth and the scissors to her saddlebags on the floor beside Logan's, then sat in a chair on the far side of the table, between Logan Trent on her right and the burly old bull buff, Ben Trent, on her left, putting her back to the large kitchen's dry sink and the hot range dueling with the mountain morning chill.

She sipped her whiskey and turned to the elder Trent. "Let's get down to brass tacks, Mr. Trent. I didn't just come here to help your son. I know Rachel could've done that."

"She still here?"

Logan glanced over his shoulder to see his pretty but weary-looking sister-in-law standing in the kitchen doorway, arms crossed on her chest as she leaned against the doorframe. She gave her father-in-law a reproving look.

"Why are you allowing this?"

Megan rose, grabbed another glass off a shelf, poured whiskey into it, and set it on the table across from her. She turned to the late Devon Trent's wife. "Come have a drink with us, Rachel. You, too, should hear what I have to say."

"Why? You're a Donovan. I won't believe you."

Annoyed, Logan glanced over his shoulder at her. "Rachel, get over here and sit down and give her a chance. If you don't believe it, you can slink back up to your room and stew in your rockin' chair!"

Eyes narrowed and framed by her brown hair, her jaw hard, she pushed off the doorframe and strode toward the chair where the proffered glass, one-quarter filled with Big Ike Donovan's whiskey, rested. She sat down, but slid the glass away from her in revulsion. She folded her arms on the oilcloth-covered table and glowered at Megan.

"Let's hear it. I have work to do." Rachel shuttled her glare to

Logan. "I don't just stew in my chair. I'm tryin' to get this place cleaned up. My father-in-law is not a neat man, and he needs a maid, whom he refuses to hire."

The elder Trent chuckled, sipped his drink, and gave his head a single wag. "She's on a tear, this one!" He chuckled dryly again.

With no further ado, Megan looked from Rachel to Ben and said, "I think this rustling syndicate is going to pit us against each other, so we wipe each other out and do their work for them. If we go to war and burn each other's ranches, they'll take all our herds, sell them to crooked ranchers and crooked stockyards, and be able to light out of the country rich men."

"Same with Dan True," Logan added.

"True?" Rachel said, frowning in astonishment.

"True," Logan and Megan said at the same time.

"I know, I know," Logan said. "He's a fat, dried-up old man and a useless lawman—one who refuses to hire a deputy, no doubt because he doesn't want anyone else to know his ploy. Who'd suspect a familiar lawman ready for retirement? He prob'ly even has himself a room picked out at an old folks' home in Three Forks, but"—Logan smiled knowingly—"he'll never use it. He's going to take his cut of the money from the stolen cattle and light a shuck and live high on the hog in Denver or San Francisco for the year or two before they turn him under."

Ben turned to Megan. "You do know we found beeves with the Triple T brand on them in one of your corrals, right?"

Megan nodded. "They found your son on our graze, too. But we didn't kill Devon. On our own *land*? Our men didn't take those cattle. They found them on our graze and corralled them, intending to take them back here. But you and your men came before they got around to it. Our men are as busy as yours, Mr. Trent."

"Pshaw," Ben said, lifting his chin and scratching the gray-brown beard on his neck. "I don't believe that. Big Ike woulda said so. Instead, he said nothin'."

"Because he knew you wouldn't believe him, just as you didn't believe him about Devon. Besides, he's as stubborn and surly as you are. He doesn't cotton to 'palaverin',' as he would call it, with men he's deemed his enemies. Frankly, he didn't care what you thought. He just makes sure all his men are armed and ready for war."

Seeing the absurdity in the situation—a long-fought war that refused to die, threatening both the Donovan and Trent spreads—Ben gave a droll smile and shook his head.

Rachel sneered at Megan and turned to the elder Trent. "They say she's a witch, you know. She's just up to her witchy tricks!"

Megan slapped the table and laughed. "How did this get started, anyway?"

"You dress like a man, ride the range like a man, drink like a man, shoot like a man, and disappear for days at a time. They say you have a coven somewhere in these mountains."

Megan turned to Logan, who smiled at her and glanced at his arm. "Maybe the witch'll get this arm to heal faster an' I can get back to findin' out who killed both her brother an' mine."

Megan lifted her glass to him. "Cheers!"

"Boss!" a man's voice called from the direction of the bunkhouse. "Riders! One is Dan True! Two is federals! The other two . . . well, they're *dead*!"

Chapter 22

"Talk about gall!" Ben Trent exclaimed, pushing up out of his chair, his face red with anger.

Logan glanced at Megan, incredulous. She returned the look, opened her hands, and closed them as if to say, *Reckon we'll see.*

Logan rose, reached for his rifle, then decided to leave it where it was. It was best if True believed none of the Trents or anyone else, for that matter, knew what the Three Forks sheriff was up to.

Logan strode through the foyer, then onto the lodge's veranda, his father following him out. Rachel came out next. Megan decided to stay inside. Her being at the Triple T might cause True to think they were joining forces, and it was best if he wasn't aware of that. He would know soon enough.

Ben stepped up beside his son atop the steps, laughed, and slapped his denim-clad thigh. "Holy blazes, how in tarnation did you haul your fat behind onto that hoss, Dan? Did you get all the way up here without *falling off*?"

True gave a wooden smile and slid his eyes to his left and his right, glancing at the two men in black broadcloth jackets over black vests and white shirts trimmed with ribbon ties. They were a natty-looking pair, complete with gold chains drooping between shallow vest pockets. One was young and tall, with sandy sideburns, while the other, to True's right, was short and somewhere in his forties. He was a seasoned, handsome man, while the young one had the look of an untested kid. The older federal's dark eyes were deeply sunk; they had a grim, worldly cast, and his thick brown mustache was touched with gray. A slight paunch pushed out from behind his vest, and he wore a pearl-gripped .45 in a cross-draw holster positioned on his right hip. A Henry rifle bristled from the scabbard strapped to the right side of his saddle. The younger man sported a Winchester rifle and an 1877-model Colt Lightning .38 revolver, nickel-plated, in a holster thonged on his right thigh, gunfighter style.

Logan would have bet he couldn't hit the broad side of a barn standing *inside* the barn.

Both men with True wore the round nickel badges of the U.S. deputy marshals, which featured a star in the center.

Both studied the old rancher dubiously.

Dan True chuckled tensely and said, "We're old friends, me an' Ben. Known each other for years."

The elder Trent returned with, "Known each other a lot o' years, but I haven't seen you sit a saddle in at least five. What's the occasion?"

True looked at Logan. "Your son wanted me to send for federals. I sent for 'em. Didn't think I'd get 'em, as they been right busy chasin' gun an' whiskey runners. These two was nearby, got the head marshal's telegram, and rode on up to help investigate this rustlin' problem." He kept his gaze, gray eyes in deep, fleshy sockets, on Logan and tilted his head slightly to one side. "You think there's quite a few, do ya, Logan?"

"I know there's quite a few," he replied.

True grinned. "All I know is we ran into quite a few *dead men* on our way up here, along the canyon trail."

"You'll find more dead in the old Tin Cup Saloon, if you want to ride that far."

"There too, eh?" True scratched his sunburned right cheek. He was fair-skinned and burned easily. His pudgy nose was bright red in the late-morning sun.

The older federal, who had a knife slash of a mouth beneath his mustache, said, "You killed those men?"

Just then, the lodge's door squawked open on dry hinges and Megan stepped onto the porch.

The young man frowned, looking the pretty Donovan girl up and down. "And who are you?"

She walked up to stand to Logan's left, holding her hand up to shield her eyes from the intensifying high-country sun. "Megan Donovan, Big Ike's favorite offspring. Not to mention his *only* offspring now." She cut Logan a quick, accusing glance.

He winced.

"Donovan?" said the older federal, scrutinizing her lithe, buxom figure more closely. He glanced at True before returning his gaze to Megan. "I understood . . . I understood the Trents and Donovans were—"

"Enemies," Rachel cut in. She stood to the right of her father-in-law, narrowing her own eyes against the sunlight. "Blood enemies," she added, glancing at Megan, who did not return her look. "They kill ours, we kill theirs."

Dan True scowled beneath the broad brim of his high-crowned gray Stetson. "So, then . . . how is it—"

"That she's here?" Rachel said, glancing past her father-in-law at her brother-in-law. "At least one of the Trent men thinks more with his—"

"Brains more than anything else," Logan was quick to cut in, and gave his sister-in-law an admonishing frown. To True, he said, "Both our families have been victims of the long-loopers. I was riding up from Three Forks yesterday afternoon when five of the devils dry-gulched me. Megan was in the area, and she backed me after I took a blue whistler to my arm here."

He glanced down at the bandaged limb.

True stretched his lips back from his small, square teeth. "That must hurt like blazes. Did it hit the bone?"

"I don't think so."

"Well, that's good, that's good. You're still young. You'll heal faster than—"

"An ugly old scudder like you would," Ben Trent finished for him with a devilish glint in his eyes, making a joke out of it, though Logan knew it was far too obvious he hated his old friend after learning he was at the head of the stock-thieving syndicate. The ultimate betrayal of a longtime friendship. They'd both come into this country at roughly the same time.

Easy, Pa, Logan wanted to admonish him. *Go easy now. No point in lettin' True know we're onto him.*

He couldn't help wondering what the federals knew, if anything, about True's position at the head of the savage syndicate.

True sensed the elder Trent's animosity, but again he chuckled, laughing as though it was all a joke between longtime friends. The federals shuttled their curious gazes between the two older men.

Ben Trent lifted his chin to look past the three men to the two horses True was trailing on lead lines. Two dead men lay belly down across their saddles, wrapped in bedrolls. Wrists were tied to ankles beneath the bellies of their horses—a dun and a steeldust, respectively.

"Came upon 'em roasting a steer for breakfast in a little canyon southwest of here." True frowned, nodding grimly. "One of yours, by the brand. I assume those two are . . . er, *were* . . . from the syndicate you think is responsible for all the rustling goin' on up in these reaches."

Logan stepped down off the porch and walked toward the two horses carrying the dead men. "Let me have a look."

"Sure, sure . . . have a look," True said, vaguely uneasy.

He turned to watch Logan part folds in the soogans, lift the heads by handfuls of hair to inspect the faces, before letting the heads drop back down against the sides of the horses. Both mounts whickered and looked jittery at having to carry their own dead riders belly down across their saddles.

Logan shook his head as he walked back up the porch steps.

"No one I recognize," he said.

"Figures," True said.

"Why'd you shoot 'em?" Logan asked his former boss.

"They went for their guns when they saw our badges," said the younger federal. "Besides, don't you shoot rustlers up here, Mr. Trent?" He smirked, knowing very well how rustlers were treated here in the Wolf Mountains, as everywhere across the West.

Logan feigned a smile.

"Well, don't leave 'em here," Ben said. "We've dug enough graves, an' there will surely be more."

True shook his head. "Nah, they ain't worth the work. We'll drop 'em in a ravine an' let the carrion eaters give 'em their send-offs."

"Where are you men headed?" Megan asked.

True shrugged. "We're on a scouting mission. These two, Bart Ramsay an' Glen Peters, never been to the Three Forks area. I'm gonna show 'em the lay of the land an' see if we can sniff out any more long-loopers, maybe the tracks of freshly rustled herds. We'll head down to Three Forks tomorrow, then ride back up with a posse and thoroughly scour the range. As long as I'm the law here, there won't be no puttin' up with 'rustlin' syndicates'"—he glanced at his former deputy—"as you call 'em, Logan."

"That's what they are," Logan said.

His father swiped his fist across his nose, scowling. "I just wonder who the head honcho is. Every 'syndicate'—as, uh, Logan calls 'em—has a ramrod."

"Don't worry," said the older federal, Ramsay. "We'll find him an' pull him kickin' an' screamin' out of his hole."

True just smiled at that. Being a lawman for so many years had taught him how to be slippery. He pinched his hat brim and swung his sorrel around. "We'll talk again as the mission progresses. Have a good day, Trents!"

The other two nodded cordially, then swung around and trotted their own mounts after True and the two dead men draped over their saddles.

The elder Trent kept his eyes on the retreating riders and asked his son quietly, "Did you really not recognize those two dead men?"

"I recognized 'em. Saw 'em both in a saloon in Three Forks a coupla months ago. They might have snagged one of our beeves, but they're not part of any syndicate. They're just two simple-minded prospectors—brothers from Oklahoma, if I remember correct."

"True killed those drifters just to try an' prove to us he was serious about runnin' down that syndicate. His *own* syndicate."

Logan sighed. "Hard to find fault with a man who shot two men dinin' on your own beef."

"No, no," Ben said. "Just doin' his job."

"He's smarter than he looks."

"Think those two federals are savvy to him?"

"Not yet. But we'll know when they figure him out, which won't be too long, the way he flaps his gums."

"How will we know?"

Megan answered for Logan as she stared after the three riders, who were climbing the forested ridge beyond the Triple T portal, the dead men's legs sticking out stiffly from their saddles. "We won't see them around anymore," she said.

The elder Trent regarded her with his brows raised, impressed. "Hey, she's smart fer a—"

"Don't say, it, Pa," Logan said stiffly. "We need her to keep her Arkansas toothpick sheathed."

Megan turned to him. "You're right smart for a Trent."

The elder Trent laughed.

Rachel turned and walked stiffly to the lodge's front door. "I'll start lunch."

Megan followed Rachel into the lodge and came back out with her rifle and saddlebags. She started down the porch steps into the yard. "I'll head home. Rosa's gonna need a break from the baby."

"Oh, I'll ride with you, then," Logan offered.

"No need."

"Yes . . . need."

"You need to rest that arm. Stay here an' climb into bed, like I told you to do."

"Ah, hell—what are the chances we'll be attacked by another grizzly?"

He went into the lodge and came out a few seconds later with his own saddlebags and rifle.

As he followed Megan, his father called behind him, "Say hi to Big Ike for me, but tell him, 'No shotgun weddin's!' "

He wheezed a hearty laugh.

Logan just shook his head.

Chapter 23

"Wait," Trent said, drawing back on Wolf's reins several miles west of the Trent ranch's headquarters.

It was just after noon, the brassy sun nearly straight up in the sky.

Megan looked at him, frowning, and checked down her pinto. "What is it?"

He lifted his chin, sniffing the breeze. "Smell that?"

"Smell wha—" She stopped and glanced at him again. "Smells like . . ."

"Charred beef."

"Where's it coming from?"

Trent pointed at where a shaggy two-track trail angled off the one they were on to trace a curving course up a forested ridge. "There's an old mine up there long abandoned by an old German killed by Sioux. They tortured him until, Pa said, he could hear the screams as far away as the Triple T headquarters. Ma didn't sleep for weeks after that. Pa thinks it was one reason she had such a rough childbirth that killed both her and my little brother."

Megan shuddered. "I remember that."

"Let's check it out."

Trent reined the roan off the main trail and booted him into a hard gallop across a sage-stippled flat. He turned Wolf onto the secondary trail and booted him into a gallop once more, hearing the thuds of Megan's galloping pinto right behind him. They gained the base of the ridge a couple of minutes later. Both horses climbed hard, following the curving two-track trail for a hundred yards through thick forest.

When they reached a relatively flat area, Trent again checked down the roan, who curveted, blowing and switching his tail. Trent stared up the trail at smoke on the other side of a wood-and-canvas shanty, which was flanked by a supply wagon bristling with picks, shovels, animal traps, and various mining tools. A mule stood off in the forest, about fifty yards from the wagon, staring nervously at the two newcomers.

"What the . . . ?" Megan said.

"I do believe we just found the camp of those two prospectors True and the federals killed." Trent sniffed the breeze once more. "That's the smell of the beef they were roasting."

He booted Wolf over to the fire. A spit and what remained of a badly charred beef haunch lay on the ground just outside the fire, which was still burning despite someone—True and the federals, most likely—having kicked dirt on it. Part of the haunch remained in the blowing, smoking coals. On both sides of the fire ring, blood streaked the grass and sage. Two battered hats lay on the ground, eight feet apart. Two rifles leaned against a large ponderosa pine—both old-model Spencer repeaters. Near the rifles lay two shell belts coiled around the holsters in which two Colt conversion revolvers resided.

Trent held Wolf's reins firmly as he gazed down at the charred beef, caked with dirt and pine needles, at the ancient Colts and equally old Spencers, and at the blood that smeared the grass around the battered canvas hats.

He glanced at Megan, who shook her head and said stiffly, "Those two didn't go for their guns, like True said. They saw the men with the badges ride up and likely froze, scared to death they were about to have the shackles thrown on them."

"True said they found the prospectors on Triple T range. This is government range."

"He wanted you and your old man to believe he was doing you a favor."

"Wonder what he told Big Ike."

"Oh, I'm sure he tried to get Ike to believe he was doing the Double D a favor as well."

Megan reined her pinto around and booted the mount back the way they'd come. "Only one way to find out!"

Trent reined Wolf around and dogged her heels back down the mountain and out to the main trail that led to the Circle Double D headquarters. They passed through the Circle Double D portal a half hour later and galloped up to the long, L-shaped, two-story lodge, smoke rising from two separate chimneys. It may have been summer, but this high in the mountains, fires were kept burning against the high-country chill every day of the year. Especially when there was an infant on the premises . . .

Trent heard the baby crying inside.

The door atop the porch opened and the short, squat, denim-clad old bull buff himself ambled out onto the porch, his mountain lion hide draping his broad shoulders, his customary scowl in place on his deeply tanned, weathered face.

"What in holy blazes?!" he bellowed, glancing from Trent to his daughter. "I was about to send out a scouting party to find and haul back your carcass, girl! I figured you'd stumbled onto a rustlers' camp, and they perforated your hide after they did only God knows what to you!"

"Sorry, Pa."

"What in the hell held you up an' "—Big Ike slid his angry gaze back to Trent—"what're you two doin' together again?" He turned his head to one side, giving them each a sidelong, suspicious look. "You two ain't startin' that old nonsense all over again, are you?"

Trent and Megan exchanged incredulous glances.

They turned to her father and said at the same time, "What nonsense?"

Big Ike waved a big, thick brown paw in front of his face as though to shoo away a pesky mosquito. "*What* nonsense? Don't give me that. Everyone in these mountains knows what went on between you two ten years back. I thought I'd finally lived down the shame, an' here you are again."

He gave them another sidelong, exasperated look. "You two didn't run to town and get married, did you?"

Trent glanced at Megan, then turned to Big Ike. "Can I call you Pa?"

Big Ike's weathered, bearded face turned red and swelled up like a giant welt, eyes flashing rage. "Why, you . . . !"

"Pa," Megan said, "did Dan True and two federals stop here a few hours ago?"

Big Ike nodded. "They found a couple rustlers carvin' up one of our beeves on Double D range. True said he thought they were *Triple T* men." Old Ike gave Trent a cutting glance. "What's goin' on, Logan? Your old man tryin' to start a shootin' war?"

Megan shook her head. "Those men were on free range, Pa. And they weren't rustlers. Oh, they stole a cow, all right, but they were just a hungry pair of prospectors. True is playin' you like a fiddle, tryin' to pitch you an' Mr. Trent against each other. He knows that for years you two have been in competition for everything, including cattle, seed bulls, grass, and even the men on your payrolls. He's takin' full advantage of that."

"Hmmm . . ."

Trent said, "He's the one orchestrating the rustling syndicate operating in these mountains. He wants to long-loop as much beef as he can an' sell it, then clear out of the mountains. He'd love nothin' so much as for you an' us to go to war an' wipe each other out, leavin' nothin' but our beef an' our horses."

Big Ike scowled, confused. "I don't get it. Why did he say—"

"That beef was on *your* land?" Trent said. "Because he's tryin' to ingratiate himself to you, just like he did with my pa. He rode over to our place with those two 'rustlers' he killed, to try to ingratiate himself to *us* against you."

Frown lines carved even deeper lines across his forehead, beneath the red knit cap he wore. Big Ike said with confusion, "I don't get it. 'In-gra-ti . . .'?"

"He's workin' both ends against the middle, Pa," Megan said. "You can't believe a word he says."

Big Ike just stared at her, as perplexed as he'd been a minute ago.

She turned to Trent. "I'll explain it to him. I have to help Rosa with the baby. You get on home an' rest that arm."

Trent drew a long breath, let it out slow. *Bossy women.* He nodded. "All right. I reckon." He reined Wolf around and glanced back over his shoulder at Megan. "Good luck!" he groused, casting a dubious look at the old man in the red knit cap standing atop the porch steps, tugging pensively at his chin whiskers.

"I'll give it my best shot," Megan said as Trent headed for the trail back down the mountain.

Trent passed the outbuildings, including two barns, two stables, three corrals, and the men working around the yard—three resetting a door on one of the big log barns—and passed through the portal with the Circle Double D brand burned into both ends. Once out of the yard, he put Wolf into a trot. The thick pine, fir, and aspen forest closed along both sides of the trail, the heavy shade contrasting with bright sunlight. He'd ridden a couple of hundred yards when he heard the rataplan of galloping hooves behind him.

He pulled Wolf to the left, curveted the roan, and looked back up the trail to see a rider galloping hard, crouched low in the saddle, down the steep grade from the Circle Double D headquarters, through the sunlight and heavy purple shadows lying thick upon the trail. Trent began reaching for his Winchester automatically, but left the long gun in its sheath as the rider rushed past him in a blur of speed, the front brim of the man's hat basted against his forehead in the wind of his passing. His batwing chaps flapped like giant wings; long sandy hair blew out behind his shoulders.

In seconds, the man was twenty feet down the trail . . . then forty . . . fifty . . . and he became a small bug in the distance. A half mile away, he slowed his steeldust and turned the gelding off the trail's right side, booted the mount into a hard run once more, and shot off across a sage-purpled flat toward a long, pine-covered ridge, another half mile from the main trail.

Trent scowled after him. *Now, where is he headed like a bat out of hell?*

These mountains . . .

He put Wolf into another trot, heading east toward the Triple T, whose headquarters lay across a stretch of open range and two miles beyond where Triple T range started. There were no demarcations—barbed wire was shunned in the Wolf Mountains for good reason to Trent's mind; it was a savage invention, deadly to man, as well as beast—but everyone knew where one range ended and another began. Men knew when to cross—when their own cattle had strayed—and when not to cross—when their own cattle had not strayed.

In the latter case, it was usually assumed they'd crossed for devious reasons and would end up adorning a stout pine bow, a hang rope knotted around their necks, "cat's cradle," as it was called in range parlance, having been played with their heads.

Trent, however, was on Circle Double D range for honorable reasons, which the men back at their headquarters knew, having seen him ride in with Megan.

These were dangerous times. No woman, not even one with a bark like the one that Megan had been born with, should be riding these ranges alone. Just too damn many of True's misfits and cold-blooded killers, who were not above ravaging a pretty woman—not even the daughter of the formidable Big Ike Donovan.

Trent rode up and over a low hill, following the trail that curved slightly at the bottom. The thudding of distant hooves sounded. He turned to see six horseback riders galloping down from a haystack butte on his right. They rode hell for leather, crouched low in their saddles, whipping their mounts with their rein ends, encouraging more speed. They rode at an angle toward the trail Trent was following.

He knew right away they were going to cut him off somewhere ahead.

Rustlers?

Not this close to the Circle Double D headquarters.

These were Circle Double D men.

Trent watched them, apprehension tickling his spine. Wolf watched them, too, flicking his ears and nervously expanding and contracting the muscles beneath the saddle.

They were roughly a quarter mile ahead of Trent, still angling to the east, toward an open piece of the trail near which a creek curved out of an aspen copse on the trail's left side.

A minute later, the six riders gained the bottom of the long, sloping decline, reined the horses to a skidding halt on the trail ahead of Trent, and turned their horses to face him, stirrup to stirrup.

Executioner style.

Well, well, Trent thought. *This oughta be interesting.*

Chapter 24

The meeting got even more interesting. Trent was familiar with all these riders, because all the Circle Double D riders joined up with all the Triple T riders during the spring and fall roundups, during which fights, some savage, often broke out on the private ranges and on the open range between them.

Paul Hyde rode in the center of the six-man pack. He was a tough, short, wiry man, with a deeply tanned face sporting a thick brown mustache with upturned and waxed ends. He wasn't the man Trent was most interested in, however. No, that honor went to the one-eyed man seated at the pack's far right end, sitting up straight in his saddle and grinning oafishly at Trent.

"Tiny" Halbert Todd was a former Indian fighter, who'd lost his left eye to a burning brand wielded by a Comanche warrior in the Texas Panhandle. He'd been a bare-knuckle fighter around the docks and seaside breweries in New York City. He hailed from Dublin, Ireland, where he'd honed the art of nose-busting, arm-breaking, and knee- and shoulder-dislocating—in short, inflicting more pain and agony than most men could take.

Hyde looked from Trent, who probably appeared as though he

had a constriction in his throat, because he did, to the big ape with the eye patch wearing the collarless pinstriped shirt, suspenders, and dusty bowler hat. Tiny Todd wore a mustache, too, but his was not nearly as refined as that of Hyde. It was thick and bushy and probably hadn't been trimmed in months. Looking at the 'stache, Trent could tell the man had had ham and eggs for breakfast. The sheen of grease told of roast the night before in the Double D bunkhouse, which was captained by a cook from Tennessee, whom Ben Trent had tried to get to work for him at the Triple T.

Big Ike had won the bidding war.

Trent thought Morgan McCallister, the fat cook who even wore his apron to town driving his rattling supply wagon, was probably the best-paid cook in the Wolf Mountains, probably even in the Bitterroots as well. That showed how competitive the two ranchers—Ben Trent and Big Ike Donovan—were. On the other hand, Trent's father probably had the best blacksmith, farrier, and equine veterinarian in all of Idaho, and, to the elder Trent, big Charleston "Charlie" Lucy was worth every penny of his sixty a month, which was a whole twenty dollars more than what the punchers were paid.

No one seemed to begrudge the big former slave his salary. Charlie kept their horses shod, their hooves trimmed; he kept the wheels and wheel rims on their supply wagons and helped the mares and cows with difficult deliveries every spring. But even if Charlie didn't routinely do all that, the regular hands wouldn't have complained, for Charlie was known for getting drunk every Saturday night and spoiling for a fight.

Like the Double D's Tiny Todd, Charlie loved nothing more than fisticuffs.

He'd learned his own "art" on the plantations of South Carolina, where the slave owners orchestrated fights every Saturday with slaves from other plantations. The raucous betting was good additional income for them, especially for the owner of Charlie Lucy.

Now Hyde turned to Tiny Todd, a big grin making the twisted ends of his ostentatious mustache rise. "Tiny," he said with feigned curiosity, "ain't this the man you been talkin' about do-si-doin' with for the past five years?"

"Yep, that's him, all right, boss," Tiny Todd said in his deep, guttural but lilting Irish accent. "One an' the same."

"What was the disagreement about?" asked one of the other men, also with feigned curiosity, stitching his brows together beneath the brim of his low-crowned, sweat-stained Stetson.

Tiny Todd's grin faded to a hateful glower as his lone eye, cast with predatory menace, drilled into Trent. "He shot the elk I had my sights on, took it right out from under ol' Tiny. Him an' the other Triple T men—they laughed at ol' Tiny." The angry lines deepened as they cut across his forehead, above his broad, lumpy, broken nose. "They had me outgunned, refused to fight me for the elk, so they thought they was the owner of the meat, held me off with their rifles while they dressed and quartered the elk and rode off, laughing." He paused, lone eye turning even harder beneath the thin brim of his shabby checked bowler. "No one laughs at Tiny."

"What do you want to do about that, Tiny?" asked Hyde, with faux curiosity. He was delighting in the confrontation.

"I wanna beat the stuffin' outta him," Tiny said with quiet menace, widening his nostrils.

"Hmmm," Hyde said, toying with an end of his upswept mustache. "That sounds fair." He glanced at the others. "That sounds fair—don't it, boys?"

"Oh, hell, yeah," said one of the other men, pursing his lips and nodding.

"Oh, hell, yeah," said another in full agreement.

"I got a full month's wages restin' on Tiny."

Another Double D rider said with a caustic grunt, "Well, who in hell would bet on *Trent*?!"

The others laughed.

Keeping his stony glare on Trent, Tiny Todd tossed his reins to the man sitting next to him and swung down heavily from his saddle. He moved forward, broad hips rolling. He stopped, then stared even deeper and with even more menace at Trent.

He punched his right fist into the palm of his left hand and said, "You gonna climb outta that saddle yourself, my game-stealin' friend, or am I gonna have to pull you down?"

"Tiny, do you *really* think I'm gonna fight you?"

Hyde chuckled and said, "I reckon you got no choice, Trent."

Trent laughed, but the laugh died on his lips. "Every man has a choice," he said, smiling. The smile faded. "Ah, hell," he said a moment later, leaning toward his left, appearing as though ready to dismount.

He straightened again, and then a Russian was suddenly in his right hand, thundering, the bullet punching through Tiny Todd's broad forehead and knocking the big man over backward. His lone eye rolled toward his nose.

The other Double D men's horses lurched with starts, as did the men themselves.

Hyde shucked his Schofield .44 from the holster riding low on his right hip, clicked back the hammer, and, cursing, aimed the hogleg at Trent. Again, the Russian thundered. Hyde grunted, triggered the Schofield wide, then dropped the gun as he thrust his right hand to his left shoulder, from which bright-red blood oozed. His horse lurched again, more violently, and Hyde cursed once more as he fell from the saddle.

The other four men had closed their hands around the grips of their own hoglegs, but left them in the leather when Trent re-cocked the Russian and slid it from right to left and back again, bald threat in his eyes.

He said, "I have four more in the wheel. One for each of ya."

They shuttled their gazes from the Russian's smoking barrel to Trent's eyes and back again.

Trent said, "Toss those guns in the brush and ride the hell outta here. You can come back for 'em later."

They nervously fumbled their pistols from their holsters and tossed them into the brush along the trail. They glanced at Hyde, who was clamping his right hand over the bloody wound in his left shoulder. He was just now sitting up, his hat in the dirt beside him, its crown flattened. The four hands glared at Trent, then exchanged enraged glowers, before spurring their horses into lunging gallops in the direction of the Double D headquarters.

Hyde lifted his hand from the wound and looked at it, grunting and cursing under his breath, showing his teeth like an angry cur, then said, "You just made a big mistake, Trent."

"You did when you and those men came galloping down that hill for me. You're lucky I pulled that shot wide and didn't drill you through the brisket." Trent booted Wolf eastward along the trail, then stopped and glanced over his shoulder at Hyde. "By the way, if you want more of this, you'll get it. But next time, I won't be so nice!"

He rammed his heels against the roan's flanks. Wolf pitched, whinnied, and thundered eastward along the trail, leaving the Double D rider sitting in the dirt, hat off, hair mussed, glaring at the man who, he didn't realize, had just spared his life.

But Trent had.

He had, indeed.

Trent galloped Wolf for a hundred yards, then slowed him to take it easy on him. There were several steep, forested ridges between the Circle Double D and the Triple T. Several canyons through which small streams slid. Trent stopped the roan often to rest him and to let him draw water.

He glanced over his shoulder to see if he was being shadowed, but he saw no one trailing him as he climbed another steep ridge and then dropped down into the broad valley where the Triple T sprawled, a few riders who'd been out moving and keeping an eye on the summer herds just then entering the headquarters from the east. Their mouths were moving as they conversed among themselves, playfully mocking each other. One of the riders,

Bryce Haruf, who'd grown up on a spread in Nevada, and was half Basque, his father a sheepherder, removed his hat and slapped it against the shoulder of the man riding on his left, Cliff Turner, the oldest man on the Triple T roll, but still a damn good cowhand.

Ben Trent didn't let men go just because they were getting long in the tooth. But every man had to prove his worth, and no man was better at that than Cliff, whose longish silver hair hung down from his funnel-brimmed black hat. A silver mustache and goatee trimmed his long, bony, sun-seasoned face. Trent could tell Cliff was laughing as he joshed the younger man.

Cliff was always laughing. His father had hired the older cowhand when Trent was thirteen, which meant Cliff had been at the Triple T for twenty-one years. That was a long stretch for a cowhand—dirty, exhausting, dangerous work—but Trent knew that Cliff, who'd never been married, though he'd sparked a few women in Three Forks, enjoyed the labor. He was not ready to hang up his spurs and man a rocking chair. That was not Cliff. He could laugh and jest with the others, but Trent had seen him shoot or hang rustlers without compromise, because Cliff knew that that's what the job entailed.

He could be grimly dutiful when he needed to be. That was Cliff.

Trent was vaguely hoping he himself had not started a range war when he'd chunked that round through Paul Hyde's shoulder.

No.

He hoped Hyde had not started a range war when he and the other riders had galloped down the mountain toward Trent. The younger Trent could not control other men. As for Tiny Todd, the evil one-eyed giant had needed shooting right there on the trail, and he'd earned that bullet. Word of that row would spread.

Good.

Men needed to know what they were getting into when they messed with a Trent.

Might save a lot of trouble later.

He left Wolf with Jim Miller, one of their hostlers, then tramped over to the main lodge, batting the dust off his hat against his denims.

"You did *what*?!" his father said, heaving up out of his office chair when Trent had told him about the dustup with the riders from the Circle Double D.

Chapter 25

Big Ike pulled the stopper out of the decanter of his favorite Scotch and half-filled a matching cut-glass goblet with the magical elixir.

He glanced over at his daughter, who was gently rocking the baby she'd inherited from a neighboring ranch widow, in the flannel blanket that their housekeeper, Rosa, had sewn herself. The child had been adopted by a nearby rancher who had been shot on his own range by rustlers; his wife had died from a fever, amid the toil of raising a child alone, a month later.

Megan had taken the child, who, she'd been told, was half-Basque and had the slightly darker-toned skin to prove it. Not long after, she'd learned from a buggy loaded with persnickety church ladies, who'd drive up from Three Forks, that they'd intended to take the baby to an orphanage in Boise. Megan knew that a ranch in the mountains would be a far better place for a child—especially one of mixed heritage—to grow up in than an orphanage in a city.

"You want one?" Big Ike asked his daughter, indicating the decanter. He still held its stopper in his hand.

Megan shook her head. "I don't want Sarah to smell it on me."

Big Ike smiled. "You're gonna be a heckuva mother to that child. And to your own as well."

Megan returned the smile. "Thanks, Pa."

Big Ike heard Rosa's voice in the foyer. "*Dios mio!*" the Spanish housekeeper intoned.

Men's voices rose. There was a groan.

Both Big Ike and his daughter stared toward the open doorway of the rancher's office, frowning curiously, apprehensively. The clomping of boots grew louder, as did the low grunts and moans of what was obviously an injured man. Big Ike had just started to rise from his high-backed leather chair behind his desk when the footsteps stopped and three men appeared in the arched doorway of his office.

One of his riders, Paul Hyde, was being held up between two of Big Ike's cowhands; the man's right arm was draped over one of the men's necks, the men's arms wrapped around his waist. Blood spotted a thick bandage on his left shoulder. Sweat beads glistened on the man's bony face, with its oddly city-style mustache. The hat on his head was dented and dusty.

"What in *tarnation*?" Big Ike said, taking three steps toward the door and stopping, fists on his denim-clad hips, spreading his booted feet shoulder-width apart. "What in the hell happened?"

"Pa!" Megan reprimanded him, glancing at the baby in her arms, who was busily sucking on a rubber-nippled glass bottle.

Big Ike returned her scowl. "She can't understand me!"

"I don't want you to be in the habit!"

Big Ike waved her off and returned his attention to his obviously injured rider, glancing at the other two men, who appeared considerably more coherent. "Rustlers?" he asked loudly.

Hyde shook his head slowly and with effort, as though it weighed as much as a rock its size. "Trent!"

"Which one?" the father and daughter demanded at the same time.

Megan sat up straight on the sofa now, the baby still sucking on the milk bottle.

"Logan," said the cowhand on Hyde's left, Norman Finlay—a tall, rangy kid, with a coal-smudge mustache.

"Why?" the father and daughter asked at the same time.

In a voice taut with agony, Hyde said, "We just stopped him to ask him what he was doin' on Double D land."

The cowhand on Hyde's right, shorter and thicker than the other, said, "He shot Tiny an' then he shot Hyde! Tiny didn't make it." The man, whose name was Burt Myers, shook his head slowly. "That's some strong poison them Trents have in their veins." Myers looked at Megan, who was regarding both men with hard eyes and pursed lips from the sofa. "I'd stay away from that one, Miss Megan. He might act sweet to you, but he's a devil!"

Big Ike scrutinized all three men skeptically. "You're sayin' he shot Tiny in cold blood, and then he shot Hyde for no reason at all?"

Hyde sputtered, then said, "Well . . . I was goin' fer my pistol, of course. He shot Tiny in the head. I figured the rest of us was next."

Megan rose stiffly, holding the baby in her arms. "You men are liars!" she said. "You started trouble on the trail, and he ended it. He wouldn't kill any man for no reason." She looked at Hyde. "He didn't shoot you for no reason, either, Hyde. You men are *liars*!"

Hyde kept his gaze on her, his jaws hardening in anger.

The other two glanced across the ailing Hyde at each other, looking sheepish.

Hyde looked at Big Ike, who looked at the two holding him up.

"Get him back to the bunkhouse," Big Ike ordered.

Finlay said, "Want us to saddle up, boss? Ride over there? I mean, if the Triple T ain't punished . . ."

Big Ike walked up to him and stopped two feet away. "If any man rides over there, he best not ride back here, because he won't have a job." He glanced from Finlay to Hyde and then to Myers. "Am I clear?"

Hyde returned the rancher's gaze, then gave two quick nods. The other two half-dragged him through the parlor to the front door.

Megan looked down at the baby in her arms. Sarah was fussing.

To her father, Megan said, "I'm going to put Sarah down for a nap. I'll be back in a minute."

Big Ike didn't say anything. He just sat staring at the open doorway in which his three men had been standing a moment before. The mental gears were grinding haltingly, troublingly, in his head.

When Megan had left his office with the baby, Big Ike sagged down in his chair. He had a stunned, pensive look. He picked up his goblet and threw back half the Scotch, sighed, and ran his hand across the blotter on his desk. He was still sitting there, holding his drink, when footsteps sounded in the hall. Megan walked back into the office, removed a goblet from a small pyramid at the edge of her father's desk, and said, "Fill me up."

Big Ike did so. She picked up the glass and sat back down on the sofa. She sipped the Scotch, then balanced the glass on her knee, looking at her father. "Do you think those three are involved in the rustling for True?"

Big Ike shrugged his heavy shoulders. "I don't know."

"You know they're lying, right?"

"Yep."

"Why would they lie if they're not involved with the syndicate?"

"Because they're simple men who've been spoiling for a fight with the Triple T for years. Because we're in competition with them and they equate that with wanting to wipe them out."

"I've been worried about this. Simple men can start a range war for no better reason than the one you just gave."

Big Ike stared down at his glass. "I know." He threw back the rest of his Scotch and refilled his goblet nearly to the brim. "I feel like my bunkhouse is filled with monsters and I have no one to blame but myself."

Just after sunup the next morning, boots thudded on the porch of the Triple T lodge. Three crisp raps followed on the door.

Ben Trent, just finishing his cup of coffee at the dining room table, across the foyer from the kitchen, glanced curiously at Rachel, who was seated across from him. She'd barely touched the poached eggs, venison sausage, and roasted potatoes on her plate. She hadn't been able to eat or sleep since Dev had died. Ben looked at the dining room door, which opened onto the foyer.

Lone Dog, with his hair traditionally braided, and clad in dyed buckskins, with his customary necklace of porcupine quills encircling his neck and lying flat against his broad chest, scuffed in his beaded moccasins out of the kitchen. The Indian, who was pushing sixty, but was still a straight-backed, handsome man, with only a little silver streaking his twin braids, slid his dark-brown eyes to his boss, a customary lack of expression on his chiseled face.

A white dish towel hung over his left shoulder. In the foyer, he swung right, brushed past a wooden figure of an elk, which Lone Dog had carved himself out of dark maple, and continued with his metronomic movement toward the front door.

He'd disappeared for a half second, but then Ben saw the dish towel fly through the morning shadows of the foyer to land on the elk's broad antlers, the towel's ends jostling as they sloped toward the floor.

Ben heard the door scrape open.

"Boss in?" a man's voice said.

No response from the aging Lone Dog. He probably just nodded—a tight-lipped man, especially in times of trouble—and then boot thuds sounded, and the Trents' foreman, Ed Ringo, appeared in the dining room's open doorway. He saw that his boss was breakfasting with his daughter-in-law, fumbled his dark-gray Stetson off his head, and held it against his chest.

He shifted his weight nervously from one foot to the other. Like so many of his ilk, Ringo felt more comfortable in a bunkhouse or on a horse than he did in what he considered fancy digs.

His voice was quiet, low. "Sorry to interrupt, boss."

"What is it?" Ben, an impatient man, said crisply.

But he knew what it was.

He'd always been amazed how closely Ringo resembled Tom Horn, who'd been a deputy sheriff under William "Buckey" O'Neill, the famous Arizona lawman, and with whom Ben had once played poker and drank in Tombstone's Stock Exchange Saloon. The notorious frontiersman was a lean, rangy man, with thin dark-brown hair and a mustache, short sideburns, and a brown-eyed gaze as expressionless as Lone Dog's.

"You got company. Mr. Donovan and three of the riders who work for him as range detectives. They're armed for bear."

In ranching parlance, the term "range detective" was usually synonymous with "regulator." Ben had a few of those himself on his payroll, though their main focus was on working the herds with the other punchers. However, when there was a rustling problem or trouble with nesters or outlaws on the run looking for a remote place to hole up, that focus broadened and Sharps "Big Fifties" were employed.

Such men were usually former outlaws themselves. Former outlaws were often worth their weight in gold, for they didn't have the behavioral restrictions that inhibited "better" men. They were often tricky rows to hoe, because the rancher who hired them had to be able to trust them.

There was a certain art in dealing with such men, but then there was a certain art in dealing with *all* men. *All* women, for that matter. For instance, Dev's widow, Rachel, while quiet, had been affable before she'd lost Dev. And she'd kept herself up. Now she was a mere shell of her former self. Ben often wondered when was the last time she'd washed her hair.

At least, Big Ike had brought only three range detectives—

unless more men were lurking on the ridge to the west of the Triple T headquarters.

Rachel studied her father-in-law closely, stonily, as Ben said to Ringo, "What's the old scudder's mood like?"

Ringo shrugged as he kneaded the edge of his hat brim. "What it's always like. I don't see no difference after . . . well . . . after last night an' Logan's thing with Hyde."

Ben said, "Send him in." He looked at Rachel. "You best go help Lone Dog in the kitchen."

"I'd just get in his way, an' he hates that. Besides, I want to know what that old devil, Donovan, has to say."

Ben gave a frustrated chuff.

Dev, why did you have to go?

Ringo disappeared, his footsteps fading. They were replaced by the increasingly loud scuffs and heavy breaths of an older man. Big Ike Donovan stood in the dining room doorway. His red knit cap glowed in a shaft of light angling into the foyer from a window in the kitchen, where Lone Dog had returned to his silent, efficient, post-breakfast toils, having grabbed his towel off the elk antlers after he'd led Big Ike to the dining room door.

"Ben," Donovan said by way of greeting, respectfully dipping his chin. "Miss Rachel."

Ben was the only one of the two who responded. "Ike . . . we got trouble?"

The competing rancher's thick, callused red hands fiddled with the soiled red cap on his head. Looking down at his black boots, he winced, then looked up from beneath his brows at the Triple T rancher. "You got a bottle?"

Chapter 26

Ben Trent rose and strode, wincing against arthritis in both knees, to a stout liquor cabinet made from oak and outfitted with a fully stocked bottle rack above and behind it.

He filled two glasses with his preferred bourbon and held up an empty glass to his daughter-in-law, who nodded with sheepish eagerness. Ben knew she drank in her room upstairs, for he'd smelled it on her. She turned her flinty eyes to Donovan, who had sat down in a chair at the head of the table, his back to the foyer, his hat on the table to his right.

Big Ike had fought Indians, rustlers, nesters, landslides, and avalanches, but he couldn't meet Rachel's uncompromising gaze.

Ben splashed bourbon into the third glass. He set the three glasses on the table beside Rachel. He left hers near her left elbow, then set one of the remaining two glasses down in front of Big Ike. He deposited the last one beside his coffee cup. He sat in his chair, slid it up close to the table, poured the whiskey into his coffee, and stirred the concoction with a spoon.

He looked at Big Ike. "Logan filled me in. He an' his roan are up on a bluff yonder, watchin' for your riders."

Big Ike sipped his bourbon and scowled. "I think I might have defused the situation." Big Ike looked at Ben. "At least, I clipped the end off, but there's still enough wick there to light."

"I'm sure your men are loyal to each other . . . as my men are loyal to Ringo. Though for a month or two, they always resent a foreman if he's one of them who gets called up from the ranks."

Big Ike had just swallowed a sip of his hooch. He choked on it, laughing, and slapped the table. He had a good laugh at his and his rival rancher's shared experience, and wagged his head.

He inhaled deeply. A sheepish cast came to his face.

"No laughing matter. Hyde howled all night. The men couldn't get him drunk enough to make him pass out." Big Ike cast Ben a warning look. "He an' they will hold a grudge."

"My son will, too. And our men are friends with Logan. They're loyal to him, as they were loyal to Devon." The older Trent son had been the overseer of the Triple T, allowing Ben to sleep in and go to bed early, not sit a saddle so much, and generally go easier on his old, arthritic bones.

"Can you handle 'em?"

"Here, yes. Out on the range or in town when they're all drinking in the same saloon . . . ?"

Big Ike took another sip of his whiskey. "Yeah." He set his glass down and glowered into the amber liquid.

Ben looked at him. "If it comes to a shootin' war, which one of us do you think'll win?"

"You."

"Oh?"

"You got a foreman. I got a cripple!" Again, Big Ike slapped the table and laughed.

Ben laughed then, too.

Rachel threw back her whiskey with the ease of a seasoned cowhand, rose from her chair, and cast each old bull buff a sharp glare, wrinkling her nose distastefully. "I'm glad you both think this is so funny." She strode angrily toward the foyer. "I'm going to tend my husband's grave."

She swung left. The door opened and closed, and she was gone.

Again, Big Ike shook his head. "I wish like heck she didn't think one of my men killed your boy."

Ben said, "You know—I don't think she really does. I don't know why I suspect this, but I think she'd just like to *believe* one of your men did it. Somehow, it gives her comfort." He shook his head despondently. "That's a tortured young lady."

"Several of my men were found dead on your land. They were trying to get our cattle back where they belong. Nothing more. That's what your Devon was doing on *my* land. I know that, and none of my men would have killed him for that. That's a silent agreement, an unwritten range rule."

The front door opened and closed. Boots thudded in the foyer. Both ranchers turned to look out the dining room door. Logan Trent glanced through the door as he turned to start into the kitchen, with his Winchester riding his right shoulder. He locked brief gazes with Big Ike. Neither man said anything. Logan glanced at his father, then walked into the kitchen, where he could be heard, talking with Lone Dog, who called him in Lakota "a grizzly at the end of hibernation"—teasing him about his endless appetite.

Since Lone Dog had come to work here at the Triple T, all the Trents had acquired a good conversational knowledge of the Lakota Sioux tongue. Dev had especially enjoyed talking around the dining room table with the old warrior, who, as a younger man working as a hostler at Fort Lincoln, had come close to getting bullwhipped at the demand of none other than Custer himself, who'd been insulted by the way the Sioux wouldn't make eye contact with him or respond to any of his orders in English.

Logan's sudden laughter pealed out of the kitchen. He said something in flawless Lakota. With his mouth full of one of Lone Dog's traditional recipes—maybe a pemmican biscuit slathered in chokecherry jam, or fry bread, or maybe the cold smoked carp both brothers had loved, and which Lone Dog had always kept in the icebox for them—Logan spewed more Lakota with mirth. Both men laughed and then Lone Dog told him to get out of his kitchen and stop messing it up as fast as Lone Dog could clean it. A traditional admonishment—and one of the few occasions Logan had seen the glint of humor in the Indian's eyes.

But then Lone Dog ordered in Lakota, "Wait—stir that stew for me first and chuck another log in the firebox." A traditional command, one that made Ben Trent long for years ago, when both his boys were young men . . . and were still alive.

"He sure gives a lot of orders for an Indian" was Ben's well-worn, phony complaint.

Big Ike turned to Ben, smiling. "Both your boys love the exotic, don't they?" He hurried to sheepishly amend his grammar: "I mean, uh . . . *loved*, in Devon's case, of course."

He grimaced and took another sip of his drink.

Ben frowned curiously. "What do you mean by 'exotic'? The Lakota?"

"The Lakota Sioux . . . the Mexican." Big Ike chuckled. "Dev could speak it as fast as she could."

"As fast as *who* could?"

"You know—the *chiquita* who runs the Yellow Flower in town. Both boys could talk to her in rapid-fire Mexican. Especially Devon, but he was with her more often . . . and longer . . . after . . . Well, you know about that . . . and about Logan lighting a shuck out of Three Forks after the trial."

"Dev was in town a lot?"

"Wasn't he? I heard he rode into town late and left early." Big Ike gave an innocent shrug and sipped his tangleleg. "He stabled his horse at several different barns, an' you know how the liverymen talk like church ladies after the Sunday service." The rancher chuckled, but there was a sudden sheepish cast to his eyes.

Ben's scowl deepened. He could feel warm blood rise in his bearded cheeks. He'd tried not to think about it much, but he'd known Dev had spent time in town—maybe too much—often driving the supply wagon into Three Forks himself. He sometimes got back late and let the other men unload and stow the supplies with Lone Dog, while he hurried back to the cabin he'd shared with Rachel.

Ben hadn't mentioned anything to his oldest boy about his comings and goings. He knew Dev was distraught about Logan's murder charge and his leaving the country to try to spare his family any more reputational damage.

And because Logan was a prideful young man who didn't like the looks and stares he'd received in town, he'd sought a new life elsewhere.

But *Dev* . . .

Ben gave Big Ike a long, incredulous stare and then turned his head to one side and said, "What, uh . . . what kind of a relationship you think—"

"Anyway!" Big Ike slapped the table, threw back the last of his bourbon, and pulled his red cap lower on his forehead. "I rode over here just to warn you if we don't want to have a war on our hands, we'd best keep our men on short leashes. No fightin' in town! I can, an' I know you can, but it don't hurt to palaver about it once in a while. You can ride over to the Double D whenever you want." The grizzled rancher grinned. "You have a free pass. I'll make sure of that."

Ben frowned again. "What about Buck?" he inquired curiously.

"I think if anyone can flush out the killer, your youngest can."

"Why do you think that?"

"Because I talked to him. An' I know he wants to stay in the mountains . . . for various reasons . . . an' he wants his reputation back." Big Ike held up a mock-cautionary finger. "But you tell him—as far as my daughter goes, no shotgun weddin's!"

He slapped the table again and laughed as he ambled out of the dining room and into the foyer. He strode, dragging his bootheels. The front door opened and closed. Hooves thudded.

They dwindled quickly, leaving Ben Trent alone with his thoughts.

Logan Trent, standing in the foyer's deep shadows near the base of the stairway leading to the lodge's still-dark second story, jerked with a start as Big Ike's hand slammed down on the dining room table and his deep-throated, wheezing laughter rose.

He lurched forward, adjusted his rifle on his shoulder, and quietly started up the stairs.

He turned his head to one side, seeing in the corner of his left eye Big Ike amble down the foyer to the front door, which opened and closed, and he was gone. Trent had just been leaving the kitchen when he'd heard his father and Big Ike mention the pretty Mexican owner/operator of the Yellow Flower in Three Forks.

Having stopped in the foyer, concealed by the shadows, he'd eavesdropped on the two older men's conversation.

Her name and Dev's name echoed in his head, as did Big Ike's telling Ben Trent that Devon had spent a lot of time in town after Logan had left. That he'd ridden to town late and left early.

As he gained the top of the stairs and bent his heels toward his bedroom, he couldn't help reflecting that the infant whom Megan Donovan was raising was dark haired and brown-eyed, with light-brown skin. Megan had told Trent that the Olsons had adopted the child from a young Basque couple from the Mexican part of Three Forks. There were quite a few Basques left in the country. In fact, Basques from France and Spain had first settled this area, raising large flocks of sheep, which the white cattle ranchers had eventually driven out.

A half-Mexican child could pass as a Basque child.

Chapter 27

A half-Mexican child could pass as a Basque child.

The revelation whispered in Logan's head as, ten minutes after he'd climbed the stairs, he descended them, rifle resting on one shoulder, saddlebags and blanket roll hanging over the other shoulder.

He strode through the foyer and glanced into the dining room.

His father remained sitting at the table, leaning forward, elbows on either side of his empty drink glass and his coffee cup. He was kneading his temples with the knuckles of both hands. As Logan passed, the older Trent looked at him.

As Logan continued toward the front door, his father yelled, "Where you goin', son?"

"I'll be back before nightfall, Pa. Got somethin' I have to do in town."

Ben Trent responded to that, but by that time, his son was halfway out of the house and pulling the door closed behind him. Logan crossed the porch and descended the steps to the yard, seeing the wheel furrows Big Ike's buggy had left in the dirt and ground horse manure fronting the wrought-iron hitchrails. The old rancher rarely rode a horse anymore. It was too hard on his back and posterior. The furrows conjured what Big Ike had told his father about the "*chiquita*" who owned the Yellow Flower in Three Forks.

He'd heard the very subtle jeering in Big Ike's voice.

The rival rancher still felt in competition with the Trents, and, of course, he still resented Logan for the deaths of his two boys, though Logan had only killed Pete, who had been trying to kill him, on his way back from Big Creek. Still, Big Ike didn't want the two outfits to go head-to-head. He and Ben Trent had ranched in these mountains long enough to know how destructive range wars could be to every rancher in the area, for they had a way of sucking in others outside the boundaries of the original conflict.

Shooting broke out randomly, savage bushwhacks, barns and lodges burned, men hanged, women ravaged, cattle and horses shot . . .

Ben Trent and Big Ike had seen it all, and while they still didn't much care for each other, they shared a violent history that wore heavily on each man. They had to tamp down their feud.

But what would happen if Big Ike learned . . .

Trent shook his head, hazing the thought out of his mind.

He couldn't jump to conclusions. He had to find out for himself.

It couldn't be true.

He couldn't imagine his older brother fathering a child with a woman outside of his marriage to Rachel.

As he headed for the stable, Logan heard loud boot thuds on the porch behind him. His father's deep, resonant voice thundered: "Where are you goin', boy? You turn around and answer me!"

Logan cursed and stopped. He turned around. The old man, in a wool shirt and crisp blue denims, the cuffs of which were tucked down into his boots, regarded his only remaining son with his thumbs hooked behind his wide brown leather belt. He was old and gray, but he was still a handsome man, straight-backed and long-legged. He carried only a modest paunch.

"You overheard." The elder Trent nodded darkly and narrowed one eye. "He wouldn't do that. Big Ike was just tryin' to drive a knife in for . . . well, you know what for."

Logan said, "He knows I didn't kill Buck. He knows why I killed Pete, though I didn't even know it was Pete I was killin', just some gutter-crawlin' dry-gulcher from the dry-gulch country I came from an' was ridin' back into. Well, here I am, an' I got some problems to iron out. Like I said, I'll be back before nightfall!"

He swung around and continued to the stable. He dropped his saddlebags near the corral gate, leaned his rifle against the fence, and entered the stable through the large, open doors. When their oldest hostler, Billy Hawkins, saw him grab a rope, Billy scowled, incredulous, and said, "What're you doin'?"

Trent walked to the door that led to the stall in which Billy had hazed Wolf after tending the roan, feeding and watering him and rubbing him down. "Goin' for a ride."

"You just came back from a ride."

Rage burst like a shotgun blast inside Trent. He swung around and shouted, "Well, I'm goin' for another one! You got a problem with that, Billy?"

Hawkins just stared, thoroughly confounded by Ben Trent's younger son. He'd known Logan for many years, and he'd never seen him act this way. Downright hateful and belligerent.

Hawkins, short silver hair bristling atop his head—in his younger years, he'd been one of the Triple T's best range riders, and had even been foreman for a number of those years—raised his hands and opened his fingers in supplication.

"All right, Logan," he said softly. "All right."

Guilt and regret instantly filled the younger man, making his stomach feel as though he'd drunk sour milk. "I'm sorry, Billy."

Trent turned toward the stable's side door, tripped the steel latch.

"Logan?"

Trent stopped and glanced over his shoulder at the aging hostler. Hawkins slowly wagged his head. "It ain't true. Whatever Big Ike told your pa, it ain't true. He's devious, Big Ike is. Oh, he can act right friendly when he needs to, but he'll still try to drive in a knife . . . especially after . . ."

Trent dropped his pensive gaze to the straw- and hay-littered stable floor and nodded. "I know." He looked at Billy Hawkins. "I know."

How had the hostler known what Big Ike had told the elder Trent?

How many others knew?

When anything involved the Trents, though, others knew.

Trent turned, strode into the stall, roped Wolf, led him outside, and tied him to a corral slat near the gate. The other seven horses in the corral gathered before them, switching their tails and flicking their ears, curious. Dust lit by morning sunlight rose around them. Ten minutes later, Trent had the roan saddled.

Wolf glanced at him sidelong, with a similarly incredulous expression as the one Billy Hawkins had just given him. Wolf gave his head a puzzled wag. He stomped one front hoof and touched the rubbery end of his nose to Trent's left ear, as if by smell he might detect what lay in his rider's heart, why Trent seemed on edge.

Horses were curious creatures; they could sense about a man what other men could not.

"Long story." Trent grunted as he swung up into the leather, with the reins in his left gloved hand. Poking his boots into his stirrups and settling himself in the saddle, he added, "We'll have us a deep palaver later over whiskey an' oats."

He clucked and heeled the mount into a gallop across the yard and through the portal in the wooden crossbar of which the Trent Triple T brand had been burned above the open end of a horseshoe. He'd ridden a mile and a half when he glanced off the trail to the right and saw five riders just then ride up a bald ridge, crest it, and drop down the far side. The last rider's horse switched its tail, and then horse and rider were gone.

Trent stared at the arching blue sky, still brassy with the morning sun, and against which the riders had been briefly silhouetted just before they'd disappeared. A wave of fresh anger burned through him. Those weren't Triple T men. Most of the crew had headed toward the western and southern ranges earlier, gathering and moving herds in anticipation of the fall gather. Counting them, too, for Ben Trent wanted an exact count so he knew how many might have been taken by rustlers.

No, the five men Trent had just seen weren't Triple T men. The only Triple T men out this way were three riders Trent's father and his foreman, Ringo, had sent out three days ago to watch over a smaller herd in Spruce Valley, by the slender, meandering Spruce Creek, where, as boys, Trent and Dev had fished and swam and gathered wild huckleberries.

The creek made for a verdant valley carpeted in long green grass.

Trent cursed.

He had to check the five riders out. If they were who he suspected they were—True's rustlers—he'd run them down, shoot them, and hang them as a dark warning to others of their ilk.

He reined Wolf off the trail and up the ridge, which sloped gently for a quarter mile before rising steeply. He stayed close to the forest, which grew along a connecting ridge to the right of a long, shallow ravine between the two rises. When he reached the crest of the ridge, he rode fifty yards down the opposite, forested side so his quarry wouldn't outline him, as he did them, against the sky.

He drew back on Wolf's reins and stopped the horse, who turned so he faced across the shoulder of the slope toward the east. Trent stared down the ridge and into a pine-stippled valley rolling off—a velvet blue-green in the intensifying light—toward a jog of blue connected ridges another two miles beyond, to the south. He put Wolf ahead, to the east, paralleling both the ridge's crest on his left and the base to his right, a hundred yards below.

As he rode slowly, he scrutinized the ground, until he picked up the faint but recent tracks of five horses angling southeastward down the ridge. He followed the tracks into the pines, spruces, and aspens and continued following them until they disappeared on the grassy, western bank of Spruce Creek. He put Wolf into the shallow water and crossed the stream, but he didn't pick up the tracks again, which meant the five riders were probably riding in the creek, following it downstream to the south, to cover their tracks.

Had they seen him on the trail, on the other side of the ridge?

Trent didn't think so.

This was just one heckuva cautious lot, which meant they were probably seasoned at what they did—stealing other men's cattle.

Trent followed the stream slowly, casting his scrutinizing gaze from the bank on his left to the one on his right. He'd ridden nearly a mile, not finding a single track, when a horse's whinny rose in the forest on his left. It came from maybe fifty or sixty yards away.

He put Wolf up the eastern bank, stopped him, stepped out of the saddle, and tied the roan, who gazed warily eastward, to a pine branch. Trent shucked his Winchester from the boot, patted Wolf's neck, silently telling the horse to stay and be quiet, then racked a cartridge into the Winchester's action. He off-cocked the hammer and began moving quietly, wending his way around the trees, along the valley's flat floor to the east, looking around carefully, wincing at the faint crunch of pine needles beneath his boots.

He walked for nearly fifteen minutes before he saw a horse standing before him in the trees fifty yards away. The gelding was not saddled. It wore only a rope halter, the frayed end of the rope trailing along the ground.

The horse, a palomino, stared at Trent stiffly.

Trent's heart quickened. He recognized the mount as one from the Triple T's remuda. It was one from Dewey Allen's rough string. Allen was one of the three men Ben Trent and Ed Ringo had sent here to keep an eye on the small herd grazing this summer range—a dozen or so steers they'd wanted to fatten up on the long green grass before the winter snows came.

Trent crept slowly forward.

He studied the ground to his left. Three sets of shod hooves angled toward him from the thicker forest in the north. The tracks were spread out, the ground churned up—old leaves, needles, pinecones, and small branches kicked out from beneath running shod hooves. The horses had been galloping hard and fast. Brass rifle cartridges lay strewn among the hoof prints, which angled off ahead of Trent and to his right.

Straight ahead of him, the palomino whickered, turned, and trotted several feet away before stopping and turning back to face Trent again, nervously switching its tail. Trent held up his gloved left hand, palm out.

"Easy, fella. It's all right."

The horse had been badly frightened.

Trent continued walking ahead and to his left, following the deeply gouged prints of the running horses. He walked a hundred feet and stopped suddenly, drawing a sharp breath, his heart thudding against his ribs.

A ring of fire-blackened rocks lay twenty feet ahead of him.

Saddles, saddlebags, bedrolls, rifles, battered hats, cooking gear, and shell belts—two with holstered pistols, two without—lay strewn around the ring. The tracks of the three running horses churned up the ground around the ring and around the large ponderosa pine from which the bodies of three men hung. The dead men's chins were dipped to their chests. Two of them were each missing a boot. They'd all been shot; blood matted their shirts. The one who still wore his boots had probably been dead when the killers had hanged him.

Bloody wounds shone over his heart and above his right ear.

His name was Kyle Coughlin, and he was tied to the same branch as Nils Latham, on the pine's left side.

Dewey Allen hung from a branch on the pine's right side; that stout bough was a little lower on the tree than the one from which

Coughlin and Latham hung. All three bodies turned slowly in the morning breeze. The ropes they hung from creaked mournfully.

Trent punched his saddle horn with the end of his right fist.

He glanced back toward the creek down which the five riders had ridden. Had three of them been members of the rustling/killing trio who slaughtered Allen, Coughlin, and Latham?

Likely.

They had to have gall to return to the scene of their crime—the cold-blooded killings of three men who'd been sent out here to watch over a small herd. They were part of True's syndicate, for sure. They must have taken the steers and, after a night of more rustling on the Triple T or on the Donovan Circle Double D, they were heading back to where they'd taken the stolen beeves.

Squeezing his Winchester in both hands, Trent stared back toward the stream. He wanted to track those five. They were likely heading to their lair, their mountain hideaway. Trent would have given his right arm to know where that was, but tracking along the stream would be futile. And if he did find the killers' lair, he'd likely be badly outgunned and would probably end up like the three Triple T men.

He'd live to fight another day.

He swung around, walked back to Wolf, tucked his Winchester in its boot, and mounted up. He galloped back out to the main trail and then swung east toward Three Forks. He'd send men and a wagon for the three bodies, the palomino, and the other two men's horses, if they could find them, if they'd hadn't been taken, too. He would do all this when he returned to the ranch from town.

First, the Yellow Flower . . .

Chapter 28

An hour later, Trent crossed the last wooden bridge along the final fork in the Wolf River and entered Three Forks.

It was nearly midday, the sun hanging straight up in the air, its brassy light sucking up the last of the morning's shadows. He wended his way through the heavy wagon, dray, and horseback traffic, pulled up in front of the Yellow Flower, and sat staring up at the window Red Maclain had broken when he'd flown back through it with Trent's bullets riddling his chest. The window had already been replaced.

Clarita didn't mess around. At least, not with her business.

Crusty brown blood still shone in the dirt fronting the building, to the right of the double swing doors.

His heart thudded angrily.

He said quietly to himself, "Go easy, Logan. Put on a friendly face. Just go in, belly up to the bar, have some lunch, and a double whiskey. Make easy conversation. Nice . . . an' . . . easy."

He swung down from the saddle and tied Wolf to one of the bawdy house's three crowded hitchracks.

Stepping up onto the boardwalk, he forced himself to smile, trying to loosen up the taut muscles of his face. Thumbing his hat up onto his forehead, he pushed through the batwings, took a few seconds to size up the place—nearly every table was occupied, but only a dozen or so men stood at the bar. Trent swung to his right, strode to the bar's left end, removed his hat, and tossed it onto the polished mahogany.

Clarita, clad in a long, low-cut, sleeveless red dress, which Trent had noticed was getting plenty of attention from the male clientele, was busy drawing beers and pouring whiskey, tequila, and vodka for the two scantily clad serving girls—one a brunette, the other a blonde—who were both pretty as sin, but flushed from exertion. Some of the brunette's hair was secured in a bun atop her head, but roughly a third had torn loose of its pins and hung like a crow's wing over the right side of her face.

As Clarita set several shot glasses and three beer schooners on her tray, the brunette kept shaking it back, with an annoyed look, but it wouldn't stay. Clarita opened her hand, set several pins on her tray, and smiled. The girl smiled back at her, swung around, and returned to the fray.

Trent gave a fleeting, crooked smile, and shook his head.

It was hard for anyone, even a married man, not to tumble for such a bewitching young lady. He hoped he had it wrong about her and Devon, though. He *really* hoped he had it wrong.

Clarita had help in the form of two male aprons, with pomaded hair, trimmed mustaches, and green and red bow ties, respectively, but she usually assisted behind the bar during busy times, like now. Trent had seen her glance his way and she gave him an acknowledging smile. He raised a hand and shook his head, silently telling her to take her time.

He was no longer in a hurry to confront Clarita about anything. When he was away from her, he somehow forgot how alluring she was, with that rich near-black hair pinned into a braid behind her head, and large gold hoop earrings dangling from her ears. Her eyes were as dark as Christmas chocolate, and they glistened in the light angling from the saloon/brothel's long, rectangular, well-polished windows running along the building's front adobe-brick wall.

She set a beer schooner, three shot glasses, and a bottle of expensive Scotch on the tray of the second serving girl—a blue-eyed blonde from a hay farm near Three Forks, whose family made a good living selling hay and firewood to the local ranchers, like the Trents themselves—then strode down the bar to Trent, hoop earrings jouncing. Her nut-brown cheeks were flushed from work. A sheen of perspiration glistened on her forehead.

She slapped her hand down on the bar in front of Trent, locked eyes with him, and curled one half of her rich, upper lip. "Name your poison, cowboy! If you make it something other than that putrid beer and cheap whiskey, I'll join you." She glanced to her left, where the two barmen, one thickset, one lanky, seemed to be getting a handle on things. "I don't pay myself enough to work this hard, amigo!"

She lowered her head and laughed.

Trent laughed, too. As always in her presence, his heart felt lighter. It wasn't beating nearly as hard and as quickly as it had been just a few minutes ago. He jerked his right glove off, slapped it onto the mahogany, and said, "Your best tequila, senorita. *Vamos!*"

She rose up onto her tiptoes to pull a bottle off a shelf over the bar. Trent sighed. That was some dress. She set the bottle onto the bar, pulled a couple of shot glasses off a near pyramid, dug the cork out of the bottle, and poured the shots, her brown eyes widening with delight. The desert-fragrant air of the tequila peppered Trent's nostrils. Clarita slid one of the shot glasses toward Trent, pulled the other one toward her, and left the uncorked bottle on the bar between them.

Trent lifted the glass to his nose, took a deep sniff, and hooded his eyes dreamily. "The heavenly scent of your home country, senorita. Residing in a bottle in Three Forks, Idaho!"

She laughed and took a sip. Lowering the glass and smacking her bee-stung lips, she said, "*Dios mio*—it makes me homesick!"

Trent took a sip from his own glass. He smiled. "Makes me homesick for it, too, and I never even lived there. Did a little prospecting there when I was still a wild-tailed youth who'd locked horns with his father, but I was raised right here in the Valley of the Three Forks and in the wild and woolly Wolf Mountains."

He took another sip of the delectable liquor. He frowned, feigning innocent curiosity. "Say, you were back there recently, weren't you? Old *Mejico*?"

Clarita nodded. A slight flush rose in her impossibly smooth brown cheeks. She lowered her cool gaze to her shot glass on the bar, one delicate thumb and forefinger wrapped around it. "A few months ago, *sí*. How did you know?"

Trent chuckled. "You know how the ranchers up there"—he canted his head to indicate the Wolfs in the northwest, beyond the three forks of the Wolf River—"like to gossip like schoolgirls at barn dances." Again, he chuckled, though he could hear the phony mirth in it. "You can't get away with much around here."

He'd learned more details about her sudden and prolonged disappearance from Three Forks via another snoopy liveryman who'd stabled Devon's horse when Trent's older brother had occasionally ridden to town at odd hours.

Trent took another sip of the tequila, which smelled like agave and Mexican sage, ancient adobe-brick cantinas crouched under red tile roofs in the hot, sandy desert, bristling with greasewood, creosote, barrel cactus, and saguaros; it evoked the strains of some ancient Mexican ballad lifting from a fiddle sawed away on in the cantina's shadows by some wiry, little man as dark as a full-blood Apache, wearing a frayed, low-crowned straw sombrero.

He'd listened to the music of such men, the emotion evoked in them by the sad songs they'd played as they'd reflected on all the bygone years—years of past lovers who were mere dust now, mingling with that of the desert they were buried under.

Trent was gradually becoming such a man now himself. A man with the sadness of building memories, of years sliding past like water in a stream . . .

"What do you mean?" Clarita said, looking up at him, hoop earrings caressing her neck. "'Get away with'?"

"Just that, everyone knows everything about everyone else around here. Now," Trent added offhandedly, "I did not miss that when I was gone. Why, all the old ranchers around here knew who I shuffled around with at barn dances before we were even done steppin' on each other's toes!" A feigned chuckle, though to his own ears it sounded as though he were choking.

"*Sí . . . sí . . .*" Clarita said, staring off, pensive.

That's all she'd needed to say. Just the way she'd said it, and that vaguely haunted look in her eyes when she'd said it, told him that what he'd suspected was true.

He cleared his throat, raw emotion having started to creep in. He was starting to feel bad, but he wasn't ready to let on. "What took you down there for so long?" he asked, trying to make the question sound innocent.

Clarita threw back the rest of her tequila, then refreshed her glass, as well as Trent's. She set the bottle back down on the bar and brushed the back of her hand across her mouth. "My aunt was sick. She lives alone on a *granja*, a little farm in the desert. Her husband died. They never had kids." Clarita gave her bare shoulders a little shrug. "She raised me after my mama and my papa died. She died slowly, bedridden, and needed someone."

Still staring down at her glass, she gave her shoulders another little shrug.

"I'm sorry," Trent said. He could tell from the sad cast to her gaze that at least that much of her story was true. She was just leaving a big part out—a big part about her motivation for leaving Three Forks for as long as she had.

But that was all right, he suddenly realized.

He wasn't even sure he wanted to know the rest.

He didn't need to know. She had her secrets. Devon had had his. He had his. Who was he to try and pry hers and his brother's out of her?

He realized he'd been staring pensively down at his own shot glass, when he glanced up to see her probing him now with her own vaguely suspicious gaze.

"What is it, Logan?" she said in a low, raspy, intimate voice. "What are you thinking about?"

"Nothing."

Frown lines deepened across her forehead. "Tell me."

Trent drew a deep breath. "I was . . . I was just thinkin' . . . I need to finish up and push on."

"Have you seen her?"

"Rachel?"

"*Sí*, Rachel."

Trent looked back down at his tequila. He nodded and asked Clarita, "Does Rachel know? Does Megan know?"

Tears glistened in Clarita's eyes. They ran down her cheeks, glinting in the midday sunlight pouring through the windows.

"Was Dev killed because of . . . this?" Trent couldn't help asking.

"I don't know why he was killed. I've always assumed rustlers. Maybe Big Ike's men. He was on Double D range."

"Ike didn't kill him."

"How do you know?"

"Ike's many things, but he's not stupid. He wants to keep that place for his daughter when he's gone. His sons are dead. All he has is her . . . and your—" He stopped suddenly, amended the sentence. "The child."

"He accepts her?"

"Seems like it."

"She is mixed blood. She is no Basque. She is half *Mejicana*. She is my and—"

"No need to say it."

"Why not? That's what you came here to find out."

Trent threw back a good swallow of his drink and set the glass back down on the mahogany. "I don't need to know. I didn't realize it when I was riding down out of the mountains, but it's none of my business." He looked at her again directly. "Unless it had something to do with why he was killed."

Clarita shook her head. "I don't think so. It was rustlers. They're all over. They're so brash. I see them in here. I know who they are. They have that look about them. Brash . . . brazen. Killers."

"True's their leader."

"I know. Like you said, everybody knows everything about everyone in this valley. In those mountains." She jerked her head back, indicating north. "Even in the Bitterroots."

"I didn't know. I think Pa suspected, but he an' True were friends . . . back when they were both young and settling this country . . . fighting the Sioux, rustlers, wildfires, drought, heavy winter snows. They both survived. That bonds men. When one goes bad, the other wants to ignore it for the sake of better times . . . a better past. Fond memories."

Clarita frowned. "*Sí.*"

"Did you love him?"

She nodded. "And he loved me. It wasn't just . . . you know . . ."

"Does Rachel know?"

Clarita looked down at her glass again. For nearly a minute, she said nothing. In the meantime, the Yellow Flower was clearing out. Lunch hour was over. The businessmen and drovers from neighboring ranches were heading back to their businesses, back to the ranges. The two serving girls looked relieved as they cleared and scrubbed the tables. The bartenders were swabbing spilled liquor and water rings from the bar, hauling tubs of dirty glasses to the kitchen through a swing door on the far side of the room. Steam from boiling water slithered through the door before it swung back shut.

Finally Clarita looked up at Trent, gave a brief nod. "*Sí*. Rachel knows. Megan as well. Rachel rode to town in a carriage one day. I saw her from my office window. I'd never seen her in town before. The way she studied the Yellow Flower I knew she knew about me and Devon."

"She keeps to herself. Always has since she came to teach school."

"I know."

"What was Rachel doing here?"

"She came into my office. She was very quiet"—Clarita shook her head gravely—"but very angry. Her eyes were dark and on fire at the same time. Do you know what I mean?"

Trent nodded.

"She threatened to kill me if I didn't stop seeing him. She"—more tears came to Clarita's eyes—"said they were trying to make a *baby*!" More tears came until she was sobbing, chin down, head bobbing. "She said she'd be damned if she'd let me take him away from her!"

Clarita grabbed the edge of the bar and bawled.

She cried for a long time.

Trent heard men murmuring behind him. Footsteps grew louder in his ears, a heavy man dragging his bootheels. A big hand clamped over Trent's right shoulder.

"Hey, Trent—why in hell are you makin' the *chiquita* cry? Who in the hell do you Trents think you are?"

Trent looked in the backbar mirror behind Clarita. The thuggish Houk Stetler, owner of a local lumberyard, stood behind him. He was a big, bearded man in his mid-thirties. Poison-mean eyes. From looking at the man, a person wouldn't know his family was prominent, his father a banker and mine owner.

Trent locked eyes with the degenerate in the backbar mirror. "Get out of here, Stetler," he said in a voice taut as wire. "Or I'll kill you."

There was the ratcheting click of a pistol being cocked.

A gun barrel was pressed against Trent's lower back, over his right kidney. "If you think a Trent can digest a forty-five pill better than anyone else, make your play." In the backbar mirror, Trent saw the man's nostrils flare.

Clarita stopped crying, but with tears still streaking her cheeks, she frowned angrily at the bearded lout flanking Trent. "No," she said. "No!"

Stetler grinned at her over Trent's right shoulder. "Oh, yeah."

Trent swung around, a blur of fast motion. He smashed his left forearm against the gun in Stetler's right hand. Stetler cursed shrilly as his .45 roared, drilling a round into the wall just above the kitchen's swing doors. One of Clarita's aprons had just been coming through the doors. As the bullet chunked into the wall above him, he yelped, ducked, and crossed his arms over his head.

Trent squared his shoulders at Stetler, smashed his right fist against the stocky lout's left cheek, driving him stumbling backward. Trent smashed his fist against Stetler's bearded face again, again, and again. The man was trying to hold his hands up to shield his face, but Trent punched through them.

Stetler fell backward onto a table that the serving girls had just finished clearing.

"Logan!" roared a familiar-sounding voice.

But Trent's wolf was off its leash.

He was drowning out the pain of his own emotions regarding Devon, Clarita, and Rachel by venting a long-harbored hatred against Houk Stetler.

Gritting his teeth, jaws hard as stone, he rammed his fist two more times into the stout man's face.

"Logan!" thundered that familiar voice once more, closer this time.

"*No!*" Clarita screamed.

Trent drew his arm back, ready to drive his fist forward once more.

He didn't land the punch.

A pistol butt slammed down against the back of his head. He dropped his right hand. His head went up, vision blurring. He felt his knees buckle. They struck the floor. He fell forward without breaking his fall.

The world went black.

Chapter 29

Trent didn't know how much later he woke to see Dan True's fleshy face staring through the bars of a cell door at him.

Grinning, rather.

An angry blacksmith pounded in Trent's head. The most painful of the pounding came from the top of his skull, where the Three Forks lawman, the sheriff of Clear Water County, had kissed him with his Colt's walnut butt.

"Still got a temper on ya," True said, and sipped from the tin cup in his hand. He swallowed, lowered the cup, and said, "Some things never change."

It took a great deal of will and a deep suppression of the agony in his battered head, but Trent sat up and swung his booted feet to the floor. Beyond True, he saw his dented Stetson sitting on the sheriff's desk. "You didn't need to hit me that hard."

"I disagree. One more punch like the others you were gifting Houk Stetler with, his old man, Willoughby, would make sure you were hung in the street outside his bank, complete with warm burritos being sold from carts and a three-piece Mexican band makin' the whole street shake!"

True chuckled and sipped his whiskey.

Trent stared at him. He didn't know why, but suddenly the man's face riveted him. True felt the heat of his prisoner's gaze. Frowning, he drew his face back, incredulous.

"What're you lookin' at?"

Trent didn't say anything.

Trent's mind had gone back to the night Buck Donovan had been murdered.

Trent was stepping out of the Yellow Flower, his right fist aching from its hard connection with Buck's face. Buck had been drunk and harassing Clarita, where she sat at a table by the piano at the back of the room, along the wall over which the stairway angled up to the second story.

"Let's go upstairs, *chiquita*," Buck had urged, nibbling one of Clarita's earlobes.

Clarita had pushed him away. "This is a private meeting, amigo!"

But Buck, often unrelenting when drunk, merely grabbed her arm, squeezing with his right hand, drawing her toward him, and closing his mouth over hers. Trent had seen it all in the backbar mirror, where he'd been standing nursing a whiskey with Cliff Turner, who was then the foreman at the Triple T. They'd come to town to pick up three stallions Trent's father had purchased from a rancher in the Bitterroots.

The horses had not yet arrived. It was late. Both men were weary from loitering around Three Forks in the hot sun and now, long after supper, at nearly midnight.

Trent slammed his beer schooner down angrily. He didn't like any man pawing Clarita like that. She'd entertained Donovan's flirtations a time or two, but that was over. She hated the man. Trent fancied her and he knew she fancied him. They'd been together for over a month, and he was already considering asking her to marry him, to allow him to make an "honest woman" out of her, so to speak; though as far as he was concerned, she could run her saloon/brothel for as long as she wanted.

Besides, she was the most honest person he'd ever known.

She was her own woman. He understood that. That was one of the main things, beyond her beauty, he'd loved about her.

He jerked Buck away from her and they'd gotten into it. Buck was so drunk that few of his punches landed on Trent. Several of Trent's blows had landed on Buck, until the fight had drained out of the man's face, crimson now with humiliation.

"Enough!" he'd shouted when Trent had moved toward him again. Buck held up his hands, palms out.

He'd stooped to grab his hat. He'd stuffed it on his head, glanced at Clarita, and, his face growing even redder, stomped out of the saloon, the batwings clattering back into place behind him.

Trent glanced at Clarita.

She didn't allow fights in her digs. She gave him a hard-eyed, reprimanding look, but a faint, grateful smile was on her mouth as well.

"Sorry," he said.

He picked up his own hat and returned to the bar, pressing his sore fist against his chest.

A few minutes later, he had a drink at the bar with Clarita. Neither mentioned anything about Buck. A hostler from one of the liveries came in and told Trent and Turner their stallions had come in. It was a fair, full-moon night, so they'd intended to drive the stallions into the mountains to the Triple T.

"See you over there," Turner had said, giving Trent a knowing smile, aware that the younger man wanted to say goodbye to his girl in private.

Turner left.

Trent went out the saloon's back door to retrieve some firewood for Clarita. Having fallen ill, the boy she'd hired as a swamper had taken the night off. After returning to the saloon, Trent and Clarita talked for five more minutes before he reached out to shield their faces with his hat and placed a tender kiss on her cheek.

Setting his hat on his head, he gave her a parting smile and left. He swung right outside the batwings and had just walked past the dark alley mouth east of the Yellow Flower, between the hurdy-gurdy house and a harness shop, when a man walked toward him.

It was Dan True.

He was fiddling with something on his right hip. Trent couldn't see what it was.

True smiled at his deputy and said, "Enjoyin' the night off, Logan?"

"What night off?" Trent had said. "I don't know what that means, Dan. Between Pa an' you, I barely sleep."

Just before they'd passed each other in the darkness, Trent had seen a long, dark smudge on his boss's left cheek, two inches above the corner of his mouth. Then True was gone . . . until True and several men who'd been in the saloon, and who had witnessed the fight between Trent and Buck, had come to the livery barn, where Trent and Turner were inspecting the three sleek stallions from the Bitterroots.

True's face had owned a pained expression.

"Sorry, Logan," he'd said, his voice trembling a little with emotion. "I'm, uh . . . gonna have to . . . *arrest* you."

"For *what*?" Trent had laughed.

"For the murder of Buck Donovan," True had said.

Now True, scowling a little defensively through the cell bars at Trent, who was staring at his former boss and seeing everything so clearly, said impatiently, "What in tarnation are you *lookin'* at?"

"You." Trent rose from his bunk and walked to the cell door. "I'm lookin' at you, Dan."

A drunk cowpuncher, looking for a privy, had found Buck lying dead in that dark alley, between the Yellow Flower and the harness shop. He'd tripped over the body, in fact. He'd run into the Yellow

Flower, saw True just then taking his first sip of a fresh beer at the bar, and had yelled for him. True and several other men from the saloon had followed the drunk puncher outside and into the dark alley, to the body of Buck Donovan.

"You, Dan," Trent repeated now. "I'm lookin' at *you*."

True stared at him flatly. His eyes flicked between Trent's.

Finally he stepped back, reached behind him for the heavy key ring hanging from a ceiling support post, then stepped forward and poked one of the four keys into the lock on Trent's door. He scraped it to one side. The lock was old and rusty and it required some effort to turn it. When the bolt clicked back into the door, True left the key in the lock.

He took one step back, unsnapped the keeper thong from over the hammer of his .44, and slid the old Schofield from the holster. He aimed the revolver straight out from his right side with his right hand and pulled the cell door slowly open with his left hand. His eyes grew flatter and flatter, colder and colder.

When the door stood wide open, there was nothing between Trent and the .44. True took one step forward, entering the open doorway and clicking the Schofield's hammer back.

Trent smiled and held his ground—he and his former boss, three feet apart, with nothing between them except the cocked six-shooter.

His smile in place, Trent said, "You gonna say I tried to escape, Dan?" He paused, raised both brows, his lips still quirking his faintly jeering, knowing smile. "Is that it? Do you think anyone's going to believe you?"

"Big Ike will."

"I don't think so. If I'm found dead in here, warning bells are gonna toll in that rancher's old head. See—he knows you're the head of the snake."

True turned his head to one side, frowning. "What's that mean?"

"He knows you're the head of the rustling syndicate. All he has to do is have his men throw in with our men at the Triple T, and then we're gonna come after you, shoot your whole crew down like the pack of marauding, calf-killin' wolves you are."

Trent paused, held True's flinty-eyed stare with the bemused one of his own. "You killed Buck."

The lawman's flinty-eyed stare grew flintier.

"It worked well for you that night, didn't it? Out of the blue, everything fell into place. You were walkin' past the Yellow Flower, makin' your usual rounds, when you saw me an' Buck goin' at it, head-to-head. You saw Buck cash in his chips. He was drunk an' beat up." Trent shook his head slowly. "He was beat up, embarrassed in front of Clarita an' the other girls. He headed for the batwings, almost sobbing.

"You hurried into that dark alley, ran maybe twenty feet inside it, slid your Arkansas toothpick from its sheath, and crouched, waiting. When you heard Buck's boots on the boardwalk—what'd you do? Whistle for him?" Trent arched his brows higher. "Said maybe . . . maybe you needed help? Fell an' hurt yourself? Or maybe you just called his name. And he came."

Trent could tell by the flush in True's cheeks, the twitch of the man's left eye, he'd guessed right with that last one.

"Sure, sure," Trent said. "You called, 'Buck,' an' he entered the alley." Trent smiled more broadly, heart thudding, knowing he was walking a tightrope and a wide chasm opened beneath him. "Buck said, 'What is it?'" Trent continued to speculate.

True dipped his chin. His lumpy chest rose and fell heavily. He squeezed the walnut grips of the Schofield so hard his hand, shiny with sweat, shook slightly. His right finger drew taut against the trigger.

"You go to hell," the sheriff said. "You think you're smart. All you Trents think you're smart. The years you worked for me, you always thought you were smarter'n me. Younger . . . wiser . . . an' you wore the big name in these parts—Trent!"

"Never use the stream you bathe in for a privy, Dan."

True ground his jaws and stepped forward. Trent took one step back, glancing apprehensively down at the .44 shaking in the enraged, frightened man's hand. His two biggest secrets had been uncovered. The chasm beneath Trent yawned wider, darker, deeper, and more ominous.

But, despite the lawman's index finger drawn back taut against the Schofield's trigger, Trent thought he still had some time.

"Pretty obvious why you killed Buck, ain't it?" he said. "Even five years ago, you had the plan in your head. Pit the Triple T against the Circle Double D. Make them go to war against each other. Finish each other. Then all the cattle from both spreads would be yours."

The glowering lawman's chest rose and fell again heavily. "Who else knows?"

"Plenty."

"Who, damn you?"

"Plenty!"

The fleshy lawman, a cauldron of his own bitter demons, took another lurching step forward and raised the Schofield. He narrowed an eye as he aimed down the barrel at Trent's head. "I'm gonna drill you one right through—"

Rather than jerk back as True had anticipated, Trent leaped forward, swung his arm up, and slammed the back of that hand against the side of True's right hand, knocking the cocked six-shooter just far enough to Trent's left that when the revolver roared, bright orange flames lapping from the barrel, the bullet whistled through the air an inch off Trent's left ear.

Trent felt the hot curl of air as the bullet passed and ricocheted off the brick wall behind him. It pinged as it clipped a bar in the cell wall to Trent's left. The sharp sound aggravated the almost unbearable ache in his head.

Trent leaped forward. As True cursed loudly and cocked the Schofield once more, again bringing the gun up to try another shot, Trent wrapped both hands around the revolver and shoved its barrel straight up. True cursed again. The Schofield had come loose in his grip as Trent shoved him backward through the open cell door. He ripped the pistol from the man's hand and tossed it across the office to his right.

The gun thudded to the jailhouse's wooden floor and slid up against the base of the far wall.

Trent clenched his fist and delivered a hammer-like, blow to True's jaw.

The lawman screamed and fell, slamming his head down hard against the dusty hardwood floor. Flat on his back, he pressed his hands into the floor on both sides of him, squeezed his eyes closed, and stretched his lips back from his teeth in misery. He blinked his eyes, trying to remain conscious. He dug the heels of his boots and the heels of his hands into the floor and arched his back.

With a great *whoosh* of air exploding from his lungs, his back dropped flat against the floor, his head turned to one side, and the big lawman lay still.

Trent stared down at him.

He could hear the man breathing, sort of groaning with each shallow breath.

He wasn't dead. He was knocked unconscious. When he woke, he'd have one heckuva headache.

The thud of footsteps rose from the porch fronting the jailhouse.

Trent scrambled over to True's gun.

He picked it up and, on one knee, aimed it at the door and cocked it.

The door opened. Clarita gasped and froze in the two-foot opening.

"Oh, hell!" Trent depressed the Schofield's hammer and lowered the gun to his side. His heart was still racing. "Don't do that to me," he said, breathless.

She walked slowly into the office. "Don't do *that* to me, stupid gringo!"

Her shocked gaze slid to where Dan True lay stretched out on his back. "*Dios mio!*" she exclaimed under her breath, splaying a hand across her chest, on the red knit shawl she wore over her sleeveless bright-red dress. "What did you do? Is he *dead*?"

Trent rose, his head and heart hammering. "He wasn't a minute ago."

Holding the lawman's revolver down low against his right leg, Trent crossed the room to True, leaned over the man, and touched an index finger to his neck.

Straightening, he said, "He's still kickin', the son of a—"

"What *happened*?" Clarita walked over to stand near Trent and the unconscious lawman.

"I'm too smart for my own britches. I don't know why I thought it was a good idea to tell him all I knew about him when he had me locked up like a hydrophobic cur and could shoot me at any time an' call it a failed escape!"

Clarita looked at him and sucked a sharp breath through her teeth. "You are just like your brother. *Impulsivo!*"

Trent looked back at her. "He killed Buck. He framed me for it, to drive a bigger wedge between us and the Donovans. Wanted us to go to war, kill each other, and save him the time an' trouble." He grabbed True around the ankles and dragged the big man into the cell through the open door. He locked it and tossed the keys behind the lawman's desk, where it would take anyone at least a little time to find them.

He turned back to Clarita. "Meanwhile, he'd have hazed our herds out of the mountains, though he's doin' it right now, anyway, tryin' to make it look like we're rustlin' *each other*!"

Voices rose outside the jailhouse door.

Trent ran to the door and placed the locking bar in the brackets to either side of it just as boots thudded on the boardwalk fronting the place. Someone tried to trip the latch; there was a metallic rattle.

"What the hell?" a man said on the other side of the door.

He rapped three times loudly on the door panel.

"Dan, you in there? Got your mail!"

Trent tossed True's gun on his cluttered desk, grabbed his own hat, gun, and shell belt off a wall peg, took Clarita's arm, and pointed at the back door. "Out! Now! You an' me!"

She ran along beside him, her slippered feet rasping softly along the dirty wooden floor. "You'll look guilty!"

"I *am* guilty!"

Once outside, Trent released Clarita's arm and said, with urgency, pointed down the rear alley in the direction of the Yellow Flower, "Go! Hurry over to the saloon, grab a few sticks of firewood from the woodpile, then head in through the rear door. You just stepped out to get some wood. And fer God's sake, try to look innocent!"

"That's not easy for a good Catholic girl. I was with a man who just broke out of jail!"

"*Go!*"

"*Sí, sí, sí!*" she intoned. Holding the hem of her dress above her ankles, she ran down the alley to the southwest.

Trent crossed the alley between the jailhouse and a barber and stopped at the shop's rear corner, peering up the gap between buildings toward the busy, dusty main drag. He wanted to make sure Clarita got clear before he made a run for Wolf, who, he hoped, was still tethered to the hitchrack fronting the Yellow Flower.

A wooden scraping sound rose behind him, from the direction in which Clarita was running.

Trent turned. Morgan Henley had just stepped out of the rear door of his grocery store and turned to start gathering firewood from the massive stack of split wood abutting the store's rear wall, framing and dwarfing the open rear door. Henley, a tall, bony man, with long, thin sandy hair tumbling to his shoulders, and wearing a white apron, stopped and turned, frowning curiously at Trent.

"Ol' Dan already let you out?"

Trent swung around and headed up the alley to the south, just as Clarita, in her red dress, disappeared through the Yellow Flower's rear door, her brown arms clutching a few sticks of split wood to her chest. The door closed and she was gone.

With a deep sigh of relief, Trent pulled his hat brim low on his forehead, smiled at the skinny grocer gawking at him, and said, "That's right, Henley," as he strode past the man. "Ol' Dan let me out for good behavior!"

He glanced behind him cautiously, then picked up his pace as he continued striding south, trying not to run.

Loud voices sounded in the break between the jailhouse and the tonsorial parlor as the postman and at least one other man headed for the jailhouse's rear door to see if they could gain entrance from that end.

Trent cursed and continued walking.

"Hey, Henley," he heard the postman say behind him, "you seen True?"

"Not lately, but I done just saw his prisoner—Logan Trent!"

Trent glanced over to see Henley pointing at him, his right arm and index finger thrust forward.

Trent ran.

Chapter 30

Trent swung into a break between two buildings north of the Yellow Flower. He cast a quick glance toward the jailhouse, then looked around the busy main drag ahead of him, at the break's far end.

Only a couple of old mule skinners, standing with three others on the boardwalk fronting the Mint Saloon, and holding soapy beer mugs in their fists, glanced at him once, then another time, before nudging each other and jerking their chins in his direction, indicating him.

Trent swung to his left and jogged off down the boardwalk, his heart lightening when he saw Wolf gazing at him skeptically from where the roan stood, still tethered to the hitchrack where Trent had tied him around ninety minutes ago.

"Howdy, boy!" Trent said, breathless with urgency as he untied the reins from the rack and, taking both ribbons in his left hand, toed the left stirrup, grabbed the horn, and pulled himself into the saddle.

He swung the incredulous stallion into the street. He glanced back toward the jailhouse to see three men, including Dan True, walk out the front door and onto the boardwalk. True held his hat in one hand, a Winchester rifle in his other hand. He was crouched forward like a stove-up old man, caressing the back of his head with the hand that held the hat. The postman and the other man were sort of leading him, arms snaked around the small of his back.

He wasn't ready to put the hat on his head yet. He was still too sore.

Which Trent could understand. The man had made a heckuva hard landing on the hardwood jailhouse floor.

Trent couldn't help chuckling as he booted Wolf into a hard run across the street and through a break between business establishments—a well-worn, two-track trail that would take him across the three forks of the Wolf River via those small wooden bridges and into the Wolf Mountains.

Sanctuary.

Or so he hoped . . .

He held Wolf to a fast trot and even slowed the horse down from that when they began climbing through the canyon that would take them higher into the Wolfs. Trent was in no hurry. True, in his condition—and probably even if he didn't have a noggin as thunderously sore as Trent's own—would take time to drag men out of a couple of the rowdier, seedier saloons to form a posse.

But first, True had to fetch his horse from the livery barn sitting kitty-corner from the jailhouse. Trent knew that True would likely gather a few of his rustlers in town, who were stomping with their tails up, taking a break from the high-and-rocky, drinking a little whiskey, playing a little poker, and taking a woman or two upstairs. Trent doubted he had much control over them. They were likely seasoned outlaw long-loopers, which meant they were wilder and woollier than True himself.

The only control he likely had was giving them a cut of the money he dragged in when he sold the stolen beef. Of course, they could just shoot him and take what they wanted, but, knowing True,

Trent figured the sheriff had a few—maybe more than a few—loyalists in the bunch.

Contrary to logic, there was, indeed, honor among thieves. After all, if other outlaws didn't trust one another, they wouldn't ride together. It was as simple as that.

Keeping a casual eye on his back trail, Trent rode higher into his home country, feeling the warmth and security of the giant arrow-shaped evergreens rising around him, stony crags rising beyond them, jutting out of ridge crests and resembling half-excavated dinosaurs. He could tell the roan felt better here, too. Like Trent, Wolf had never liked town. The farther they rode from Three Forks, the lighter the roan's mood seemed to grow, until he held his head high, and, with his mane jostling and glistening in the high-altitude sunshine, he shook his head with a flourish, whickering contentedly and giving his tail a few cheery switches.

The horse paused once to playfully paw a front hoof at a flat rock behind which a young rabbit crouched, teasing him the way young rabbits will do. The rabbit ran, kicking out its rear legs tauntingly, and disappeared into some cedars and twisted roots bristling at the base of the canyon's north wall. Wolf gave another whicker, shook his head, and continued climbing higher into the mountains he called home, too.

Trent grinned, feeling better, despite the complications he knew his visit to town had just brought.

No one had witnessed what had happened in the jailhouse.

Of course, True would tell everyone he'd tried to escape and had assaulted him—a prison offense. It would be Dan True's word against his. And even though Logan was, indeed, a member of the respected Trent family, he knew a good many people in the area still believed he'd killed Buck over Clarita.

A darkness seeped into him.

Was it a darkness similar to the one that had compelled him to leave Three Forks?

Would he ever be able to call the Valley of the Three Forks, the Wolf Mountains, the Triple T, his permanent home again?

A smile crept slowly across his face.

He'd be damned if he wouldn't make it so.

For another hour, he followed the curving trail that sometimes rose gradually and sometimes steeply, glancing occasionally behind him. Still, he was in no hurry. He crested a ridge, started down the other side, and stopped. He curveted the horse and turned to stare up at the top of the ridge littered with rocks, gnarled cedars, and dwarf spruce. Men's voices from the opposite side of the ridge touched his ears. He heard the occasional clang of a shod hoof off rock.

A horse whinnied.

A squirrel chittered nearby.

Trent looked up at a ponderosa straight ahead of him, ten feet off the trail, and saw a squirrel hunkered on a bough of the pine, glancing at him and chittering angrily, then turning his attention to the ridge crest and continuing to chitter angrily. The squirrel had unwanted guests.

Trent gave a dry laugh, knowing such guests included himself. He said, "Let 'em come, fella. Let 'em come."

He booted Wolf straight ahead, along the shoulder of the slope he was on. He came to a tall, rocky scarp, rode around behind it, and booted Wolf up the scarp's backside. Twenty feet from the top of the outcropping, in a small copse of pines and aspens, he stopped Wolf, dismounted, and slid his Yellowboy from its sheath. He patted the roan's neck, silently instructing him to stay and be quiet—no whinnies or nickers—then climbed the steep incline to within ten feet of the top. He stopped in an area of mossy rocks of all shapes and sizes, and small twisted pines.

Ahead of him, a shelf of rocky granite also dusted with moss rose sharply. He climbed to it, stopped, pressed his shoulder against the side of the formation, and doffed his hat. He stared through a V-shaped notch in the scarp. From here, he could clearly see the trail as it dropped from the top of the ridge he'd just ridden over and disappeared into heavy forest beyond. The trail dropped from his right to his left, roughly fifty feet away from him.

The clomp of hooves gradually grew louder, as did the voices of the men pursuing him. The hoof thuds grew even louder as True's posse climbed the ridge's opposite side. Soon Trent heard the squawk of tack and the jangle of bridle chains.

He stared through the notch toward the crest of the ridge ahead and on his right. When the first rider appeared at the top of the ridge, Trent jerked his head down. He waited. After half a minute, he edged a look back through the notch.

The riders were on the trail beneath him now.

Dan True led the pack, though his head had to be killing him, same as Trent's head was killing him. They were two stubborn skirmishers; both men wouldn't rest until they'd settled their differences with a bullet.

Trent counted the men as they passed on the steeply sloping trail beneath him. There were an even twenty. Trent recognized only two as men who lived and worked in town—a livery hostler named Tate Hollister, clad in pinstriped blue overalls and a shapeless black felt hat, and Frank Thoren, the alcoholic, chubby, fat-faced owner of one of the seediest saloons in town called the Wet Whistle. Something told Trent that True had found his other posse riders in the Wet Whistle and in another sleazy, dangerous watering hole, the Rio Stiletto Cantina and Gambling Parlor, which sat one door down from the Whistle.

They were True's rustlers—the entire twenty-man bunch. That's how many that, judging by the tracks Trent had found here and there in the mountains around the Triple T and the Donovans' Circle Double D, remained of the pack after he and a few of the hands from the Trent ranch had turned several others toe-down. The dead men's carcasses were now likely being cleaned every night by carrion eaters, including owls, eagles, mountain lions, bears, and coyotes. There were likely some wonderfully savage, proprietorial fights occurring nightly over such delicacies—as the bones of the dead rustlers—while the stars twinkled magically in the dark firmament above.

Ah, life . . . sweet life!

That all the long-loopers—or a good chunk of them, anyway—had all been in town together told Trent they must have recently made a sale to corrupt ranchers and could afford a few nights out before heading back to the mountains to long-loop one or two rounds of Trent and Donovan beef, as well as a few from the smaller outfits peppering the area.

Or maybe they were done. Maybe this was as far as they wanted to take it.

Who knew?

When the posse had passed below Trent and disappeared in the thick forest sliding up around the trail, dense and dark, Trent donned his hat, rose, and walked down the steep ridge to where Wolf waited, watching him skeptically, reins drooping to the ground carpeted in short, light-green grass and sage.

"Well, ol' fella," Trent said as he slid his Winchester into its scabbard, "those fellas aren't followin' my trail. The trace is too rocky and too many other horsebackers and ranch wagons pass on it daily for even the best tracker to follow only one set of prints. But True's assumin' I'm headed home, back to the Triple T."

Trent crouched, wincing at the pain in his head, and straightened, the roan's reins in his hand. "And you know what?" He smiled like the cat that ate the canary. "They'd be right."

He swung up into the leather with a grunt against that unceasing throb in his skull, and added, "But they think I'm *ahead* of them. Not *behind* them. That's where they're wrong."

Wolf gave a low nicker.

Trent booted him down the incline and into the pines and aspens at the bottom. He swung left and rode back down onto the trail, checked Wolf down and sat straight-backed in the saddle, pricking his ears to listen intently.

There were only the somber voices of the first of the night birds.

The rustle of the breeze in the mixed forest.

He glanced at the sky. It was getting late, but it was summer, which meant he had a couple hours of light left. He'd follow the bunch to the Triple T where they thought they'd likely get the drop on Trent's father and his hands. By the time the posse reached the headquarters, the ranch staff would be wandering in small, weary packs into the Triple T yard from the scattered ranges. The hands' minds would be distracted by the anticipated clang of the cook's iron triangle and the succulent meal awaiting them in the galley end of the bunkhouse.

Now sure that the posse was at least half a mile ahead of him, Trent smiled.

Yeah, they were ahead of him.

If all went as planned, Ben Trent would be ready for trouble. The old frontiersman was always ready for trouble. His son was always ready as well. Both their lives had been filled with enough of it. Trouble had been a good teacher.

Trent would follow the syndicate into the yard, and he'd have the drop.

His wily father would call the shots—and, oh, what shots they'd be.

Trent heeled Wolf forward along the trail to home.

Chapter 31

Ben Trent took a sip of his beloved Scotch, which he'd had sent by clipper ship all the way from his ancestral home, though he had never been to Scotland himself. His grandparents had moved from Scotland just after the Creek War, and they'd settled in the wild frontier of Tennessee, where they'd raised Ben, and his five siblings—only three of whom had reached adulthood—as well as goats, sheep, horses, three milk cows, and a moderately sized herd of beef cattle.

An adventurous lot of Scots, Ben thought now as he set his glass on the polished cherry table beside the overstuffed leather chair he sat in, across from Big Ike Donovan.

Donovan sipped his own Scotch and smacked his lips. "Elixir from the old home country—eh, Trent?" He chuckled. "My own preferred tangleleg is *uisce beatha*." He smiled. "That's Gaelic for—"

"Yes, I know," Trent said with a smile of his own. "'The Water of Life.'"

Big Ike chuckled, wheezing. Age had laid waste to his lungs, as it had to several other things in him, as it had to Ben himself. Ike couldn't sit a saddle anymore. That's why he rode over here—a repeat visit only a day after the previous one—in his leather-roofed buggy, a handsome Morgan in the traces. Four of his most gun-handy riders had accompanied him, acting as bodyguards, for they knew that members of the rustling syndicate, led by Dan True, had left signs of their having recently been in the area.

Those signs were several more missing Circle Double D cow-calf pairs.

That's what Donovan had come over to discuss with Trent.

They hadn't gotten to the topic yet. It wasn't the way of the Scotch or the Irish to hurry into things. They needed to drink a little—possibly more than a little—of their favorite hooch from their native lands. It opened them up, took away some of that British reserve.

Ben took another sip of his drink and was about to open a humidor on the table beside him when a voice called from the front of the house: "Riders, boss! Twenty of 'em. Led by True an' armed for bear!"

Trent and Donovan exchanged meaningful glances.

"Well, I'll be hanged." The Irishman brushed a hand through his gray goatee, frowned at Trent, and said, "Trap?"

The Triple T rancher placed his gnarled, arthritic red hands on his chair arms and pushed himself to his feet. "Let's go see. Maybe we can get this little misunderstandin' finished right here before dark!"

As the two old men moved uncertainly from Trent's office, Donovan, dogging his neighbor's heels, said, "What do you suppose he's up to—True? Kind of late for a lead swap, ain't it?"

Trent nodded as he passed Lone Dog standing, customarily stiff and formal, in the kitchen's open doorway from which, as usual, succulent supper smells originated, laced with the aroma of freshly split pine and oak, the latter providing a longer burn. Whatever the Lakota was cooking, Lone Dog had been cooking it slowly since noon, basting it frequently with whiskey, butter, and brown sugar.

Probably an elk haunch.

That was about the only thing that could distract Trent, however briefly, from the fact that the enemy was in his yard!

"Must be a posse," Ben said as he stepped out onto the porch, where three of his men stood, side by side, dressed in chaps and dusty Stetsons, Winchesters in their hands, grim sets to their faces.

Flanked by a number of hard-eyed, trail-dusted men, also holding Winchesters, Dan True pinched his hat brim to the two old ranchers and then held up that hand, palm out. He sat his steeldust gelding roughly twenty feet out from the base of the porch steps. "Now, don't go jumpin' to conclusions," he said. "We don't want trouble. We just want your son, Ben. He did a bad, bad thing!"

The lawman, if you could call him that anymore, leaned forward in his saddle and jutted out his chin.

Ben scowled as he walked forward to stand atop the porch's broad front steps. Big Ike stepped up to his neighbor's left and gave a dry chuckle, casting Ben a jeering grin. "What's he done *now*?"

Ben didn't respond to the jab. He knew that he and Big Ike, being competitive neighbors, could never truly bury the hatchet. At the moment, however, they were in the initial stages of combining their armies to go after the rustlers who were threatening both their spreads.

Maybe all were sitting their horses before the Trent lodge now?

Impossible. Or was it?

They all had the look of rustlers, sure enough. Ben didn't really know what an individual rustler looked like. He just recognized one when he saw him. True, himself, had that flat-eyed, conniving look now. This was the first time Ben Trent had recognized it.

Maybe he was getting too old for this job.

Maybe it was time to turn it all over to Logan. Not only the day-to-day operations, but everything else as well. Ben wasn't sure he could trust himself any longer with anything by way of running a sprawling ranch with hundreds of head of cattle, a good-sized remuda, and a hefty payroll.

He knew one thing, though.

He could kill Dan True right here and now. He didn't go anywhere without his pearl-gripped Colt, which resided on his right hip in its worn but comfortable black leather holster. Big Ike wore his own pistol for the cross-draw in a soft, brown leather holster on his left hip. The grips of a second gun—an ivory-handled, six-shot pepperbox revolver—jutted from a large pocket.

Ben wore a wool-lined elk jacket that fell to his thighs, and over which his holster and shell belt were buckled.

Trent glared at True from beneath the brim of his high-crowned black Stetson. "I'm waiting," Ben said flatly, flaring one nostril.

"I had to arrest him for assault and battery at the saloon. When I had him over at the jail, locked up in a cell, he assaulted and battered *me*." True angrily flung out an arm and pointed an index finger, narrowing one eye. "Hit me so dang hard I'm still seein' double! Now, that there is an offense that'll get you prison time!"

To Ben's left, Big Ike said, "Best not look in a mirror, then, Dan. You sure as blazes don't wanna see two of *you*!"

A couple of True's hard-bitten rustlers chuckled.

True cast them a hard look over his shoulder. That silenced them; their mocking smiles disappeared. One cleared his throat contritely.

Ben Trent bent over, laughing.

Several of his own men, who'd ridden back to the headquarters during the past hour, stood around in front of the stables and bunkhouse, holding rifles. A few of them laughed, too.

True raised a gloved fist at them. Two laughed harder.

"He ain't here," Ben said. "Besides, you know I let my sons fight their own battles." He turned his head to one side, narrowed one eye, and added, "Do you know that rustlin' is a *hangin'* offense, Dan?"

"I do. Who you need hung, Ben?"

Ben Trent glanced at Donovan, jaw hard, an angry flush rising in his cheeks, clomped down the porch steps, more awkwardly due to age and arthritis than he'd have preferred, and strode into the yard, in front of True, mounted on the steeldust. The gelding stretched its neck to give the rancher a cautious sniff. Horses always knew a person's intentions by how he smelled. Trent had learned some of the same art from them.

On Dan True, he could smell the hate for the Trents. His resentful jealousy of his old friends, Ben and Ike.

"You, Dan," Trent said, and glanced around at the hard-faced rustlers flanking him, spread out so they were at least six, eight feet apart. They needed room if it came to shooting. They'd ridden here expecting that, Trent knew, and they were just overconfident enough that they believed they could win a shooting war here at the Triple T headquarters. That probably came from killing several of Trent's riders and stealing respected men's cattle.

"We ain't afraid," announced one of True's men, flanking Dan on his right. "You may have some cold steel on your roll, but we're harder." Holding his Henry repeating rifle, the sandy-mustached man thumbed himself in his chest with his left hand.

Ben laughed at him.

Then the rancher stepped forward and came up alongside True's horse. He stared up at the so-called "lawman" of Three Forks. Again, he narrowed an eye.

"Who killed my son, Dan?" He lowered his voice, but kept his cold gaze on True. "Was it you?"

True shook his head. "Ben, it hurts me to hear that from you. Why, we was friends once. You an' me am' "—he glanced at Big Ike, still standing atop the porch steps—"an' Ike. We tamed these mountains together."

"Then you had to go an' untame them," Big Ike said, a fierce scowl on his face, miniature bayonets of pure hatred stabbing out from his hard, lake-blue eyes.

"You go to hell, you old rascal!" True said, holding the reins of his nervous horse firmly in his gloved left hand. In his right hand, he held an 1873 Winchester carbine. He aimed it at Trent's chest, but his eyes lacked resolve. His right index finger lay slack against the trigger.

Trent suddenly realized why True had been so bold as to ride out here with his entire contingent of rustlers. Not only was he overly confident with such gun-adept killers backing his play, but deep down, he didn't think his old friends would kill him.

Ben said tightly, "You killed Buck an' framed Logan for it to broaden the wedge between the Triple T an' the Circle Double D."

Big Ike shook his head slowly. "You only weakened it."

Ben glanced at his own dusty riders on the porch behind him and in the yard around the bunkhouse and stables. At the moment, he had about twelve men on the place. He and his foreman, Ed Ringo, had sent his riders all over Trent's vast range earlier that morning. Some might not be back till midnight.

That was all right. What Trent lacked in current manpower, he made up for with fury and the hot drive for revenge.

Just then, the lodge door rasped open. Dev's widow, Rachel, stepped out through the opening, holding her own carbine in one hand straight out from her right hip. She moved up to stand beside Big Ike. Her pale face, framed by her dark hair, was expressionless. Her eyes teemed with emotion, however. Raw, unspoken emotion.

Rachel could never express all the torment in her heart and soul.

Trent had never seen a person grieve so hard. Not even he had known that kind of inner agony when his men had brought Dev's body back from where they'd found it when he'd been chasing strays on Double D range. Trent had drunk a whole bottle of Scotch and bawled himself to sleep that night. But in the morning, hearing Rachel screaming down at her and Dev's cabin through the lodge's open windows, he'd calmly walked to his office, scribbled out the telegram for Logan, and sent a man to town on a fast horse with orders to fire off that cable.

Ben was jolted out of his reverie when Dan True leaned forward in his saddle, poked up his hat brim, and leered at Rachel. "Your army's gettin' purtier, Trent!"

Still without expression, Rachel rammed a round into the Winchester's chamber, raised the rifle, and pressed the rear butt plate against her shoulder.

"Wait now!" True screamed, raising his gloved hands and leaning far back in his saddle.

She didn't wait. The rifle bucked and roared. The lawman screamed again as the .44 round ripped his hat off his head.

True yelped and ducked. His fine gray hair was harassed by the breeze. Every horse in his bunch jumped and whickered. The men held tight to their reins and saddle horns, cursing, cutting sharp, apprehensive looks at the woman standing atop the steps in a white blouse and a long green wool skirt. Big Ike had whipped his head to her in shock. Now a slow smile broadened his mouth framed by his patchy, unhealthy-looking beard.

His red knit cap glowed in the late light.

Trent had whipped his head around to look at Rachel, too. She still held the rifle to her shoulder, staring down the barrel at the indignant Dan True scowling back at her. Pale smoke slithered from the barrel. She lowered the rifle slightly, briefly, to rack another round into the chamber.

Trent looked in the opposite direction to see all the hands who'd been standing around down there come running toward the lodge. Several who'd just ridden into the headquarters on tired, dusty horses shucked their own rifles from their scabbards, leaped out of their saddles, and came running as well, some jacking live rounds into the chambers of their long guns.

When they were all standing in a semicircle on the north side of the suddenly wary-looking pack of rustlers, Ben said, "You men, ready your rifles to blow every one of these bottom-feeding devils out of their saddles!"

"You got it, boss," said a tall rider with long, curly blond hair tumbling to his shoulders. That was "Whiskey" McMasters, always ready for a fight. He wielded a Spencer repeating rifle—he preferred the old-model rifles in the fashion of the older frontiersmen, though he was only twenty-eight. He'd been raised in the Arkansas mountains, where things and people were slow to change, and the old traditions ruled.

He smiled as he aimed down his old .56, showing his teeth beneath his blond mustache as he grinned, always eager for a foofaraw, as they say. Especially with rustlers. He knew the men before him were all rustlers. He'd probably glassed several of them out on the ranges and had been slavering in anticipation of such an encounter. Whiskey was the kind of puncher Trent was always looking for. Feisty, gun-handy, and loyal as a cur dog rescued from the poverty of some raggedy-heeled town's back alley.

Trent turned to the full-blood Indian among them. The only difference in appearance between Crow Stillwell and the other men were his mud-black eyes, and coarse, straight black hair hanging down his back. He was clad in a sweat-stained, collarless cream shirt and snakeskin suspenders.

"Crow," Ben said, glancing from the Indian to two other men aiming their rifles at True's riders, "I want you and Shatterly and Kelly to dig through these men's saddlebags. Haul out any coins or greenbacks or, hell, even gold dust, and toss it over here on the ground by me!"

Ben Trent peered down the slope to the youngest and tallest of his three hostlers leaning in the doorway of one of the stables, arms crossed on his chest, a smile on his face.

"Jim," he called, "bring a gunnysack!"

Miller turned and disappeared into the stable's purple shadows.

The sheriff looked in exasperation and fury at the Triple T rancher. "What in the hell are you doin', Ben? You're gonna . . . *rob us*?"

"Oh, hell, no," Ben said. "I'm not a robber. I'm just bettin' your men are carryin' every dime they made rustling beef out of these mountains in their saddlebags. What else would they do with it? Maybe bought a few drinks, a few meals, a couple girls, but . . . nah, they're packin' the bulk of it. They figured it would be safest on *them*. Rustlers don't trust banks or anything else." The rancher gave a cunning smile, shook his head. "Nah, it'll all be in their saddlebags—every dime of it—mine an' Ike's!"

Big Ike grinned broadly.

Ben turned to the hard-faced men flanking True, holding rifles, several barrels aimed at Ben.

"First, the preliminaries." The rancher narrowed his eyes, which turned dark with menace and cold-steel threat. "I want every rifle and every pistol you men got on 'em in the dirt over here in ten seconds. When the time's up, if any of you haven't lightened your loads, me an' my men are gonna lighten the loads of your horses, drag you off into the sage." He jerked his chin to indicate a flat stretch of sage-stippled ground between the Triple T headquarters and the base of a forested mountain a hundred yards away. "Got it?"

"The hell you say!" barked a man near the rear of the rustler pack.

A rifle barked loudly, echoing off the near ridges.

The man who'd just announced his defiance yelled incoherently as his black hat tumbled off his shoulder to lie in the dust beside him. A ragged hole appeared in its crown. The man lowered his head, raised a gloved hand to the back of it, then pulled the hand down to look at it.

Blood glistened in the early evening light.

All heads, including Trent's own, swiveled to see the tall, broad-shouldered, muscular figure of Logan Trent step out from between two spruces at the edge of the yard, his Yellowboy jutting straight out from his denim-clad right hip.

The younger Trent moved slowly forward, catlike. He stopped and smiled.

"The hell *I* say." Logan stared at the hatless rustler, who sat slump-shouldered in his saddle, glaring at Trent, while rubbing the back of his bullet-grazed head. "When I say it again, that bullet's gonna be two inches lower." He dipped his chin slightly and furled his dark brows. "An' you're gonna look mighty funny without your head on your shoulders!"

Chapter 32

Logan gestured with his Winchester.

His left arm hurt like blazes after the day's exertions, but he had both hands wrapped around the rifle and, so far, he managed to hold it steady. "Throw 'em down!" He glanced at the Triple T waddies standing to the left of True and his cattle thieves.

"You men—if they haven't thrown down their pistols and rifles by the time I get to ten, empty their saddles!" Logan started counting warily, his heart beating faster with each second. "One . . . two . . . three . . ."

True and his men glared over their shoulders at him, defiance in their hard, flat eyes.

"Four . . . five . . . six . . ." Logan maintained a cold, even expression.

But he knew it wasn't going to work. These men knew that once they'd been relieved of their guns, they'd be hanged. They had nothing to lose. Ben Trent and Big Ike would play cat's cradle with their heads. Both ranchers had reputations to maintain.

So did Logan.

"Ah, hell, boys!" True slid his revolver from its holster. He held it out over the left side of his saddle as though he were going to drop it.

"Seven . . ."

Still holding the Colt out over the left side of his saddle, True glanced over his shoulder at Logan. He smiled. That's when Logan, who anchored his feet to the ground, bracing himself, knew all hell was about to break loose.

Dan True glanced at the hard-faced rustlers around him. His sinister smile in place, he said, "There ain't but only one choice, fellas." He turned forward way too quickly for a man his size and age, and extended his pistol at Ben Trent, clicking the hammer back. "Shoot the hell out of 'em!" he bellowed.

Logan stared in wide-eyed horror as True aimed his revolver at his father.

The pistol bucked and roared in the rogue lawman's hand, orange flames and pale smoke lapping from the barrel.

"*Pa!*" Logan shouted.

But Ben Trent had been faster than True.

Having anticipated the rustling leader's move, he'd snapped up his own Colt and, stretching bearded lips back from his teeth in a snarl, aimed the weapon up at a slant from his right shoulder. His own gun thundered a half-an-eye wink before True's. The crooked lawman jerked back, and to one side, in his saddle, clamping his left hand over the right side of his neck as his own slug tore into the ground six inches in front of the porch steps.

True's horse reared and whinnied, swinging around abruptly.

True lunged forward to grab his saddle horn, somehow making the maneuver, and managed to stay saddled as the horse galloped hell for leather through what was now a smoky battlefield, while his own riders and the Triple T and Double D men returned fire with rifles and pistols at the rustling snakes.

Horses screamed, wheeled, and danced as men fired from their saddles, shouting curses. Men from both factions dropped, screaming.

Logan tried to draw a bead on True. His Yellowboy roared once, twice, three times as bullets fired at him by the rustlers whistled through the air around his head and thumped into the ground near his feet and just beyond him. As the rogue lawman approached the ranch portal with the Triple T brand burned into either side of the wooden crossbeam, he glanced over his shoulder and, still clutching the right side of his neck with his gloved left hand, shouted, "Come on, boys—live to fight another day!"

His steeldust galloped under the crossbeam and a thirty-foot stretch of open, sage-stippled ground, then started up the ridge to the southeast, soon concealed by the darkening pines, spruces, and aspens. Out of the corner of his left eye, Logan saw the man flee, his horse kicking up dust behind him. Logan was busy returning fire on the rustlers, who shot at his father's men, but then they jerked their horses around and aimed at Logan.

The younger Trent shot two riders quickly, one after another.

Bang! Bang!

One, crouched low, gritting his teeth, galloped toward him, leveling his carbine at Logan's gut.

He and the other man dropped from their saddles, firing their rifles wide and cursing. In less than five seconds after True had fled, his proverbial tail between his legs, three, four, five of his men flew off their horses, grunting and yelling loudly. One of the men Logan had just shot struck the ground to the left side of his horse, dust wafting around him.

The man, tall and cinnamon-bearded and suddenly hatless, had just turned onto his left shoulder, extending the rifle he'd somehow managed to hold on to in his violent fall, at Logan. Before he could get the shot off, his gelding, crow-hopping and dancing three feet off the ground, whinnying shrilly, his tail arched, kicked his down rider's head with his iron-shod, right rear hoof.

The man grimaced, then flew six feet from where he'd landed. He dropped his rifle and rolled, his thin cinnamon hair hanging long and straight from around the large bald spot on the top of his head, dancing around his shoulders. He rolled up onto his side and lay, quivering, as he died from one heckuva badly cracked skull.

Blood glistened above his left ear.

Logan dropped to a knee and quickly jacked a fresh round into his Winchester's action. A bullet cut a burning line across the outside of his ribs on his right side, just as he aimed the Yellowboy up at a slant from his right shoulder. It burned devilishly, but the bullet hadn't done much damage. Most of the rustlers—those who'd survived the sudden, savage, loud, and bloody lead swap—were galloping down the slope toward the headquarters' eastern portal.

Logan jerked his right index finger back against the Yellowboy's trigger and smiled coldly, and with great satisfaction, as his bullet punched into the throat of the man whose bullet had just grazed his right side. The man lowered the smoking twin Schofields in his hands. He held on to the gun in his left hand, dropped the one in his right hand, and jerked that hand to his throat.

Blood oozed from between his fingers.

He stared in horror at Logan, opening and closing his mouth wildly as though trying to yell something coherent, but was unable to find any words. Only two seconds after Logan's .44 round had torn the man's voice box out the back of his neck, his dun stallion dropped his head, dark-brown mane jostling wildly and glistening gold and salmon in the dying light. The horse buck-kicked sharply, rear hooves stabbing at the sky, and the now-voiceless rider flew straight up and over the dun's head.

He struck the ground and rolled, grimacing, and turned toward Logan, extending the Schofield, which remained in his left fist. Logan racked another round quickly and finished the blond-headed man with a bullet through his brisket, between the flaps of his black wool-lined leather vest.

Logan tried to rack another round, but there were none left to rack. He'd fired them all. The empty copper casings glinted in the dirt around his boots, near the furrows the rustlers' bullets had torn into the dirt and finely churned horse manure of the yard.

An empty rifle wasn't as bad as it could have been, for just then he saw the last rustler galloping out through the eastern portal, leaning low in his saddle, holding his left arm over his obviously bullet-plundered belly. As the man's black horse passed under the portal, the wind tore his black hat off his head, and it bounced along the trail behind him, before angling off and falling still. Horse and rider lunged across the short stretch of open sage, then disappeared into the forest climbing the near-dark ridge.

Cackling laughter rose to Logan's left.

He turned to see Big Ike Donovan slumped back against the steps of the Triple T lodge, clamping his left hand over the thigh of that denim-clad leg. Blood oozed out from between his gloved fingers. From the jubilant expression on his gray-bearded face and the twinkle in his wide blue eyes, one would never know he'd been shot.

"You see that, Ben? Took down over half o' them rannies and them still alive are in so much agony they're likely thinkin' about turnin' around and beggin' us to finish 'em!"

The old bull buff threw his head back and roared at the sky.

Meanwhile, Ben Trent was flopping around on the ground eight feet from the lodge's steps. He was flapping his arms and driving his booted feet into the ground as Rachel, crouching beside him, her smoking rifle in her left hand, was trying to pull him to his feet.

"Are you all right, Ben?" she yelled, grave concern in her eyes. "Maybe you should stay down!"

"Stay down, Pa!" Logan heaved himself to his feet and, holding his Yellowboy down low in his right hand, ran toward his ailing father.

As he did, hoof thuds thundered along the slope behind him.

"Pa!" came a young woman's shout. "*Pa!*"

Logan turned to see Megan Donovan galloping toward the lodge from the portal on the west side of the yard, hair whipping across her shoulders. She held her Winchester in her left hand, held her reins in her gloved right hand, eyes round and dark with horror as she thundered past Logan, stopped the pinto near her still-roaring father, and fairly leaped out of the saddle.

She dropped the pinto's reins and knelt beside Big Ike.

She pried her father's hand up off the wound in his left thigh, scrutinized the bloody hole, and bunched her lips in a grimace. "You're hit. You're hit bad, Pa!"

"Ah, hell," Big Ike said, adrenaline still washing through the veins of the spirited oldster, who probably hadn't been in a fight like that in ten years. "I been cut worse shavin' after a night o' drinkin'!"

Untying the blue bandanna from around her neck, Megan glanced across her left shoulder at Logan, who was jogging toward his own downed father.

"What happened?" she yelled.

"True an' his riders come callin'. They were after me, but . . ."

Logan shook his head, crouched, and hooked his arms under the ones his father was still flapping, winglike, an unwieldy bird trying to gain his feet.

"Here, Pa," he said. "Here!"

With a grunt, he heaved old Trent to his feet.

Breathing hard, Ben steadied his feet beneath him, then bent forward, hands on his knees, trying to catch his breath. Supporting the old rancher with her right arm snaked around his waist, Rachel glanced at Logan.

"I don't think he's hit. I don't see any blood on him."

"Ah, hell, I ain't hit," Ben said, still bent forward and gasping for air. "I just got my feet entangled and dropped like a damn drunk on the Fourth of July!"

He lifted his head to glance over at his rival. "Just like the old days—eh, Ike?"

Ike laughed as he continued to lean back against the lodge steps.

"Just like the old days." He shook his head, a dreamy light washing into his blue-eyed gaze.

Megan tossed a worried look at Logan. "He's hit bad! The bullet's still in his leg!"

Logan said, "Let's get 'em into the house." He gave his father a nudge with his left shoulder. "Come on, Pa. Into the kitchen. Ike's hit. We gotta get that bullet out, an' you need to sit a spell. You mighta broke somethin' and don't even know it."

"Ah, hell," Ben said, straightening. "All I broke was the notion I still got some fight left in these old bones!"

"You got some fight left in ya, Ben. You got True runnin' like he seen himself in the mirror, and you drilled two more. I took a couple outta their saddles, but one o' the varmints snuck off a shot just as he hit the ground!"

"Come on, Pa," Logan said as he and Rachel helped him up the broad porch steps.

Ahead of them, Lone Dog was holding the lodge door open, a double-barrel shotgun in his weathered hands. Both maws were sending up curls of pale smoke. He'd joined the fight. The Triple T was his home, too.

When he and Rachel got the elder Trent seated in the kitchen, Logan went back out to the porch and helped Megan hoist her father up. Snaking their arms around the old man's waist from either side, they managed to get him hobbling up the steps, grunting and wheezing against the pain he was just now feeling in his injured leg as the excitement of the fight gave up some territory.

"Easy, Pa," Megan said, casting a concerned look across her father's broad chest at Logan. "Easy does it."

Again, Lone Dog held the door open for them. He was no longer holding the Greener. They passed through the front door and into the big kitchen off the foyer and eased Ike into a chair at the table's far end, near Ben. When they'd gotten Ike seated, Lone Dog grabbed a bottle off a shelf and set two short water glasses on the table before each man.

"What happened to the tall ones?" Ben asked the Indian, a vaguely ironic cast to his gaze.

Despite his pain, Ike chuckled. He watched dreamily as Lone Dog half-filled the short glass before him, holding a towel in one hand beneath the bottle as he did, as though he were pouring fine champagne in a toney San Francisco saloon. Meanwhile, Rachel and Megan went to work, stoking the stove and setting water to boil. Rachel pulled Lone Dog's sewing kit down from a cabinet on the kitchen's far end, to the right of a large window growing darker as the sun continued to sink.

"Unless you need me for somethin'," Logan said to Megan, "I'm gonna check on the men."

She nodded as she unwrapped a small rawhide wallet containing a spool of catgut and two needles of different lengths.

"Turn him over to Lone Dog," Logan added to Rachel as the Indian pulled a chair up close to the ailing Ike's left leg and began using a shears from the sewing kit to cut through the neckerchief Megan had tied over the wound. "He's been doctorin' our riders for as long as I can remember. Has a good twenty, thirty bullets lined up on a shelf in his room"—he smiled as he cut a look at the Lakota Sioux—"like trophies."

Typically, Lone Dog said nothing. He lowered his head to carefully inspect the wound, then employed the shears once more to cut the bloody denims away, giving him better access to the ragged hole in Big Ike's leg.

Logan asked him to see to the riders in the bunkhouse when he was. Again, the Indian merely nodded and continued his slow, purposeful work. Logan wasn't worried. He'd known a good many bona fide medicos in his life, but none better than the self-taught Lone Dog.

Logan went outside and picked up his Yellowboy from where he'd set it on the ground. Glancing at the men still helping the wounded riders toward the bunkhouse—one of the wounded hopping on his good leg as he dragged the other along the ground, cursing under his breath—Trent plucked fresh .44 rounds from his cartridge belt and punched them through the Winchester's loading gate.

He started walking toward the bunkhouse, muttering.

This was bad here in the yard. Real bad.

But it was going to get worse for True and the other rustlers who'd survived the initial battle.

Much worse.

Guns barked in the distance, from the direction of the eastern ridge, totally dark now after the sun had set.

Logan gave a wolfish smile.

True's men were shooting the wounded.

Chapter 33

Logan checked on the Triple T riders.

There were four wounded. Five lay dead in the yard between the bunkhouse and the lodge. One of the wounded included Mike Tracy, Ben Trent's first lieutenant, the dangerous former gunfighter from Oklahoma, who sat on his lower bunk, his shirt off, a nasty wound on his right side, halfway between his gun belt and his shoulder. The healthy men—several more had recently ridden in from off the range—were scrambling around to get the wounded men's bleeding stopped.

None of the wounds looked mortal, thank God.

The Triple T foreman and Ben Trent's first lieutenant had finished off the three rustlers who lay wounded and howling, then headed for the bunkhouse.

Logan told Ringo that Lone Dog would be down when he was finished with Big Ike inside the main lodge.

"Hold down the fort, Ed. In an hour or so, Lone Dog and the girls are likely gonna need help carryin' Ike upstairs to a bedroom. I'm ridin' out." He turned to the door.

Ringo placed a hand on his arm, turning him back around. "Where you goin', boss?"

"After them vultures—where else?"

"*Alone?*"

"Best alone. They'd detect more than one shadower. The fewer horses and riders, the better. I'll be all right. I think I know where True is headed, if he even makes it. Pa sent a blue whistler across his neck. Hard to know how deep it cut."

"Let me ride with you," Ringo urged, toying with an upswept end of his ostentatious mustache and slapping his left side with that hand. "I'm fit as a fiddle."

Trent shook his head. "You been in the saddle all day. The men here need you. Besides, like I said, one person can go quieter, have a better chance."

He opened the door, stepped out, and drew the door closed behind him.

He was about to chew off a glove to whistle for Wolf, but stopped. The horse stood near a large cottonwood, thirty feet away from him, and to the right. Wolf was slowly switching his tail and cropping grass growing around the base of the tree. Earlier, Trent had left the roan in a ravine off the northwest corner of the Triple T headquarters, intending to get his so-called shadowers—True's men had never realized until it was too late that *he'd* actually been shadowing them—in a whipsaw with his father's riders, several of whom he'd known would be at the headquarters that time of the day, with others to follow.

The confrontation had become a bloody battle—one that had been coming sooner or later. He wished he'd been able to get word to his father earlier, so he and his men could have been better prepared. But even if he had, the result would have been similar—dead and wounded men on both sides. It was either going to happen in the mountains or here at the Triple T.

Didn't much matter.

The results would have been the same.

The price of doing business with savage cattle rustlers.

Trent walked over to Wolf, patting his loyal roan. He slid his rifle into the saddle scabbard and tightened the stallion's saddle cinch. "Thanks for comin', boy," he said, grabbing the roan's reins and toeing a stirrup. "Hope you got a little rest out there. We got a few miles to go."

He reined the horse around and booted him toward the headquarters' north portal.

They galloped through the portal, across the flat beyond, and up the ridge through the dark forest pushing up close around the trail. He held Wolf to a trot; even with a thumbnail moon, the trail was dangerously dark, more in some places—where the trees were closer to the trace, for instance—than in others.

Also, he was wary of a possible bushwhack.

He didn't think True and his men would hold back on shooting anyone from the Triple T who decided to shadow them. On such a dark night, most smart men wouldn't be doing what Trent was doing. But Trent was chomping at the bit to get to the rustling killers before they had time to light a shuck out of the area.

Also, he had a pretty good idea that True was with the man or men who'd killed Devon. He'd killed Buck Donovan, hadn't he? He couldn't take the chance that True would ride free after that assault—not just on Dev, but on his father and all the Triple T stood for.

Justice.

Rough justice, for sure.

But justice, just the same.

When he was within forty-five minutes of Three Forks, he swung onto a secondary trail branching off the main trail to the right, descending sharply. He'd sent men again to collect the dead men's horses. He didn't know for sure, but he'd always figured this was an old trail used by Indian hunters, and then had probably become a prospectors' trail long before the main trail from town to the mountain ranches had been cut by wagon traffic. It was a rugged trace, but it was a shortcut to town, and one on which he wouldn't have to be worried about being dry-gulched by True's men.

No one took this trail anymore.

No one but himself and Devon when, on the way to town for supplies, they'd wanted a little "adventure."

The trail crossed a good trout creek, which had a deep, bone-splintering-cold swimming hole. The stream's source was a spring up high in the mountains. They'd stopped at the spring many times over the years while they'd hunted elk, moose, and bear in those higher reaches. The spring was a gash in a pitted, mossy granite wall on the side of a mountain. The water ran out of it like from a pump to flow nearly straight down for fifty yards before it turned and continued dropping at a lesser angle.

Trent and Dev had dared each other to jump in the swimming hole, and then, clambering out of the water, they'd point and jeer at the rather humbling effects the chilly dips had had on each other's, um, manhood.

Trent stopped at the creek now, cupped the skin-numbing water up with his palm, and chuckled.

Boys.

He sat back on his bootheels and turned to Wolf, who was drawing water beside him. "You remember ol' Dev—don't ya, boy? Weren't he a caution!"

He mounted back up, crossed the creek, and kept descending the mountain toward Three Forks spread out in the valley beneath him, surrounded by and bisected by the three serpentine streams the valley was named after. This late, all he could see of the streams was the pale-yellow moonlight reflected off their surfaces, glinting like the skins of black snakes.

He'd ridden another hundred yards, following the switchbacking course, when the clang of a shod hoof striking rock rose from the dark slope above him. He jerked back on Wolf's reins, and instantly his cross-draw Russian was in his right hand, his thumb ratcheting the hammer back.

His heart quickened as he studied the slope cloaked in high-country darkness, relieved here and there by the faint, dull wash of moonlight.

Hooves thumped. The thumping grew louder.

On the trail straight above him, a horse blew. Tack squawked. He saw the shadowy figure of a horse and rider cross the shoulder of the mountain from his right to his left, turn when the trail switched back, and ride steadily toward him, dropping at the severe angle, the horse chuffing with each downward lunge.

A familiar female voice said, "Don't pull that trigger, Trent. It's just me."

Trent sighed in frustration, depressed the Russian's hammer, and returned the piece to its holster. "Why are you followin' me? You said I wasn't *that* much fun."

Megan reined her pinto to a halt before him. The pinto and Wolf touched noses, switched their tails in friendly greeting. *Why can't men . . . and women . . . be more like horses?* Trent reflected.

"Killin' True and the rest of his snakes *will* be fun," she stated.

Trent opened his mouth to respond to her.

But before he could speak, she added with her own brand of strained patience, "I have as much reason to kill those bottom-feeding thieves as you do. So, no, I'm not gonna turn around an' take my purty behind home."

"I never said you had a 'purty behind.'"

"Besides, you should know me better than that, you Trent idiot!"

"How's Ike?"

"Lone Dog was just plucking the bullet out when I left to follow you. Someone needed to back your fool hide. What's wrong with your men?"

"They follow orders."

"I reckon I'll find out how Pa's doin' when I return to the Triple T."

Megan placed a hand on her hip and shook her head. Her eyes bored into his. "You'd be *sooo* dead without me around, Logan. You really should suck up some of that go-it-alone pride."

"I don't have time for this!" Trent swung Wolf around and booted him down the mountain toward Three Forks, Megan following close behind on the pinto. Trent leaned forward and said into Wolf's pricked ears, "Harpy."

The roan snorted.

"I heard that," Megan said.

Trent and Megan stopped their horses a hundred yards south of the mostly sleeping Three Forks. It was between ten and eleven at night, and deadly silent.

Even at night, this silence was unnatural. It wasn't *that* late.

They walked into town after wading across two of the three forks of the Wolf River, then ran crouching through a break between a feed shop and a gunsmith's shop. Trent stopped and pressed his left shoulder against the right front corner of the feed shop.

Before them, and perpendicular to them, was the town's main thoroughfare, Bitterroot Avenue. Eighty percent of the town's businesses lay along the avenue, including the Yellow Flower, which was two blocks away to Trent's left. The Yellow Flower was on the opposite side of the street, which was lit here and there by glowing oil pots that sent sparks straight up in the quiet, dark air, causing shadows to slide this way and that on the dusty street, to fairly dance when a vagrant breeze, whispering down from the mountains, picked up.

The Yellow Flower was one of the few businesses that betrayed any life. Another of those few was a saloon along the street to Trent's right, to the southeast. A couple of cowboys sat in front there, in tipped-back chairs, sipping beers and talking in desultory tones.

Watery lamplight angled down on the wooden boardwalk and

hitchrack fronting the watering hole and on the two cow ponies tied to the hitchrack, heads hanging, still as statues.

The Yellow Flower's two large windows, one on either side of the batwing doors, also shed light onto the boardwalk, two stock tanks fronting two hitchracks. Nine horses were tied there, six to the hitchrack nearest Trent and three more to the one beyond it.

Trent recognized True's steeldust. It was one of the three mounts tied to the hitchrack beyond the first. The horse was just then drawing water from the long tank in front of it. One of the other horses craned its neck to chew at something on its left hip, between the cantle of the saddle and the saddlebags and bedroll. The third horse made no noticeable movement.

A man stood on the boardwalk between the horses and the batwing doors.

He looked around cautiously, then raised his rifle and poked the barrel down the back of his shirt to, like the horse, scratch an itch. Trent gave a dry chuff, then looked around the front of the saloon/brothel, to the left and right of the lone sentinel.

He saw no one else out there.

Over his right shoulder, Megan said quietly, "What's goin' on?"

"A scratch fest."

"Huh?"

"They're expecting me." Trent bunched his lips with annoyance. "True knows me too well. He knew I'd come."

"He knew *where* you'd come."

No little sarcasm in the young woman's voice.

Trent had no response to that, so he said nothing. It was often best to say nothing.

Not her way, however. "That train has left the station, eh?"

Trent pulled his head back into the alley. He turned to Megan and shoved her several steps straight back into the break's deeper shadows. "You stay here. I'm goin' in there"—he gave her his coldest, most commanding look, though he doubted it would work—"alone."

"Nope." She shook her head, pursing her lips and sucking in her cheeks. "In case you hadn't heard, *that train* has left the station, too."

"All right," Trent warned.

He went jogging back down the break in the direction from which they'd come. He made his way north along the alley. In the cool night air, the nasty stench of something dead lay—heavy and cloying. Trent picked up his pace, striding down the dark alley that lay behind the business establishments lining the west side of Bitterroot Avenue, to his right. Stables, woodpiles, privies, and stock pens swept past on his left. In one such pen, hogs drowsed in the shadows, grunting.

Something caught Trent's left eye.

He stopped, turned, and gazed down at something gleaming in the moonlight at the base of the hog pen. Something small and shiny. It was partly hidden by the stick of a new cedar twisting up out of the ground beside it.

"What have we here?" Trent muttered, bending down and picking up the object of his curiosity, wrinkling his nose against the stench that was even keener here.

He held the object up, close to his face, and squinted down at it.

His blood chilled.

It was a U.S. deputy marshal's moon-and-star badge—nickel plated, washed in silver. The brown specks on the face of the nickel-plated tin were blood splatters.

With an expression of deep revulsion, Trent slowly straightened his legs, rising. He peered into the pen. Too dark to see much, just a few patches of black horror strewn about the pen, along with a badly flattened black Stetson. The stench of death threatened to suffocate Trent. He looked at the blood-splattered badge in his hand again, dropped it, and fought back the urge to vomit.

The two deputy marshals who'd been summoned to help with True's rustling problem had come to a bad end, as Trent and Megan had feared they would.

They must have figured out who the head of the Wolf Mountain cattle rustling was. The syndicate's inside man. The mess in the hog pen was the result.

Fighting down another vomiting spasm, swallowing hard, Trent shook his head to rid his mind of the ugliness in the pen and the stench around it. He strode to the edge of town, far from the oil pots, and ran through thick darkness as he crossed Bitterroot Avenue to its other side. Ten minutes later, he hunkered in the shrubs abutting the stable that flanked the Yellow Flower, the upper-story windows of which shone with guttering candle- and lamp-light.

A wagon, its tongue drooping to the ground, lay between Trent and the Yellow Flower's back door. Silhouetted by the light seeping through the cracks around the door, a bearded, big-gutted man stood. He was dressed in a striped serape, a funnel-brimmed Stetson on his head, a rifle held up high across his chest.

A cigarette glowed between his lips as he drew on it, then exhaled the smoke through his nostrils, the glow fading from the coal.

Trent looked at the gap between the wagon and the Yellow Flower's rear wall and the closed door that stood in the center of it, behind the guard. A good twelve-foot distance between the wagon and the guard. Even if the man turned away, it was unlikely Trent would be able to sneak up on him, thrust his bowie knife into his back, and angle it up to stop his heart before he could call out.

Giving a fateful grimace, Trent heaved himself to a standing position. As Dev used to say, "No point in overthinkin' it."

He walked away from the stable and around the back side of

the wagon parked in front of it. He stopped at the wagon's far rear corner and thumbed the rifle's hammer back. The stubby sentinel swung his bearded face to Trent sharply, eyes widening, the quirley dangling from the left corner of his mouth.

Trent aimed the Yellowboy straight out from his right shoulder.

He didn't say anything. Neither did the other man.

A hunting owl screeched in the distance. A coyote howled from a far-off ridge.

Crickets gave their ceaseless ratcheting cries.

Trent stepped forward until he was three feet away from the sentinel, who reeked of sweat and whiskey. Trent said quietly, "Do we understand each other?"

The sentinel gave one slow nod, his dark eyes grave beneath the brim of his weathered hat.

"What's goin' on in there?" Trent pointed his Winchester at the dark rear door outlined by lamplight from within.

"They're waitin' for you."

"How's the girl?"

"She's okay."

"Downstairs or upstairs?"

"Down."

"Have they hurt her?"

"Not last I was in there."

"Is she tied up?"

The man nodded. "In a chair facin' the batwings." He drew a deep breath. There was a trill in his voice as he said, "You gonna kill me, Trent?"

"Do you want to die?"

"Nope."

"If I ever see you in these mountains again—*anywhere* again—I'm going to gut-shoot you an' hang you."

The sentinel sighed.

Trent reached forward, took the Spencer from the man's hands, and tossed it over the wagon and into the brush beside the stable.

"Just get it over with," the sentinel said.

"I'll give the orders." Trent flipped the Yellowboy around in his hands and smashed the brass butt plate against the lumpy sentinel's forehead.

He collapsed in a heap. He gave one last groan before lights out.

Chapter 34

Trent looked around carefully as the crickets chirped and the coyote continued its mournful howl from some night-shrouded ridge in the distance, somewhere south of Three Forks.

The night itself seemed despondent, its heart broken.

A breeze muttered in the shrubs beyond the wagon. Otherwise, nothing, no one, moved.

He was alone back here behind the Yellow Flower. No one else had heard the sentinel's collapse on the hard-packed ground. The rear door, at the head of the well-worn path angling off toward the privy, remained closed.

Flipping his Yellowboy back around, squeezing the rifle in both hands, Trent edged a look around the brothel's left rear corner.

He peered up the break between buildings toward Bitterroot Avenue cloaked in darkness. Nothing moved in the ten-foot-wide gap. Holding the Winchester up high across his chest, he jacked a round into the Yellowboy's action, off-cocked the hammer. He slinked like a cat around the building's corner, crouching, trying to make himself as small as possible.

He'd taken one step into the gap, heading for Bitterroot Avenue at the mouth of the gap, when a shadow moved in the weak lamplight shed by a front window. It moved on the boardwalk fronting the adobe-brick building. His heart quickening, Trent backed around the brothel's rear corner, pulling his head behind it just as he saw a man's hatted, silhouetted head poke out around the Yellow Flower's front corner ahead of him.

"Hey, Fletch—all quiet back there?"

Trent's heart beat even faster. He pressed his right shoulder up taut against the brothel's rear wall, licked his lips, and said in a raspy voice, trying to disguise his own, "Yeah, all quiet!"

The man at the building's front corner lowered his head slightly. A match flared to life in his cupped hands. The orange light flickered across the flat planes of the man's face as he lit a cigarette. Smoke wafted around his silhouetted head; the end of the cigarette glowed.

He lifted his head and said just loudly enough for Trent to hear, "I don't think he's comin'. Wish he would so we could get this over with an' move on, but I don't think he is. True thinks if he comes, he'll come alone, have it out, just him an' us. For his brother an' the girl, but I think he'll wait till mornin' and come with others. Others he's got *left*, that is!"

He wheezed a devious laugh.

Trent wheezed out his own laugh, hoping he sounded at least somewhat like the lumpy sentinel, Fletcher, whom he'd just tattooed with his Winchester's rear butt plate.

"Anyway . . ." the man at the mouth of the gap said, tired and bored, and pulled his head back in front of the building.

His shadow moved on the boardwalk again, dwindling as he moved off toward the brothel's far end.

Trent drew a deep, stress-relieving breath and let it out slowly. He scrubbed sweat from his brow with his shirtsleeve, then took his rifle in both hands again, stepped into the gap, and began making his way once more through the dark break toward Bitterroot Avenue. He probably should have taken Ed Ringo's advice and brought a rider or two along to back him. However, he doubted he would have come as far as he had if he hadn't come alone.

With backup, there would have been more opportunities to be detected.

That meant more opportunities for Clarita Ortiz to be caught in a cross fire.

Despite his mixed feelings for her now—considering her dalliance with his brother, a dalliance that had produced a child, a dalliance that had been the ultimate betrayal of Dev's wife, Rachel–he didn't want to see Clarita dead.

He wanted True dead.

He wanted to be the one lone man who dumped the vermin in a deep ravine, food for the coyotes and crows.

It was True, Trent was sure, who'd murdered Dev, just like he'd murdered Buck, trying his best to finally ignite the long-brewing war between the Trents and the Donovans.

Trent slowed his pace as he approached the front of the Yellow Flower. At the corner, he removed his hat, dropped it on the ground beside him, to his left, and, holding the Winchester low in his right hand, edged a quick glance around the building's corner to the front, where lamplight slanted out through the windows on either side of the batwing doors and over the doors themselves.

The other sentinel—a tall, stoop-shouldered man wearing a cream sombrero from which longish, light-brown hair fell, hanging down over his shoulders—just then stopped at the building's far end.

He started to turn back around, pausing to scrutinize the street before him, beyond the tied horses. He drew on the cigarette and blew the smoke into the darkness. He yawned, then continued walking toward Trent's end of the brothel and into the light shed by the windows and batwing doors.

Trent drew his head back behind the Yellow Flower's front corner.

He pressed his back against the wall behind him, once again taking the Winchester in both hands, squeezing it, heart thudding.

The dance was about to begin.

The fiddlers were finishing tuning their fiddles, the piano player his piano.

The boys were moving away from the walls toward the timid girls on the opposite side of the proverbial room.

Death was at hand.

Trent clicked the rifle's hammer back with his thumb.

Boots thudded on the boardwalk over his right shoulder.

He thought the sentinel, somewhere in his early thirties, was just then passing the batwings.

The boot thuds grew louder as he approached Trent, who was standing stiffly back behind the brothel's corner.

The man was close to Trent, now that Trent could hear the faint crackling sound of the paper as the man drew on the quirley. The smoke peppered Trent's nose.

The man's shadow grew large on the end of the boardwalk to Trent's right.

It then faded into the scuffed toes of the man's dusty boots. They had a few splatters of blood on them from the dustup at the Triple T headquarters. Trent lifted his gaze a little. The man held his smoldering quirley in his left hand, an old-model Winchester carbine in his right, the barrel angled across the gold buckle of his cartridge belt.

No point in *overthinkin' it.*

Trent stepped forward, squared his shoulder at the smoking sentinel.

The man's eyes snapped wide. He opened his mouth. The quirley tumbled out of it to land on the ground at Trent's feet, sparking. With savage fury and an enormous strength one found in hard-working men from the mountain ranches, Trent rammed the butt of his rifle into the sentinel's gut.

"*WhooAHHHHHH!*" the man exclaimed on a great explosion of air from his lungs.

Trent grabbed the man's rifle out of his hands before he could drop it on the boardwalk and make a noise that might be heard from within. Trent tossed it into the brush on his right. The sentinel dropped to his knees. His hat tumbled off a shoulder, revealing a tangled mess of sweat-encrusted, thick sandy hair and a deep gash above his right temple.

A bullet graze. Also relatively fresh.

Fury engulfed Trent as he remembered the horde who'd dogged him from Three Forks to the ranch, because he'd broken out of True's jail.

After rustling so much of his father's beef.

The gall!

The man kneeling at Trent's feet grunted and groaned, trying to breathe, grinding his forehead into the edge of the boardwalk.

Three savage blows of the Winchester's stout rear stock against the back of his head finished him. He stopped trying to suck air into his battered lungs. With one last groan, he rolled over onto his side, blinking quickly before his lids opened wide, his eyes rolled back into his head, and his lower jaw fell slack in death.

Trent stepped around him, took three quick steps along the boardwalk, and crouched to peer through the window right of the batwings.

"Good God!" he said.

He pushed through the batwings, drawing the Yellowboy's hammer back to full cock. He aimed straight out from his right shoulder at the men—fewer of them, now that Trent had further culled their herd—who grabbed their rifles and leaped from their chairs. They had been playing cards at two round tables pushed together near a stout ceiling support post.

Clarita Ortiz stood atop a square table to the men's left.

A rope was wrapped around her neck. The end of the rope was attached to a wagon wheel chandelier, three feet above her head. Her hands were bound behind her back. A white bandanna was wrapped tightly over her mouth, tied at the back of her head.

Her feet were bare beneath the hem of her long, sleeveless, cream-colored gown embroidered in the Mexican style. Her hair had been piled in two buns atop her head. The highest bun had most likely been loosened in her struggle against True and his remaining rustlers.

It hung down over her right ear, part of it resting atop her right shoulder.

She stared at Trent in horror, her brown eyes bright with tears.

She slid her eyes to her left, where Dan True stood with his back to the bar, a smirk on his face, a bloody white bandage stretched across the right side of his neck. His rifle lay on the bar to his right. He had a hand on it. When Trent had first entered the place, the rogue lawman had started to reach for it. He'd thought better about it when he saw the big, rifle-wielding Trent take three long strides into the room and stop, batwings clattering into place behind him.

Rage in his eyes. The promise of bloody death.

To the six men holding their rifles, which they hadn't cocked yet, Trent said, "I'm not even gonna tell you to drop those long guns. You know you'll die, anyway. That's the cost of doin' business with the Triple T. The cost of treating senoritas so shabbily."

He glanced at Clarita, sobbing behind the gag tied across her mouth.

In the corner of his left eye, Trent saw True snap up his rifle.

Trent shot him in the upper left thigh.

True yelped and dropped to his right knee, tossing away the rifle and clutching the thigh from which dark-red blood oozed like a geyser.

Trent ejected the spent cartridge, which went smoking over his right shoulder to clatter to the floor behind him. He rammed a fresh round into the Yellowboy's action as the men, apparently seeing their opening, snapped up their rifles.

A thickset man, with a coal-black beard and high-crowned black Stetson, was fast. Before Trent could line his sights up on him, the man had his own rifle aimed at Trent's guts. His broad mouth quirked a wolfish grin inside his beard.

"Logan!" a woman's voice screamed behind him, beneath the thud of bootheels and the clattering once more of the batwings.

The scream distracted the black-bearded rustler and the others, who turned their heads slightly to Trent's right . . . to where Megan Donovan, true to her defiant form, had just strode into the saloon, aiming her own rifle straight out from her right shoulder, that cheek pressed up snug against the long gun's rear stock.

She and Trent shot the black-bearded man before he could snap off a single shot.

He cursed and flew backward, bleeding from the twin wounds in his chest.

The others cocked their rifles, three aiming at Trent, two aiming at Megan.

Only two got off shots before Trent and Megan shot them all, jacking and firing, jacking and firing, watching in droll satisfaction as the last of the rustlers leaped and danced in a bizarre pantomime of one of those ballet shows performed from time to time in an opera house. Only, these fellas were screaming like schoolgirls after a boy dropped a snake through the half-moon in their privy door.

Trent had just fired his last shot when he saw the table Clarita was standing on suddenly slide out from beneath her feet.

She gave a muffled scream behind the gag in her mouth as she dangled in midair, the rope above her head creaking as the slack left it suddenly and it grew taut as wire. Clarita's brown eyes widened in horror as she swung on the deadly rope.

Trent turned to where Dan True lay on the floor fronting the bar, his left leg extended straight out before him. With that foot, he'd nudged the table out from beneath Clarita. As he clamped his hand tightly over the bloody wound in his thigh, the crooked lawman grinned cagily up at Trent, who shot him in his right shoulder, laying the man out flat.

"*Ohh!*" True cried, resting his head back against the brass footrail running along the base of the bar, panting. "Oh, you devil!"

He removed his hand from his thigh to clamp it down hard across the oozing wound in his shoulder.

Trent tossed his rifle to Megan, who caught it one-handed.

He lurched forward, slid a chair beneath Clarita, whose eyes were growing steadily, horrifyingly dim. He leaped onto the chair and shucked his bowie knife from the buckskin scabbard on the right side of his cartridge belt. He grabbed the senorita around her waist with his left arm, lifting her to put some slack into the rope, then sliced through it with the bowie's razor-edged blade.

Clarita fell limp in his arms, as slack now as the rope he'd just cut.

Her head slumped down over his right shoulder.

She wasn't moving. He didn't think she was breathing.

Had her slender neck snapped?

"Clarita!" he yelled, laying her down on the table she'd been standing on and cutting the gag away from her mouth. "Don't you die on me, senorita!"

She moaned, turned her head a little, blinking, sobbing.

Alive!

To Trent's left, Dan True wheezed with laughter.

Trent unholstered his cross-draw .44, walked over to True, and clicked the hammer back. True stared up at him, at the gun he held steady in his hand, down the barrel of which Trent aimed, narrowing one eye as he planted the sights on True's left knee.

No point in gifting such a demon a quick death. Might as well make him hurt some more.

True squirmed a little, looking down at the knee Trent was aiming at. "No . . . now . . . *you* . . . Just get it over with, Logan!"

"Did you kill Dev?"

True stared up at him, his eyes at once bright with misery and dark with . . . what?

Deadly secrets?

"You killed Buck," Trent said. "I remember it now. I see it in my head. Buck layin' dead in that alley, stabbed. Then you came walkin' down the boardwalk . . . with blood splattered on your cheek."

"You prove it!"

"I don't have to prove it. I know!" Trent pressed his cheek up tight against the Yellowboy. "You killed my brother, too. Just couldn't get the greed out of your head. All that land . . . all that beef . . . two dead ranchers. All their men dead . . . all their buildings burned. All their cattle . . . *yours*!"

True raised his hands, palms out in supplication. The glint of jeering joined the brightness of misery in his eyes. "You really wanna know?" he asked.

"No!" a girl screamed.

Trent turned to where Clarita was now sitting up, resting her back against the stout ceiling support post abutting the table she'd been standing on when True and the other rustlers had been about to hang her.

Trent frowned at her. Megan, standing beside her, frowned at her, too.

"No," Clarita sobbed, slowly shaking her head, tears streaming down her cheeks. "No . . . please." She jerked up her chin to gaze sharply, imploringly, at Trent. "Enough!"

"No," Trent said, deeply confused, horrified. "It . . . wasn't you. I won't believe that!"

Clarita raised her knees, rested her forehead against them and sobbed, her hair completely down now and hanging thickly against the sides of her head, over her arms, and covering her from her shoulders to her elbows. She raised her hands to her head, squeezed, and said in a little girl's voice, "No."

"She didn't kill him," True said in a cold, even voice, his pain-bright eyes boring into Trent's.

"I did," Clarita said, grinding her forehead against her knees. "I killed him. It was me!"

"Nah," True said. "It wasn't her. Leastways, not really."

"No," Megan said, staring down at Clarita before her. She shook her head, then turned to Trent. "I was out riding that day. I saw movement in a crease between wooded buttes below me . . . on Double D range. Devon was riding along the trail down there, leaning out from his saddle, following tracks. Rustlers' tracks, no doubt. They'd hazed Triple T beef across our land, picking up a few of our beeves along the way."

Trent turned to her, scowling, thoroughly befuddled. "So . . . ?

"Devon stopped suddenly, dismounted, dropped his reins, and walked into a copse of aspen and pine, looking at the ground, still following the rustlers' tracks. He was in those trees for maybe five minutes when another rider rode up behind him, stopped."

She turned to glare down at True, resting his head back against the brass footrail once more. She drew a deep breath, let it out slowly. She shook her head, glanced at the sobbing Clarita.

"It was her," Megan said.

"It was me," Clarita said, slowly shaking her head from side to side, forehead still pressed against her knees. "It was me. I killed him." She jerked her chin up, stared brightly, desperately at Megan. "Megan, stop, *por favor*. For all the saints in Heaven!"

"It wasn't her," Megan said softly, quietly, gazing back at Clarita. She turned to Trent. "It was *her*. Not Clarita, though she wants to take the blame for what she . . . what *they* . . . did together."

"*Who*, then*?*" Trent urged in exasperation.

True looked up at him, his eyes flat now, but his mouth corners quirking a self-satisfied smile. "We were out there, too. We were movin' beef we'd stolen, me an' some fellas. We seen Devon comin'. Then we seen her. She stopped her horse, swung down, and disappeared into the trees . . . behind her husband."

"*What?*" Trent said in disbelief.

"Sure," True said, flinching as a particularly sharp pain spasm assaulted him. Blood had pooled thickly on the floor beneath him. He didn't have much time left. He knew it. "Can't really blame her," he said beneath Clarita's pleading screams of "No! No! No!"

as she rammed the ends of her small fists against the table on either side of her. "*No! No! No!*"

Megan turned her bereaved expression to Trent. "Rachel."

She paused, then sobbed once herself, into her own hand. She lifted her head again, sniffed. "She couldn't bear the fact that her husband . . . a man she'd loved nearly all her life . . . whom she wanted to have a family with"—she turned to Clarita, who had rolled onto her side and was openly bawling, grinding the knuckles of her left fist into her temple—"had a child with another."

"No," Clarita said. A quiet, desperate, defeated plea this time. She was overrun with grief and self-recrimination. "No . . . *por favor*. Please stop!"

To Trent, Megan said, "Rachel confessed it to her." She glanced at the despondent woman. "Clarita never tells anything to anyone. She just listens. And she knows everything. But when she learned that I was raising her baby, she told me. She wanted me to know. It was too great a burden for her shoulders alone."

"No," Clarita said again, crying. "No!"

Again, she banged her fists against the table.

Megan lowered her head and sobbed.

Trent turned to True.

The man lay back against the brass footrail, head turned to one side, his eyes open but unblinking.

Dead.

Trent lowered the .44, depressed the hammer, returned the piece to its holster.

He turned, began walking toward the batwings. He needed some air. His heart was a heavy stone in his chest. He couldn't feel it beating. Part of him wondered if it had stopped. If it would ever beat again.

He paused beside Megan, swept her hair back with his hand, planted a tender kiss on her cheek. "Don't worry."

She looked at him, brushing tears from her cheeks with the

backs of her hands. "You won't," she said hopefully, beseechingly. "You won't—"

"Tell anyone?" Trent shook his head. "Hell, no. She's been punished enough. Not only betrayed by the man she loved. But she was so hurt by him she had to kill the man she loved, to boot. And blame others to cover her tracks. If that doesn't kill a person, especially a good person like who Rachel really is, I don't know what will. She could be in prison for thirty or forty years . . . and never be punished the way she's bein' punished now."

"Oh, Logan," Megan said, looking up at him, smiling at him. "I love you so much!" Her voice broke with emotion.

"Well . . . you know how I feel about you."

"How?" she said, more tears running in streams down her cheeks.

"You got the purtiest behind in these mountains."

Megan laughed.

Trent took her hand and squeezed it.

He glanced at Clarita. She'd stopped crying and just lay on her side, staring in shock down at the table beneath her, knees drawn to her chest, not saying anything.

"Let's get her to bed," Trent said to Megan. "Then let's head on home an' see about Ike."

Megan raised her brows. "Home? You mean the Triple T."

"I mean *home*. Our home . . . once we're married and merge our herds, our graze."

Megan's lower jaw dropped. Her mouth opened. Her eyes were bright again.

Again, Trent smiled. "Now, that," he said, "is one way to win a war against a blood enemy—ain't it?"

She threw her arms around his neck and buried her face in his chest.

TURN THE PAGE FOR AN EXCITING PREVIEW!

The Longest-Running Western Series Ever!

In this gun-blazing adventure from the bestselling Johnstones, mountain man Smoke Jensen reckons he can stop a romantic rivalry from turning into a bloodbath—but he's dead wrong. . . .

JOHNSTONE COUNTRY. WHERE CUPID SHOOTS TO KILL.

As a happily married man, Smoke Jensen is glad his courtin' days are over. Especially when two blond beauties open a dress shop in town—and a big can of worms along with it. It doesn't take long for the comely Caldwell sisters to catch the eyes of Sugarloaf ranch hands Pearlie and Cal. But the boys've got competition. Their romantic rivals are a pair of roughneck cowboys who are also trying to win the girls' hearts. And willing to fight dirty. Smoke might find it all amusing—if it weren't for the rash of crimes that broke out as soon as those pretty heartbreakers showed up. . . .

Cattle rustling. Train robberies. Stagecoach holdups. It looks like the work of seasoned outlaws, not a pair of dressmakers. Sure, the Caldwell sisters might be trying to swindle money out of Smoke's ranch hands, but mastermind an outlaw gang? Doesn't seem likely. But it's true.

Their stepfather is the notorious jailed outlaw "Whisper" McReady. His stepdaughters are running the gang while he serves time. And when the gang leader busts out of jail, all hell breaks loose. Whisper McReady may not be able to holler since he was shot in the throat. But he's screaming mad over the girls' mishandling of his gang.

And now he's taking control—not just over his gang, but the whole town of Big Rock.

Over Smoke's dead body . . .

Chapter 1

The tunes coming from the town hall in Big Rock, Colorado, on this late spring evening, were sprightly. What the musicians might lack in talent, they made up for with sheer gusto. The couples swirling around the floor inside the hall, which had been cleared for dancing, seemed to be enjoying themselves.

Smoke Jensen definitely enjoyed having his beautiful wife, Sally, in his arms as they went through the steps of a waltz.

"You're doing very well," she told him. "You must have been practicing."

"You mean I haven't stepped on your feet any, so far," Smoke said.

Sally laughed. "Honestly, Smoke, I don't recall that you've ever stepped on my feet. You've always been a fine dancer. I was just teasing you."

"I guess I'm just naturally graceful," he said with a smile directed down at her lovely face, which was surrounded by waves of thick, lustrous dark hair.

They made an attractive couple—that was for sure. Smoke wasn't classically handsome. His features were too rugged for that.

But his face had a clean-cut appeal under his ash-blond hair, and his muscular shoulders were unusually wide. His body had an undeniable aura of tautly leashed power and speed, like that of a mountain lion.

Or like that of a man known to be one of the fastest, deadliest gunfighters west of the Mississippi, which was exactly what Smoke Jensen was.

Most of the time, though, including tonight, he was mighty happy to put aside that reputation and just be a successful rancher and the husband of the former Sally Reynolds.

The daughter of a wealthy family from New England, she had been trying to contribute something to the world by serving as the schoolteacher in the rough frontier town of Bury, Idaho, when they met.

She hadn't known it at the time, but he was there to rain down Colt-flame and death on the men responsible for the killings of several of his loved ones: his father, his brother, his first wife and their infant son. Those tragedies seemed to have burned the goodness and mercy out of Smoke Jensen, leaving only the need for revenge.

That was what he'd believed at the time, anyway. Over the years since they'd gotten married and established the Sugarloaf ranch, west of Big Rock, Sally had taught him different, taught him that a core of decency, courage, and loyalty remained inside him, and together they had nurtured that core and made him into the kind, decent man he was today.

Kind and decent, but still faster on the draw and more accurate with his guns than just about anybody who had ever ridden down a Western trail.

Smoke wasn't thinking about that tonight. He was just enjoying dancing with his wife and looking forward to visiting with his many friends, most of whom were here in attendance at the town social.

He was even looking forward to drinking some of the punch that was being guarded by several ladies to make sure no mischief-making cowboy tried to spike it.

As the group of guitar-strumming musicians at the front of the room continued playing, someone tapped Smoke on the shoulder. He and Sally paused, and Smoke looked over at a well-dressed, sleekly handsome man somewhat older than him.

"May I cut in?" Louis Longmont inquired.

"I don't know," Smoke said. "Are you planning on stealing my woman away from me?"

Longmont chuckled. "I doubt if the Seventh Cavalry could succeed in stealing Sally away from you, Smoke. All I have in mind is a dance."

"Well, if the lady doesn't object, I don't."

"The lady doesn't object," Sally said with a smile of her own.

Smoke handed her over to Longmont, who swept her away with the other dancers. Still smiling, Smoke walked toward the wall on one side of the room where a number of men, who weren't dancing, were standing around talking to one another.

One of them, also older than Smoke, but considerably more weathered than Louis Longmont, grinned and greeted him by saying, "How'd you manage to get away?"

"I wasn't trying to," Smoke told him. "Louis cut in."

Sheriff Monte Carson nodded sagely. "He always did have an eye for the pretty ladies."

Monte and Louis were two of Smoke's staunchest friends. Before Monte had pinned on a star, he had been mostly on the other side of the law, working as a hired gun. In fact, it was one of Smoke's enemies who had brought him to the area before Big Rock even existed. Monte had soon realized that he was on the wrong side of that conflict, however, and had backed Smoke's play instead.

Louis was also noted as a fast gun, but he was a gambler, first and foremost, and had lived a wandering, dangerous life before settling down in Big Rock and opening the town's finest restaurant and saloon.

Both men had fought side by side with Smoke many times. He would trust them with his life, without hesitation. Even more importantly, he would trust them with Sally's life.

"I saw Cal earlier," Monte went on. "He looked mighty down in the mouth."

"That girl he was sweet on wrote to him from back East. I think she must have found another beau and was letting him know. He's been moping around ever since he got that letter from her."

"That Bolton girl? What was her name? Hannah?"

"Susannah," Smoke said.

"That's a shame. Cal hasn't had much luck where gals are concerned, has he? I'd almost say the boy's snakebit."

"He's young. He'll get over it."

Calvin Woods was one of the hands who worked for Smoke on the Sugarloaf, but he wasn't just one of the crew. He had become almost like a member of the family, along with Smoke's foreman, Pearlie Fontaine. Pearlie regarded Cal sort of like a little brother, and Cal certainly looked up to Pearlie. They were good friends, as well as top hands. Smoke figured he couldn't get along without them.

He looked along the wall and spotted both men sipping from cups of punch. Cal looked just as disconsolate as he had been for the past few days, and it appeared that Pearlie was trying to cheer him up, without having much luck at it.

Maybe Cal shouldn't have come to town, Smoke mused. Seeing those happy couples swooping around the dance floor might just remind him of the girl he'd lost.

Smoke hoped he wouldn't start any trouble before the night was over, just to let off some steam.

* * *

"Dang it, Cal, you've had your heart broke before, and lots worse'n this, too," Pearlie said as he clapped a hand on his young friend's shoulder. "I know it stings pretty bad for a spell, but you'll get over it."

"Yeah, you're right, I know that," Cal managed to say. "At least, Susannah's doing fine, even if she did decide to stay back there where her father's sending her to school. She didn't die or anything. As big a Jonah as I am when it comes to romance, she ought to consider herself lucky she didn't get hit by a bolt of lightning."

"You ain't a Jonah in romance or nothin' else. It's like breakin' ornery horses. You're gonna get throwed from time to time, and that's just the way it is. And what's the best thing to do when you get throwed?"

"Get right back on the horse," Cal muttered.

"That's right." Pearlie cast a speculative eye across the big room toward the unattached ladies sitting in chairs along the wall on the far side. "And I spy a couple o' likely lookin' fillies right over yonder."

Cal followed Pearlie's gaze and saw two young women sitting by themselves. Both had blond hair, and they looked enough alike that Cal figured they must be sisters. There wasn't enough difference in their ages for them to be mother and daughter. They were both in their twenties, he estimated.

"You're talking about those two blondes?" he asked Pearlie.

"Yep. They're mighty pretty, ain't they?"

"Well, a fella would have to be blind not to see that," Cal grumbled.

"I reckon they must be new in town, too," Pearlie went on. "I don't recollect ever seein' 'em before, do you?"

Cal thought about it and then shook his head.

"We don't know everybody in Big Rock, though. The town's growing all the time."

"Sure, it is, but answer me this: If you'd laid eyes on a pair of gals as good-lookin' as those two, you'd remember it, wouldn't you?"

Despite his determination to continue moping, Cal felt his interest perking up.

"I suppose I would," he admitted.

"Well, then, let's go ask 'em to dance."

"I don't know if that's a good idea."

"I ain't *suggestin'* we ask 'em," Pearlie said as he took hold of Cal's arm in a firm grip. "I'm *tellin'* you, and I'm your boss, remember?"

"Smoke's my boss," Cal objected, "and, anyway, we're not on the ranch right now."

"Maybe not, but I'm still older an' wiser than you, no matter where we are. Come on."

Cal gave up and allowed Pearlie to steer him around the crowd of dancers in the middle of the room. They had to go almost all the way to the entrance to find enough empty space to cross over to the other side.

While they were doing that, the musicians—four guitarists and a chubby man with a big bass fiddle—reached the end of a song. As the dancers paused, the leader of the group stepped up and announced in a loud voice, "We've got a real treat for you folks tonight. You all know Len here."

He waved at another of the guitar players, a handsome, curly-haired young man who gave the crowd a shy smile.

"He's a good cowhand, but what you might not know is that he's a mighty fine singer, too. Len, step up here and give these folks a song!"

The young man seemed a little reluctant, but he moved up in front of the other musicians and said, "Evenin', folks. If you don't like this, feel free to chuck rocks at me and I'll hush up."

With another shy smile, he strummed the guitar he still held and broke into a lively song about a cowboy from Texas and a beautiful senorita with a red, red rose in her hair. The other musicians briskly accompanied him, and people began dancing again.

Pearlie and Cal reached the far wall and started along it toward the spot where the two attractive blondes were sitting.

"Uh-oh," Pearlie suddenly said. "Looks like a couple other rannies got their sights set on those pretty little mavericks. Hurry up, Cal. We don't want those boys slappin' their brands on 'em before we get a chance to."

Cal saw what had caught his friend's attention. Two men were walking from the back of the hall toward the blondes, and judging by the intent expressions on their faces, they had the same objective as Pearlie and he did.

"I know those hombres," Cal said. "They ride for the Three Sevens, don't they?"

"Yeah, maybe, but it don't matter. They ain't cuttin' in ahead of us."

Pearlie tightened his grip on Cal's arm and urged him along at a faster pace. The two cowboys coming from the other direction must have noticed that because they quickened their steps as well. All of them were almost running now.

At that moment, several older ladies inadvertently blocked the path of the pair from the Three Sevens ranch. They had to stop or run into the women, and they were chivalrous enough to throw on the brakes. Both men scowled darkly at the delay, but there was nothing they could do.

That gave Cal and Pearlie time to reach the young women first.

Pearlie put his right arm across his stomach and his left arm behind his back and bowed. Cal thought he looked ridiculous.

"Howdy, ladies," Pearlie greeted the young women. "Or maybe I ought to say 'good evenin',' since we ain't out on the range. Ain't this just the finest town social you ever did see?"

The older blonde smiled up at him and said, "It's very nice, Mr. . . ."

"Fontaine, ma'am. Pearlie Fontaine." He put a hand on Cal's shoulder. "And this here is my good friend, Calvin Woods."

"Just Cal is fine," the younger man said with a nod.

"My name is Violet Caldwell," the woman said. "And this is my sister, Daisy."

Violet's hair was shorter and curved fetchingly around her face. Daisy's blond curls tumbled freely around her shoulders. Both wore simple but elegant dresses that displayed their graceful figures to fine effect.

"It's a plumb pleasure and an honor to meet you ladies, Miss Caldwell," Pearlie said. "Cal and me, we was hopin' you'd do us the even greater honor of consentin' to have a dance with us—"

Before he could go on, the two cowboys from the Three Sevens spread finally reached the spot, and they definitely didn't look happy.

"You and Woods just mosey along now, Fontaine," one of them said with a scowl. "These ladies are fixin' to dance with Jasper and me."

"Chuck's right," the man called Jasper said. "You two are hornin' in on our range."

Violet Caldwell arched an eyebrow and said in a chilly voice, "Excuse me?"

"Don't pay any attention to him, ma'am," the first cowboy said. He glared at his companion. "A mule kicked him in the head when he was young, and he ain't been quite right since."

"Oh, no!" Daisy Caldwell said. "How terrible." She leaned forward and spoke to Jasper slowly and clearly, as if she were talking to a five-year-old, and not a particularly bright one, at that. "I'm sure it must have hurt."

Jasper flung a hand out dismissively and said, "Oh, he's lyin'! I never got kicked in the head by a mule or nothin' else." He attempted a smile, which probably was supposed to be charming, but actually looked a little grotesque. "But I reckon seein' how pretty you are felt a little like bein' kicked in the head, ma'am."

Pearlie said, "You boys might as well just trail your twine,

Hendryx. Miss Caldwell and the other Miss Caldwell are gonna dance with me and Cal."

"We haven't heard them say that," the first Three Sevens cowboy responded hotly.

"Well, we got to 'em first." Pearlie nudged Cal. "Tell these varmints that, Cal."

Cal ignored the urging and instead said to Daisy as he held out his hand, "Would you like to have this dance with me, Miss Caldwell?"

As the younger of the sisters, she was only two or three years older than him, Cal thought, close enough to his age so as not to matter.

She laughed and said, "It's nice to finally be asked politely. Of course, I'll dance with you, Mr. Woods."

She started to reach up and take Cal's hand.

Before Daisy could complete the gesture, the first rival cowboy, whose name was Chuck Dade, Cal recalled now, moved in quickly.

He grabbed Cal's shoulder, jerked him around, and threw a punch, which crashed solidly against Cal's jaw.